DEEP WATER

A TOM ROLLINS THRILLER

PAUL HEATLEY

INKUBATOR
BOOKS

Published by Inkubator Books
www.inkubatorbooks.com

ISBN (eBook): 978-1-83756-567-2
ISBN (Paperback): 978-1-83756-568-9

For Aidan

1

It's a sunny day, hot, and there's a new arrival to the worksite.

Tom Rollins has been working construction in Newark, New Jersey, for the last three months. It's early August and they're in the middle of a heatwave. It's early morning, only a half-hour into the work day, and it's already sweltering. Tom loads broken concrete into a wheelbarrow. He feels a drop of sweat run from his temple and down the side of his face. He pushes the hard hat back from his forehead and wipes his forearm across his brow. The heat is due to break in a week, and he's looking forward to it.

Tom is a labourer. It's a straightforward job. He loads and unloads. He clears debris. He builds up and takes apart scaffolding. Tom likes the work. It keeps him busy. He's never been afraid to get his hands dirty.

He spotted the new arrival when he arrived this morning. A young guy, clearly shy, clearly nervous. He kept to the far side of the parking lot, away from everyone else. He wore torn jeans and an old shirt, Tom noticed. Clearly here to work. When Neal, the site foreman, arrived, he went straight to the young guy and took him into his cabin to run through health and safety rules and sign the necessary paperwork before he can begin.

They emerge an hour later. The new arrival is introduced to Tom briefly by Neal. "Rollins, this is Dennis."

The younger guy holds out his hand. "Dennis Kurtley." He's early twenties, though there is a taut quality to his face, visible lines around his eyes, like life has prematurely aged him. He wears a nervous, earnest smile. He doesn't have the swaggering bravado and confidence of a seasoned site worker. His cheeks are gaunt and he's clean-shaven, like he came here today looking to make a good impression. His hair is shaved short around the sides, and Tom would guess that under his hard hat it's neatly combed.

Tom takes his keen handshake. "Rollins," he says. "Tom."

"Which do you prefer?" Dennis says.

Tom shrugs.

"He's gonna be labouring with us too," the foreman says. "Keep an eye on him. Make sure he's not gonna get himself or anyone else hurt. And give him a kick up the ass if you see him slacking." Neal turns back to Dennis and winks. "And if there's one guy on this site you don't want to kick you up the ass, it's Rollins. Trust me. I've seen him in action."

"Ignore him," Tom says. "He's just trying to scare you."

The foreman laughs, then takes Dennis away to show him around the rest of the site and introduce him to the others. Tom gets on with his day. He doesn't spend much time with the others. He keeps to himself. Does his work and goes home to the small apartment he's renting. Sometimes he'll stop off at The Corner Spot, the bar where Melissa works. It's a popular watering hole for the other site workers, too, but Tom goes there alone. Usually, though, he either goes to Melissa's place or she comes to his. All to say, he doesn't spend a great deal of time socialising with his coworkers.

When he first started, he got a few sideways glances, like people recognised him but they couldn't place why. Tom's face has been flashed in the news. The most recent occasion was about a year ago, when he was in San Francisco. For nearly all of twenty-four hours, he was the nation's most wanted man. But the news cycle moves on fast, and that was on the other side of the country, a whole different coast. The people of the site couldn't remember where they knew him from, and they didn't probe him, and they all moved on with their lives.

Tom wheels his barrow of broken concrete to the dumpster and unloads it. Labouring is a lot of heavy lifting. He still does his daily push-ups and goes for an occasional run, but he hasn't felt the need to hit the gym or lift much heavier. His muscles are getting an adequate daily workout.

It's an hour until lunch. The day is getting hotter. There's little respite from it.

As Tom wheels the barrow back across the site, he spots Dennis. He's not alone. There's a few guys close to him. Tom slows, keeping an eye on the situation. He recognises the men talking with Dennis. He doesn't like them. He's never had any trouble with them, but he knows their type. Workyard bullies. There are two sycophants that hang around Bud Myers. Bud is a big guy. Burly, barrel-chested, and with thick forearms. He has a bushy black beard and curls of hair that cascade from under the rear rim of his hard hat. Tom puts down the wheelbarrow and takes a couple of steps closer so he can hear what's being said.

"I'm not after any trouble," Dennis says, holding out his hands. "I'm just here to work."

Tom notices how they've cornered Dennis under a recently constructed wall, out of view of Neal and the other supervisors.

"We never said we were looking for trouble," Bud says, glancing at his two followers. "Neither of you heard me say we were looking for trouble, did you?"

"Didn't hear nothing about any trouble, Bud."

"Not to my ears."

"That's what I thought," Bud says. "No, what I remember saying is that's a fine pair of gloves you've got. That's a fine hard hat. It's all fine and clean-looking gear. And you see my friend here." He jerks a thumb toward the man on his right. "His gear's all worn out, ain't it. I mean, my own gear's long past its best, but me and you aren't exactly the same size." He laughs his gruff laugh. "But you and my friend here, you match up real close. I'm just suggesting that, since it's your first day on *our* site and all, maybe it would be a real nice thing for you to gift all that nice new gear of yours to one of your co-workers." He leans in closer, intimidatingly close. "It would keep you in our good books, new boy."

Dennis's jaw clenches. He swallows. He looks between the three men. It's clear he doesn't want to back down, but at the same time he doesn't want to get into trouble within the first few hours of his new job.

"All right," he says through gritted teeth, and he starts to take off his hard hat.

Tom strides up to the group. "Don't take your hard hat off when you're on the site, Dennis," he says. "That's a rule, and a firm one."

All four pairs of eyes turn in Tom's direction. Tom sees how Bud's face sours. He's a bully, and like most bullies, he crumples upon confrontation.

Tom looks Bud and his two friends over. "This where you're supposed to be right now, Bud? Could've sworn I saw the three of you working on the other side of the site."

Bud inhales deeply, his nostrils flaring. He juts his chin, his beard pointing toward Tom. "Just introducing ourselves to the new guy, Rollins."

"Shouldn't take too long, huh? You've got a real short name."

Bud bristles, but he won't do anything. He knows he can't cow Tom. Knows Tom isn't intimidated by him. He grunts. That's why he's stayed away from Tom since day one. "I suppose you're right," he says. He looks at Dennis, then at his two sycophants. "Then I guess we're done here."

Bud and his two followers throw one last glance back in Dennis's direction, then turn and leave the spot, heading across the site. The sycophants look back over their shoulders toward Tom and Dennis, but Bud strides on without turning his head. Tom watches them until they're out of sight.

Dennis clears his throat. "Uh, thanks," he says. "Rollins, right?"

Tom turns back to him. He nods, once, and says, "Or Tom. Whichever you'd prefer."

"Okay. Listen, thanks, man. I don't know what their problem was."

"Don't worry about it," Tom says. "You're new. They're just hazing you." Tom returns to the wheelbarrow.

"Did they...did they haze you when you first started?" Dennis says.

Tom lifts the handles of the wheelbarrow. "No," he says, then winks at Dennis and returns to his work.

2

———

It's lunchtime. On a hot day like today, most of the workers sit around in the flatbeds of their trucks, shooting the shit for the half-hour they get to eat. On cooler days, they go into one of the cabins. No matter the weather, Tom sits apart from them. He takes his lunchbox and goes to the second floor of the condominium they're building and sits with his legs dangling, looking out over the busy nearby road leading into the city of Newark. He has a peanut butter and jelly sandwich, a banana, and a protein bar. He sees how some of the other guys eat entire rotisserie-cooked chickens or sandwiches with a full wedge of brisket jammed into them, maybe a small cake or a candy bar to chase it and a bottle of soda to wash it all down, but Tom doesn't want anything heavy. He's never had a large appetite. He can get by on the minimum.

He hears movement behind him and he looks back to see Dennis. The kid freezes when Tom spots him.

"Is it, uh, is it all right if I sit with you?" Dennis says.

"Sure," Tom says, turning back around. "So long as you're okay with heights."

Dennis sits down next to him. He peers over the edge. "It's not so high yet, but I think this might be my limit."

"Gonna be six floors," Tom says. "Not too much higher to go now."

Dennis cranes his neck back, looking up, as if imagining it.

"You worked in construction long?" Tom says.

Dennis looks back down. "Uh, no," he says, opening his lunchbox. He has a chicken sandwich that he must have grabbed from a gas station on his way in. "Uh...this is my first job, truth be told."

"Ever?" Tom says.

Dennis nods.

"How old are you?"

"Twenty-four." Dennis takes a bite out of his sandwich, avoiding Tom's questioning eyes.

"Did you go to college?"

Dennis snorts. "I wish."

"Then what's the story? You're holding out on me, but you don't have to be coy. I'm not gonna judge."

Dennis swallows. "You sure about that?"

Tom waits. He watches Dennis. He lets him talk in his own time.

Dennis sighs. "I dunno... I mean, we've only just met. I appreciate what you did for me with Bud and the others, but I'm not so sure I should just go ahead and give you my whole life story straight off the bat."

Tom shrugs. "Suit yourself."

They eat in silence for a while. Tom takes a long drink of

water, feeling the sun beating down on the back of his neck. It's going to be a sluggish afternoon.

Dennis breaks the silence first. "Have *you* worked in construction long?"

"I've been here about three months. I've done construction work before, though. I've done a little bit of everything."

"Oh yeah? You're not from New Jersey, are you?"

Tom shakes his head. "New Mexico."

"Oh really? What brings you all the way up here?"

"I go where the road takes me. I was nearby, in New York, and I figured I'd swing by and spend a little time in Freehold."

"Freehold..." Dennis repeats, thinking on why the name sounds familiar. His face brightens. "You a Springsteen fan? Is that why you went?"

Tom smiles. "You better believe it."

"What did you do out there?"

"Just took it all in."

"Cool. What's your favourite Springsteen album?"

"That's a tough question." Tom considers for a moment. "It used to be *Darkness on the Edge of Town*, and it probably always will be, but I've been listening to a lot of *Born in the U.S.A.* and *Born to Run* lately. Reckon those are the three I go back to most."

"I've always been partial to *The River*."

"Another good choice. *Nebraska*, too – that's another classic."

"Okay, I see what you're saying," Dennis laughs. "It's a tough question to answer. I mean, I listen to a lot of rap mostly – Wu-Tang Clan, Public Enemy, Run DMC, De La Soul, A Tribe Called Quest – you know, the list goes on and you get the point, but I've always had a soft spot for The Boss."

"The way I see it, if you're from New Jersey, it has to be in your blood. Like if you're from Memphis, you've probably got a fondness for Elvis. Sinatra in New York. Or, further afield, Liverpool, for The Beatles."

"Could be," Dennis says. He opens a can of soda and takes a long drink. "You said you go wherever the road takes you. What's that mean? You're a vagrant?"

"In a way," Tom says. "But a vagrant implies that I beg. I don't beg. I work. And I have savings. I've always been able to support myself. But yes, I move around a lot. I don't tend to stay in any one place for too long."

"Are you on the run or something?"

"Not for a while now."

Dennis isn't sure how to take this, but he laughs briefly like it's a joke. "Then how come?"

"Why not?"

Dennis ponders this question. "I guess I don't know. I've always been in New Jersey, my whole life. I can't really imagine going anywhere else. I mean, I couldn't if I wanted to. I don't have any money." He chuckles, though there isn't much humour in it. "But you like doing that? Just moving around, going job to job, never really having a home?"

Tom feels like there's a deeper meaning behind Dennis's questions, but he doesn't probe it right now. Dennis is building to something, he can feel it. Maybe telling the story he didn't feel like he could share earlier. "I'm not sure I've ever known anything else. I joined the Army straight out of high school, and I feel like I've been on the move ever since."

"The Army – oh man, I could tell," Dennis says. "I thought so. You've got that look about you. I figured you must've done something like that once upon a time – either military or police."

"I look like a cop?"

"No, it's just the way you carry yourself. The way you handled those three guys." Dennis pauses for a long moment before he continues, like he's wrestling with something. "I didn't mean any offense when I asked if you were a vagrant. You don't look like a beggar or anything, and I don't think there's anything wrong with that. I...I used to beg. I had to. That's how I got by."

Give a person long enough, and they'll tell you everything about themselves. People like to talk, even the guarded ones. If they can find out enough about you, they'll soon tell you everything about them. Tom guides him gently. "You were homeless?"

"Kind of," Dennis says, chewing his lip, deliberating how much he wants to share. "I mean, there were places I could stay. Friends who would let me couch surf for a few nights. And there were shelters. But...ah, man. I probably shouldn't tell you this."

"That's up to you," Tom says.

Dennis takes a deep breath then blows it out, his shoulders sagging, his body caving in on itself a little. "If I tell you this...will you promise not to tell anyone else on the site?" He looks at Tom, and his eyes are glistening and earnest.

"I promise," Tom says.

"I, uh, I was an addict. For a long time. I was hooked on crack, but really I'd take anything I could get my hands on. I even tried heroin a couple of times, though that was harder to get hold of. But crack was my lady. Man, a good day for me was if I could just spend the whole twenty-four hours smoking up, then passing out on whatever was passing for a mattress back then." His face twists as he recalls, and he shudders. "There's times...there's times when I just want to go back to that, you know? I just want to find a hovel to curl up in and smoke all my problems away and let the world go by in a blur. And then there's other times, like right now – the majority of the time now, thankfully – that I look back and I can't believe that I used to live like that. And I just feel so...so *dirty*. So ashamed."

Tom listens without judgement. "For how long?"

Dennis blows air again, casting his mind back. "Twelve years, I guess. But I'm clean now. I don't even touch alcohol or cigarettes. Too much risk, man. I know what I'm like, and it's a slippery slope. I'm totally Straight Edge, and I have been for two years. It's hard sometimes – *really* fucking hard – but I don't want to go back to that."

"Twelve years," Tom repeats, subtracting in his head. "And you've been clean for two. You started when you were ten?"

"Around then, yeah." Dennis runs a hand over his mouth. He looks to the ground below, at the other men on their lunch break. "It was when I was in the home. This one kid – he was a few years older than me – he got hold of some and snuck it inside, let a couple of us try it with him. After that, for a long time, I didn't think there was any going back after that. Dead by thirty, I always thought."

"The home?" Tom says.

"Yeah – the orphanage."

"I'm sorry to hear that."

"My dad died before I was born. Brain aneurysm while he was out riding his bike. Total freak thing. And then my mom died when I was eight. Turned out she had a heart defect. Never even knew. Her whole life, she was a ticking time bomb. Doctors checked me out to see if I had it too, but I got the all-clear." Dennis rolls his eyes.

"My mom died when I was nine," Tom says.

Dennis looks at him. "What got her?"

"Cervical cancer."

"Man, that's rough. I'm sorry."

"So you were on your own after that?"

"Yeah," Dennis says. "No other family. I belonged to the state, right up until I was eighteen, then they shook my hand and sent me on my way."

"They never knew about the crack?"

"Maybe they did, but they never said anything. They weren't paid enough to deal with the kind of shit we were doing."

They sit in silence for a moment, the story hanging between them. Dennis looks like he already regrets sharing it.

"Why'd you get clean?" Tom says.

"I'd known for a while there were only two ways out," Dennis says. "You either get clean, or you die. I'd seen too many of my friends die. Too many girlfriends, too. I wasn't gonna be another one." His face darkens and he momentarily trails off, memories coming back to him, overloading him. "I wasn't gonna be just a statistic. I wanted to do something with my life. I wanted to make something of myself. So I went to rehab, I got clean, and the counsellors and the nurses – they could see I was taking it serious. I *wanted* to be there – I'd checked in of my own accord. I hadn't been forced. And I was putting in the *work,* man. It ain't easy to quit something you've loved for twelve years. But anyway, they could see I was serious, and they were serious in turn. They helped me out as best they could. They got me onto courses and shit. And that's how I got here. A friend of a friend of a friend of one of the counsellors knows Neal, and he put in a good word for me, and here I am."

"Does Neal know all of this?"

"I asked them to keep it quiet," Dennis says. "I think maybe this friend of a friend of a friend could guess – I mean, when a counsellor says they know a kid who needs a helping hand, it's probably not hard to work out, right? But if the foreman knows, he's never said anything. You're the only person I've told."

Tom looks at Dennis. An orphan ex-junkie, trying to make his way, trying to make something of himself.

Tom recognises something in him. There's a familiarity. It comes to him. He doesn't see *himself* in Dennis. He sees his brother, Anthony. After their mother's death, Tom kept moving. He kept busy. He found his own ways to cope. Anthony didn't. He couldn't. He stayed stationary, and then after Alejandra died...

And now he's in Chicago, doing God knows what.

But Anthony could have gone down this path. He could have gone down the same dark route that Dennis did. He almost did, time and again. Would he have pulled himself out of it, as Dennis has? Tom doesn't know. All Tom knows for sure is he should have been there for Anthony when he was younger, when they were both still children. He's cleaned up enough messes for him over the years, but he should have been stronger for him long before the first mess ever came along.

When he looks at Dennis, he sees a reflection of Anthony. He sees an Anthony that could have been.

"You swear you won't tell anyone?" Dennis says.

"I promised, didn't I?" Tom says.

Dennis nods. There's guarded relief on his face.

"What are you doing tonight?" Tom says. "After we finish here."

"I don't, uh, I don't have any plans," Dennis says. "Grab a TV dinner, probably. Watch a movie or something."

"The first half of that sounds depressing," Tom says. "Come with me, we'll eat together. There's a bar I know does decent food."

"A bar?"

"Don't worry, you won't drink and neither will I," Tom says. "And there's someone there I'll introduce you to. Melissa."

"Melissa. Is she your girlfriend?"

"I suppose you could say that," Tom says. "We've been dating. You'll like her."

"I don't want to put you out."

"It's not putting me out. I made the offer. And it beats a TV dinner."

Dennis laughs. "All right. Sure."

Tom starts to rise. The half-hour is up. "Great," he says. "Then I'll see you at five. I know where to find you."

Melissa Ross is a tall woman, only an inch shorter than Tom, with an Amazonian build and a mane of long red hair. Her skin is pale and her face has a light sprinkling of freckles on her cheeks and across her nose.

She's pouring drinks for regulars in The Corner Spot when Tom and Dennis walk inside. As the bar's name suggests, it's located on the corner of a block in the Iron-bound neighbourhood. The walls are wood-panelled, and behind the bar they're covered in Polaroid snapshots of the loyal regulars and some posters of local bands, as well as a couple of movie posters for *On The Waterfront* and *The Wrestler*. Melissa has told Tom that these two are the owner's favourite movies, and it helps that both are set in New Jersey.

There are booths lining the walls, and a dozen tables in the centre of the room. It's a weeknight and not too busy, with only half of each currently occupied. At the bar there are only a few men, raising their glasses to Melissa after she's poured them. Tom thinks a lot of these old guys come here to admire her as much as they come for the drinks and the companionship. One of his first nights in town, he heard a guy refer to her as 'statuesque'. Tom doesn't disagree, and so long as the men keep their hands to themselves, there isn't any problem. Not that Tom would need to get involved. Melissa doesn't need him to fight her battles. It's one of the things that first drew him to her. She's tough. She can more than capably handle herself.

Other than her physical attributes, Tom also admires her mind. They're able to talk with each other. She's an avid reader, particularly of crime fiction, and Tom has read enough of it to be able to converse with her at length about Richard Stark, Raymond Chandler, John D. MacDonald, and Don Winslow, among others. She watches a lot of movies, mostly older ones, black and white, but sometimes early Technicolor, too. Movies with Jane Russell, Gregory Peck, Rock Hudson, Marilyn Monroe, or more schlocky fare with Vincent Price. And of course, she likes music, too. They go to shows together, unsigned, unknown rock or country bands playing in dingy bars in bad neighbourhoods.

The point is, they can talk together. They don't just need to be in the bedroom to have a good time. They're compatible. Their silences are comfortable. Sometimes they go to the gym together, too, spotting each other with the heavier weights.

Melissa knows that Tom isn't staying in Newark forever. He's made it clear that his time here is temporary, though he doesn't know exactly how long it'll be. She knows too, as he does, that despite this they'll remain on good terms. Should their paths ever cross again after his departure, they'll still be friendly. Tom will always be welcome in her home, and if Tom were ever to get one it would be likewise for her.

Tom and Dennis go straight to the bar and take a seat. Melissa's face lights up when she sees Tom. She wears tight jeans that cling to her muscular thighs and accentuate her narrow waist, and a denim shirt that she's tied into a knot at the front. "I see you've made a friend," she says, tilting her chin toward Dennis.

Tom makes introductions. "Dennis is working down at the site with us," he says. "Today was his first day."

"And Tom here has been keeping you right?" Melissa says with a playful smirk.

"Uh, yeah, I guess so," Dennis says.

"What are you drinking?"

"Just a soda, please."

"Dennis is two-years clean," Tom says. "I assured him this isn't the kind of place that's going to try and change that."

"Of course," Melissa says. "Same for you, Tom?"

"Just a water for me. And we'll take a couple of cheese-burgers."

"You got it."

While Melissa takes the order through to the chef, Dennis glances around the bar. His movements, Tom has noticed, are often furtive, his shoulders hunched, as if forever concerned about who might be nearby or trying to creep up on him.

"You ever been here before?" Tom says.

Dennis turns back around. "No, I don't think so," he says. "At least, I don't remember. But I've spent most of the last decade over on Clinton Avenue and closer to there. I never really ventured out this way."

Tom knows the area. "It's only twenty minutes away."

"Yeah, when you drive. But when your one focus in life is

to get high, it might as well have been the other side of the country."

Melissa returns and brings them their drinks. "Ten minutes on the burgers," she says. She turns her attention onto Dennis, her green eyes sparkling. "How come I've never seen you around, Dennis? Are you new in town?"

He shakes his head. "Lived here all my life," he says. "I just didn't usually come by this way."

"And today was your first day on the site?"

He nods.

"How was it?"

"Yeah, it was – it was fine. It was good."

"Can I expect to see more of you?"

"I reckon you will," Tom says.

Melissa points a finger in the air in Tom's general direction while she leans closer to Dennis. "See that? That's a stamp of approval. Tom here doesn't give those out to too many people."

A woman makes her way up to the bar and Melissa goes off to serve her. Tom takes a sip of his water.

"You can get a drink if you want," Dennis says. "I'll be fine. Just don't light up a pipe in front of me and we should be okay."

Tom looks at him. Dennis is smiling nervously, and Tom sees that he was making a joke. Tom smiles back. "I'll do my best," he says. "And it shouldn't be a problem. I've managed to stay away from it this long."

"I'm serious, though – you can get a beer if you want. Don't let me stop you."

"I don't drink that much," Tom says. "Rarely, in fact. I come to bars to pick up information. That's how I found out about the job on the site. Did you meet Eddie today? He was in here and we got talking, and that's how I made the team."

"Do many of the guys from the site come in here?" Dennis says.

"I've seen most of them occupying booths at one time or another."

Dennis deliberates before he asks, "What about Bud?"

Tom takes another drink and nods. "Sure," he says. "I've seen him in here a few times, too."

Dennis looks concerned.

"Don't sweat him," Tom says. "You've got nothing to worry about from Bud or his minions."

Dennis doesn't look so sure, but soon after their burgers arrive. Melissa hangs around and talks with them some more. She has an affable manner, a friendly demeanour that quickly wins people over, sets them at ease and makes them comfortable, and before long she has Dennis smiling and laughing.

The television is on above the bar. Tom glances toward it. It's the news. The volume is too low to hear what's being said. They're out at Monmouth Beach, talking to a woman called Tessa Maberry. The banner along the bottom says she's part of a group protesting the proposed construction of a new marina out that way. Tom doesn't know if they're being successful or not. Judging from the background, where there are no workers or diggers, where the area hasn't been cordoned off, he would guess they're doing well so far.

Tom realises Melissa is trying to get his attention. He looks at her. She nods toward Dennis. "Something has him spooked," she says.

Tom looks at Dennis. He's holding onto his burger, but he's chewing his bottom lip. Tom glances back into the bar.

He sees the cause of Dennis's consternation. Bud has arrived, along with his two followers from the site, and a couple of other friends, too. Bud has seen them at the bar. He's grinning until Tom looks his way. The grin fades, but he winks and then takes a seat with his friends in a booth. Bud is the biggest of the five men. Tom knows the two from the worksite aren't anything to worry about. He doesn't know the other two men, but they look like they've come straight from work, with grease and oil slicks staining their clothes and dirt still under their fingernails. Tom guesses they're mechanics.

He turns back around. "Relax," he says to Dennis. "He's seen you. So what? I won't lie to you, he might be stupid enough to try something, but I'm right here with you. I've got your back."

"Someone you're having trouble with?" Melissa says.

Tom gives her a brief rundown of the altercation from today.

"How likely is he to try something in here?"

"I guess that's up to him," Tom says.

Bud comes to the bar to order for his table. He leans on the countertop and angles his body toward Tom and Dennis. "Sure is nice to see the both of you again," he says.

"Sure is something," Tom says.

Bud grunts.

"I hope you're behaving yourself, Bud," Melissa says.

Bud straightens and holds up his hands. "Do you believe everything your little boyfriend says, Mel? I'm a stand-up guy. You know that."

Melissa arches an eyebrow. "Do I?"

Bud chuckles gruffly and starts carrying the drinks back to his booth.

"I think I'm gonna go," Dennis says.

"You can," Tom says. "But if you do, you're always gonna be running away from Bud, and others like him."

Dennis stays where he is, looking down at his plate, deliberating.

"I'm not saying you have to make a big gesture," Tom says. "I'm not saying you have to go over there and offer to take Bud outside. Sometimes the best way to show your defiance, especially to a bully, is to do nothing at all. Just stand your ground."

Dennis looks at Tom. Slowly, he nods. He picks up what's left of his burger and he resumes eating.

Tom and Dennis remain in the bar for a couple of hours, talking with Melissa in between her serving drinks and taking food orders. During that time, Bud and his friends order more drinks, and they get louder behind them. Bud laughs, and Tom notices the way Dennis flinches when he does, as if the laughter is directed his way. And maybe it is. Tom ignores him, ignores the whole table, and he tells Dennis to do the same.

But after a while, when the group are coming up for drinks, they start coming in twos and threes, and they crowd Tom and Dennis. They nudge Dennis, knock him with their elbows and shoulders and feign ignorance, like it was all just an accident, until eventually it comes to a head and one of them spills his drink in Dennis's lap.

Tom stands. "I think that's about enough," he says.

Three of the men are close. One of the mechanics spilled the drink. The other mechanic is present, and the third man is from the worksite. The other sycophant from the worksite and Bud are still at the booth, but Bud's head rises at the sound of Tom's voice, and a gleeful smile splits his face. He starts to stand. This is what he's been waiting for. He approaches.

"I saw that," Melissa says, gesturing toward the mechanic who spilled the drink. "Get out. All of you."

Bud ignores her. He's only got eyes for Tom right now.

"Take your friends and go," Tom says. He's not intimidated by the numbers. He knows this is what Bud is counting on.

Bud is grinning. He's almost vibrating with excitement. "Now why would we wanna go and do a thing like that, Rollins? We ain't on the worksite anymore."

Tom glances around, making sure to keep Bud in view in case he tries anything. Other people in the bar are watching. The other people at the counter have backed off, giving the scene a wide berth. Bud's two coworkers flank him closest, but the mechanics are spread out, one to Tom's right and the other further away to Tom's left, closest to Dennis still. Dennis is looking back at the five men, eyes wide. It's clear he's not much of a fighter and won't be able to provide much in the way of support, not that Tom expects he'll need it. The only real threat from these five is their numbers. Individually, they don't pose him any kind of danger. They just think they do.

"I'm not gonna tell you all again," Melissa says. "Leave now, or you're looking at a ban."

Bud and his friends ignore her. Bud takes a step closer to Tom. He leans down, leans closer. "A ban would be worth it."

Tom smiles at him. "Show me what you've got."

Bud's confidence falters a little, his eyes flickering toward his friends, but he can't back down, not now. He's gotten too close. He knows what he needs to do. He takes a swing. Tom anticipates it. He blocks Bud's right with his left forearm, and drives his own right hard into Bud's chest. He doesn't aim for his face. Catching the hard bones of Bud's thick skull would risk breaking his fingers, dislocating his knuckles, fracturing his whole hand. So Tom hits him in the chest, close to his heart, and Bud's eyes bulge and his breath catches, and before he knows what's coming next, Tom places a boot into his stomach and kicks him away. Bud hits a table and goes over it, dragging it down with him.

The other four men are moving, but Tom is already moving with and against them. One of the mechanics swings at Tom with the bottle. He ducks it easily and drives a fist into the man's crotch, doubling him over. Tom rises with an uppercut that takes him off his feet. Tom spins toward one of Bud's workmates from the site. He's lunging. Tom lifts a knee into his midsection and quickly follows through with a punch down and across his jaw. It feels like he dislocates it.

Out the corner of his eye, he sees how Melissa grabs one of the mechanics from behind, the one who spilled the drink onto Dennis, and drags him over the bar. She dumps him on the ground and starts stomping.

Tom looks at the man who remains standing, Bud's other follower from the worksite. He looks at his four fallen buddies, then he looks at Tom. He turns and runs away.

Bud is pulling himself up, using the edge of the toppled table to steady himself. His head turns, watching his follower flee. He turns back to Tom.

Melissa is done with the mechanic she hauled over the bar. She drags him out, marching him toward the door. She bodily throws him out onto the street. Melissa wheels on Bud and the other two men. "Do I have to give all of you the same treatment?"

Bud stands slowly, rubbing at his chest. His eyes are

locked on Tom. "You got lucky," he says. "That was a cheap shot."

"Then take another swing," Tom says.

Bud is hesitant. He looks at his two friends on the ground, struggling to push themselves back up.

Tom takes a step forward. Bud winces and takes a step back. "Get your friends and go," Tom says. "You go anywhere near Dennis again, and next time I'm gonna see your blood."

Bud swallows. He holds up his hands as he side-steps toward his friends. He's done. He doesn't want any more trouble. He pulls them to their feet and helps them to the door. Melissa holds it open for them. "I don't wanna see any of you again for at least a couple of months," she says as they pass. She slams the door shut behind them.

She returns behind the bar and hands Dennis some napkins to dry himself with. Tom sits back down on his stool. Melissa looks at him. She wears a mischievous smile. "Have you been making more friends, Tom?"

4

The Penney Pharma offices are located in Atlantic City, an hour and a half south of Monmouth Beach. Lee Giles drives the Cadillac Escalade north, its rear and side windows blacked out. The A/C is blowing, keeping them cool against the heatwave outside. Behind him sits James Penney, the CEO of Penney Pharma, a position inherited from his father, who founded the company, after his retirement seven years ago.

James resides in Monmouth Beach with his wife, Scarlett. James is fifty-six, and his wife is younger than him at forty-two. James is a scrawny thing. He wears glasses and has thinning hair, and he never manages to fill out his suits, even when they're fitted. Lee, on the other hand, is an ex-Navy SEAL and has maintained the physique he built back in those days. He stays in shape with a healthy diet and regular trips to the gym, and he makes sure to visit the shooting range at least once a fortnight to avoid getting rusty.

After he left the SEALs, he found there wasn't much in the world for him. The government, the whole country he'd served seemed willing to forget him. Friends he'd known from back in the day had gotten into black ops security work, occasionally dabbling in mercenary work, and after a couple of years running with them, he was recommended for an opening as the personal head of security for the CEO of Penney Pharma. It pays well. It pays better than the military ever did.

Scarlett Penney is the antithesis of her husband. They're the kind of couple where people would wonder what she's doing with him, but of course, the obvious answer is the money. Scarlett would probably admit it herself.

Like Lee, she keeps herself healthy. She's got an hourglass shape that she maintains through daily laps in the indoor pool, and hours spent on the treadmill and the elliptical. Her skin always has a healthy tan from sunbathing by the beach out the back of their home, and her blonde hair is bleached naturally lighter from these same sessions.

Lee smiles to himself, thinking of Scarlett, thinking of her body, but his thoughts are interrupted by James leaning forward and asking, "Do you think there'll be more of them today?"

Lee takes a deep breath. "Could be, sir," he says. "Seems like there's at least one or two more every day."

"But it's got to end eventually, right? They've got to give up and go home?"

Lee doesn't answer. He understands James's nervousness. He needs to get the marina built, and he needs it built soon. His shareholders and board of directors are all breathing down his neck. They lost their hook-up south of the border after the government started clamping down on the cartels manufacturing and sneaking opioids into the country. Penney Pharma has taken a financial hit since then. They need it fixed. They need a new hook-up to make Sentit B the way it's supposed to be. The marina was supposed to solve all of these problems.

And now, thanks to the activists, they have a new set of problems.

James is a nervous man, and rightfully so. He's not a strong man. He's not a born leader. He inherited his position, and it's obvious to anyone who knows him. He needs people like his wife close by, people who can tell him what it is he's supposed to be doing.

They reach Monmouth Beach and Lee slows as they approach the house. Sure enough, the protestors are outside, and they recognise the Cadillac. They start to flood into the road, about two dozen of them, waving their signs and their banners. Lee gets on his radio. "We're approaching," he says. "Clear this mess."

His men hurry out from the grounds of the Penney mansion and start roughly manhandling the protestors, grabbing them and throwing them aside, clearing them from the road until Lee is able to get through and pull onto the long driveway, his men following him in and closing the gate behind them. Lee parks up close to the house and gets back on the radio. "I expect you all to keep a closer eye on things going forward," he says. "They shouldn't have been able to block us like that."

Assorted apologies come through the radio, but Lee ignores them. He accompanies James into the house.

The mansion is beachfront property. The exterior is a cooling white, and the inside is decorated Mediterranean style. The Penneys put a basement in, Scarlett wanting a pool where she could swim her daily laps in peace away from other people that might be on the beach. The gym is down there, too. The house has five bedrooms, and there's a guesthouse out back. This is where Lee lives. At night he leaves his windows open just a crack and falls asleep to the sound of the lapping waves.

Scarlett is waiting for them in the kitchen, seated at the granite island, a glass of red wine in front of her. She wears a low-cut red dress with a high hem, ostensibly for the heat, but Lee reckons it's because she knew he was coming. He smiles to himself at this, and he has to stop his smile from getting too wide when he looks upon her. Her tanned shoulders are bare and muscular, her long blonde locks cascading over them. She comes around the island when they enter the kitchen. Her legs are long and taut, and Lee can see the muscles rippling in her thighs when she moves. She leans back against the counter, one bare foot crossed over the other. She looks James up and down.

"You look like you've had a bad day," she says. "You look like shit." She spares Lee a brief glance, a nod, and an almost disinterested, "Giles."

"Mrs. Penney," Lee says.

James goes to her, arms wide, but Scarlett subtly slips away, moving back around the island and to her glass of wine. She takes a sip. "Well?" she says.

James runs a hand down his mouth. He blows air. "It's just, it's this Maberry woman," he says. "First the cartels, then the FDA, and now *her*. It's all mounting up."

Scarlett doesn't look at him. She circles a finger atop the island. She waits for him to continue.

James takes a seat opposite her. He doesn't send Lee away. "She's coming at us with lawsuits now," he says, his tone almost pleading, as if begging with Scarlett will somehow get Tessa Maberry to back off. "She's trying to get an injunction to stop the building of the marina completely."

"Oh?" Scarlett says, sounding bored, still not looking up at her husband.

"They're saying it would disrupt the habits of local wildlife," James says. "Sealife, too."

Scarlett doesn't speak for a long time. She takes another drink. Her face is impassive, unreadable. It's impossible to know what she's thinking.

James keeps talking. He wants her input. He wants her to tell him what he should do. "If we don't build this marina," he says, "and if we don't start it soon, we could lose everything. Our profits are already falling. If we're not careful, the FDA are going to start getting more suspicious than they already are. I'm losing sleep over this. I can barely eat, and I've always got this horrible acid reflux that won't go away."

When Scarlett finally looks up and speaks, it isn't to James. It's to Lee. "Giles, you've looked into this woman, haven't you?"

"Yes, ma'am," Lee says.

"Remind me about her."

"Tessa Maberry," Lee says. "African-American. Twenty-six years old. She's from here in Jersey – grew up in Trenton and currently lives in Newark. She started her career as an activist while attending Ramapo College. And she's effective. Has a history of success on her various environmental ventures – she's prevented the building of factories, condos, the list goes on. She's also responsible for the investigation into at least two high-ranking government officials for taking bribes."

"And how's she hitting us currently?"

"Every angle," Lee says. "Obviously there's the protestors

out front, but there's also the group down the road where the building of the marina is proposed. She's organised them so that there's always at least half a dozen people present, preventing any ground-breaking from occurring. And now she's coming at Penney Pharma with various court cases, which will no doubt tangle the company up in years' worth of litigation, further prolonging the building of the marina."

"And bankrupting us in the process," James adds quietly, bitterly.

Scarlett ignores him. "And I heard something recently about a private detective. Is that correct?"

Lee smirks. She would have heard about the private detective from James. "That's correct, ma'am. She hired him to look into Penney Pharma. To look into the production of Sentit B, particularly. If he'd found out too much, that could have been disastrous for us."

"But in that case you would have silenced him, isn't that right?"

"Of course. Luckily, it didn't come to that. My men were able to apprehend him and nip that problem in the bud. I scared him off personally."

There's the faint flicker of a smile at the corner of Scarlett's mouth, but she suppresses it for now. She looks back to her husband. "There," she says. "We're all up to date. Now what are we going to do about it?"

James starts stammering. He can't answer. He looks back at Lee.

"If Mrs. Penney has any ideas, I'd be open to hearing them," Lee says, knowing this is exactly what she wants to hear.

She nods once, demurely, and then she speaks. "It seems to me that all of our problems revolve around this one woman – Tessa Maberry. The rest of them – the group in front of our home, the group at the marina site – they're not really a concern. A bunch of unwashed hippies doing as they're told, nothing more. *Tessa* is the brains. They don't have any organisational skills. They need *her* for that."

James is listening closely. He tilts his head when she pauses. "So...so what are you suggesting?"

Scarlett sighs, like she's disappointed in him. "If we get rid of the head, we get rid of the rest of them. The marina can be constructed. Our biggest problem right now isn't the protestors, or the cartels, or the FDA, or even the potential court cases. It's Tessa Maberry. If she's gone, everything else falls into place."

"Get *rid* of her?" James says.

Scarlett sighs again. She looks pointedly at Lee before she turns back to her husband. "Perhaps you should leave us," she says.

James looks back over his shoulder toward Lee, as if scared of what his wife means.

"I'm not so sure you have the stomach for this conversation," Scarlett says.

James is pale. He swallows. But he nods. Slowly, he rises to his feet and steps away. He shuffles where he stands for a moment, not looking at either of them. "I'll...I'll be in my office."

James leaves them. Scarlett motions to the seat opposite. "Take a seat, Lee," she says. "And let's work out how we're going to resolve this little problem."

5

The heatwave has broken. The days are still bright, but thankfully cooler.

It's been a few weeks since Tom beat down Bud and his friends at The Corner Spot. Bud has been on his best behaviour since then. He and the other two have given Tom a wide berth on the worksite. They stay as far away from him as possible. They stay away from Dennis, too. No one hassles him.

Tom has taken Dennis under his wing. They don't hang out every night, but they spend a lot of time together. Every day on the site, they have lunch together. A couple of weekends, they've gone out on a rented boat and fished. Melissa drives the boat. Her father was a fisherman and he'd take her out when she was younger. As she got older, he showed her how to pilot. He'd let her drive him out while he sorted through the nets with his crew.

Tonight, after work, Tom and Dennis are not going to the bar. They're not going out on a boat. They're not going to hang out in either Tom or Dennis's apartment. Instead, they're going to Melissa's place. She doesn't live far from The Corner Spot.

Dennis is nervous. He's fine around Melissa, but tonight there's going to be someone new. Someone Melissa wants to introduce him to.

"I don't think I've ever been on a date sober," he says as Tom drives them over.

They went home after their shifts. They've showered and changed their clothes. Tom has picked him up in his Toyota en route. "Then don't think of it as a date," he says. "Just be your usual charming self."

"Am I that charming?"

"Some people find that deer-in-the-headlights look endearing."

"Should I start scowling like you do?"

"I scowl very rarely."

"You scowl all the way across the worksite."

"I'm lifting heavy things. And I don't want anyone to talk to me."

"All right, maybe it's more of a frown."

"My dad used to always say he could never tell what I was thinking because I was always frowning."

Dennis laughs. "So some things never change."

Tom shoots him a side-eye.

"What's Stef like?" Dennis says.

"I've only met her a few times," Tom says. "But she seems nice. She's about a year older than you."

"How does Melissa know her?"

"Stef worked in the bar while she was in college. They've kept in touch."

"Melissa knows a lot of people."

"I guess that's what happens when you're friendly and

personable." Tom grins. Dennis laughs.

They reach Melissa's building and head inside. Stef Awad is already there when they arrive. She's short, with long dark hair, and she stands when they enter. She embraces Tom and then shakes Dennis's hand.

"I, uh, I'm sorry I didn't bring anything," Dennis says, looking from Stef to Melissa. "I feel like I should've brought something, but I wasn't sure what."

"Relax, Dennis. We don't need anything," Melissa says. "I'm well stocked."

Dennis scratches the back of his neck. "I thought about bringing a bottle of wine, but, uh, I don't drink and, uh, I wasn't sure what kind was good."

"Oh, you don't drink?" Stef says. "Neither do I."

This statement seems to put Dennis at ease. Tom notices some of the tension leave his shoulders. He actually smiles. "Oh really?"

"Yeah – well, I mean, I'm Muslim, so I never have."

"Yeah? That's really interesting. But I thought Tom said you and Melissa worked together at the bar?"

"Would you drink at your workplace?" She raises her eyebrows playfully.

"I suppose I wouldn't. What do you do now?"

"I'm a vet."

"Oh wow. That's really interesting too."

"Tom," Melissa says. "Do you want to come help me in the kitchen?"

Tom follows her through, leaving Dennis and Stef alone to become better acquainted. Hidden in the kitchen, Melissa looks pleased with herself.

"They're hitting it off," she says. "I knew they would. You know, this is my first time playing matchmaker. I think I'm pretty good at it."

"Don't get carried away," Tom says. He inspects the food. Melissa is making spaghetti.

"Stef is vegetarian so I'm doing the sauce with mushrooms," she says. "It's nearly ready. And hey, I'm serious. Befriend some other single guys on the site. I'll go through my contacts, get them hooked up."

Tom looks at her. She laughs and nudges him with her shoulder.

Tom and Melissa take the food through when it's done cooking and they find Dennis and Stef on the sofa together, focussed intently on one another and locked in conversation. They break it off to come and eat at the table with Tom and Melissa. It's clear that they're getting along. They're enjoying talking to each other.

The evening rolls on. There's laughter and storytelling, until they realise it's gotten late. Stef checks the time. It's after eleven. "Oh, man," she says. "Time flies when you're having fun, huh? I better go. I have work tomorrow."

"I'll call you a taxi," Melissa says.

Stef waves off the offer. "No, that's okay. I'll walk. It's not far, and I'll enjoy the fresh air."

Tom can see how Dennis deliberates, how he's not ready for the night to end just yet. They've made a connection. He doesn't want to lose that so soon. Briefly, his eyes settle on Tom. Tom tilts his head toward Stef, encouraging him to just say whatever he's thinking.

Dennis steels himself. Tom sees how he sets his jaw and balls his fists as he turns to Stef and says, "I should get going, too. I can walk you back, if you'd like?"

"Didn't Tom drive you here?" Stef says.

"Yeah, but I'd like the exercise, too. The fresh air. And I

can always catch a bus or call an Uber if I don't feel like walking *all* the way back to my place."

Stef smiles at him, showing off her perfect white teeth. "Okay," she says. "That would be nice."

They say their goodbyes and Stef and Dennis leave together. When they're gone, after Melissa has locked the door behind them, she spins toward Tom. She points her thumb back over her shoulder. "I did that," she says.

"Yes, you did," Tom says. "Congratulations. Don't let it all go to your head."

"It's too late," she says, stepping closer and draping her arms around his shoulders, leaning her face in close to his. "I'm reliving my childhood fantasies of when I'd read *Emma* and watch *Clueless*. I'm playing the matchmaker." She kisses him lightly and then turns her head, looking around the apartment without letting go of him. "Well, the kids are gone and it looks like we have the place to ourselves. And I don't see you in any hurry to leave."

"I don't see you trying to get rid of me."

She laughs, then she kisses him again, longer this time. Tom picks her up, and she wraps her strong thighs around him. He carries her through to the bedroom.

6

L ee has had to be patient.

He's had to wait for Tessa Maberry to be alone. He's had to wait for her to return to her apartment in Newark. He'll hand it to her – she doesn't expect everyone else to do the dirty work for her. She doesn't organise and then disappear. No, she's down there on the ground level, getting her hands grimy with the rest of the protesters. She's slept in tents and on hard ground with no cover at all. She's led the chants. She's held hands in the blockade. The only time she left was to talk with the lawyers and the media.

All to say, she remained in places where Lee and his men couldn't get to her. He told a couple of his guys to stay in Newark and watch her building. They've told him they haven't seen anyone else come or go. She lives alone.

This, at least, is good news. And what makes that good news better is that now, finally, after three weeks, she's finally returned to that apartment in Newark where she lives alone.

"Looks like she's finally taking some time for herself," Lee says to Graham and Rich. They've accompanied him from Monmouth Beach. These are the men he trusts to help him silence Tessa Maberry once and for all.

"Probably came back for a shower and a soft bed," Graham says. He's in the front, behind the steering wheel. They're parked, watching the building. Rich is in the passenger seat beside him and Lee sits behind. They came here in a nondescript black Ford that they bought cheap from a scrapyard a couple of states away. Lee has sent the two guys he had watching the building home. They've been here a while. They've earned the break.

"Even a hippy's gotta have a shower sometime," Rich says.

"She looked pretty clean to me," Graham says.

"Gotta look good for the cameras," Rich says. "God knows she's been preening in front of enough of them."

"Well, y'know, she looks good enough for the cameras."

"Oh yeah? You got a bit of a thing for the enemy, Graham?"

"I wouldn't say that. I'm just saying that I wouldn't turn my nose up, y'know?"

Rich shakes his head, purposefully turning his nose up. "No, man. Black chicks don't do it for me."

Graham laughs. "You don't know what you're missing, man. Just imagine those dreadlocks she's got, bouncing on your face while she's on top of you."

"Hippies don't do it for me, neither."

Graham laughs again.

Lee lets them talk. He's not listening. He's watching the building. Watching the lights on the sixth floor where Tessa's apartment is. He hasn't seen her pass by the windows, but he knows she's in there. He studies the rest of the building. The entrance is at the front, opposite where they're parked, and at the back is a fire exit. If the fire exit is opened it sets off an alarm. There's also a fire escape at the rear of the building. Lee and Rich are going to be the ones heading inside. Lee intends to use the fire escape to exit the apartment.

Soon, they'll move in. It's already quiet out here. It's late. They're getting close to midnight. There's a few other lights on in the building, but not many.

And then, as if he's willed it, Tessa's lights go off. "All right, look alive," he says. "Lights out. Focus up and watch the front, make sure she isn't about to leave. So long as we don't see her go, we give her twenty minutes, then we head inside."

Graham and Rich fall instantly silent at his command. They're all business now. They watch the front of the building as instructed.

Lee's team has a mix of backgrounds. Graham is ex-Army and Rich was in the Air Force. Not all of his people are ex-military. He has former security guards, some ex-cops, even an ex-boxer and a couple of MMA fighters. All people looking to make more money than they were earning in their past professions. Lee can understand that motivation. It's why he's here, after all. Working for Penney Pharma, working directly for James Penney, pays very well indeed.

Lee has trained them all up to his level. As close as he can get them, anyway. He's the only ex-Navy SEAL on the payroll, and he's made it clear what he expects from each of his men. He's not been afraid to learn from *them*, either. He's held training sessions where he's let the ex-cops take the lead, giving instructions on tactical driving and other key skills. He's had the fighters show off close-combat techniques. If one of the ex-soldiers has turned out to be a better shot than Lee himself, he's had the sharpshooter bring the others up to speed. Lee's men are well-rounded. He expects them to be sharp. The only issue is, they haven't had many occasions to put these lessons to the test. It's an easy job for the most part. That's why Lee pushes them so hard. He doesn't want them to get soft and complacent.

The twenty minutes pass. The lights remain off. Tessa has not attempted to leave the building.

"All right, if she went to bed, then she should be sleeping by now," Lee says. No more lights have come on in her apartment. It's in darkness. He's confident it's bedtime. He pats Rich on the shoulder. "Let's go. Graham, you get into position. Earpieces in, radios on. You both know the frequency."

Lee and Rich get out of the car and head toward the building. A moment later, they hear Graham start the engine behind them and slowly move the car around to the rear.

The door into the building is electronically locked. The inhabitants use key fobs to get inside. Lee and Rich have come prepared. Rich pulls a screwdriver and a keypad override from his pocket. He unscrews the keypad cover and then hooks up the override. He gets the door open. Lee holds it and waits for Rich to put the pad back into place.

They go up to the sixth floor on foot, making sure the stairwell and hallways are clear on their way. They are. The building is quiet. They get to Tessa's door without any issues. There are no security cameras inside, so they don't need to cover their faces. They knew this in advance, too. Lee's men have done their research.

The doors inside the building, leading into the apartments, are locked with regular keys. Lee has brought a kit. He drops to a knee and picks Tessa's lock while Rich keeps watch. Lee hears the satisfying click that lets him know the door is now unlocked. He shuffles back so Rich can take point. Rich already has his Glock in hand. Lee puts the kit away and pulls out his own. He follows Rich into the apartment. They move fast, quickly closing the door behind them to prevent the light from the hall spilling inside.

They know the layout of the apartment. They've seen the blueprints. It's not a big apartment. It won't take them long to reach Tessa. There's a small hallway, and there'll be a door on the right leading to the bathroom. Beyond the door at the end of the hall, the main part of the apartment is all open plan. It's a bedroom-living room-kitchen combo. To their right will be the kitchen area, which means that Tessa's bed will be in the area to the left. Once they get her subdued, they can take their pick of how to do this. They've considered hanging her, making it look like a suicide, but Lee doesn't think that would be believable. She's too active, too visible, too well known for it to be conceivable that she would suddenly up and end it all. So they need to be careful with the direction they take. They've considered force-feeding her pills and making it look like an accidental overdose, but again they can't be sure of her history with drugs. What Lee is thinking is he'll inflict some head trauma, then dump her body in the bathtub, shower running, and make it look like she's slipped and fell. A perfect crime. The scene will speak for itself.

They make their way to the door, guns held low and ready. But then, suddenly, they hear something. A repetitive, grating buzz, like an alarm clock. They both freeze. It's hard to tell where it's coming from. Rich looks back at Lee. Lee looks around the small hallway, searching for its source. He thinks it might be on the other side of the door, where Tessa is. He looks down at Rich's legs. He has to squint. He pulls a small flashlight from his pocket and shines it down, thinking at this point, with the mystery noise, a bit of light won't make much more difference.

He spots the cause. There's a tripwire, too thin to see in the dark. Rich's left shin is pressed against it, setting it off. Lee pulls him back. The alarm stops.

In the sudden stillness, they can hear movement on the other side of the door, within the main room. Lee keeps the flashlight on. He pushes Rich aside and bursts through the door and into the room. He holds his Glock up, prepared for what he might find. All that blasts him in the face is a cool gust of air. He quickly finds where it's coming from.

Tessa is at the window. She's thrown it open. She's in her pyjamas, barefoot, but she's fleeing out onto the fire escape. She glances back briefly and sees Lee, but she doesn't hang around. She set the tripwire, rigged it up to an alarm. Lee wonders if the windows are similarly covered. If the whole apartment is rigged. She's right to be paranoid. She clearly has her escape route plotted out.

She clears the window. Lee doesn't panic. He gets straight onto the radio. "Graham, she got the drop on us," he says. "She's on the fire escape. She's coming your way. Be ready for her."

7

The conversation has continued to flow between Dennis and Stef. The journey to her building is not a long walk – just twenty minutes from Melissa's. They draw it out, despite the late hour, walking as slow as they're able. The night is clear and cool, and they barely pass anyone else along the route.

"I have to make a confession," Stef says.

Dennis feels his heart beating a little faster, worrying about what she might be about to say. He tries to diffuse his sudden alarm, cracking a joke. "You're secretly a serial killer?"

He's glad when she laughs. It makes him feel better. "It's not as serious a confession as that."

"That's a relief. Okay, I feel like I could handle anything now."

"Well, I just wanted to say that when Melissa invited me tonight, I was concerned about the kind of guy she was so insistent I meet. But she said Tom vouched for you, and that was promising."

"I'm glad I have Tom's stamp of approval, at least."

"You have mine now, too," she says, looking straight at him, a small, sweet smile playing on her lips.

"I'm – I'm glad to hear that," Dennis manages to say, feeling tongue-tied.

"Don't get nervous," she says playfully. "You've been doing so well so far."

Dennis laughs. "Okay, well, I guess I have the same confession to make. I was nervous about coming along, but Melissa isn't really someone you can say no to."

"Try working with her," Stef says. "And plus, when I worked there, I answered to her. Imagine having her as your manager." They laugh together. "I'm joking, I'm joking. I love Melissa, really. She's very sweet. She's like the big sister I never had."

They pause on a street corner, and Stef suddenly looks disappointed. She nods toward the building opposite. "This is me," she says.

Dennis understands her disappointment. They cross the road, walking slower than they have up to this point. Dennis can feel that Stef is waiting for him to say something. Waiting for him to take the lead, perhaps. "Would you like to meet up again sometime?" he says, getting the words out fast before he can overthink them. "Maybe...maybe just the two of us next time."

"That sounds nice," Stef says. "I'd like that." When she smiles at him, Dennis feels a lightness in his chest. Feels butterflies in his stomach. He smiles back, always. It's contagious. "Just the two of us, without the chaperones. Let me get your number and we can firm these plans up."

Dennis is glad he's able to pull out his cell phone without fumbling it. They exchange numbers.

"Do you have far to go?" Stef says, opening the door to her building.

"No, not really," Dennis says.

"Do you think you'll call a taxi, or an Uber?"

"I'll see how I feel after a few blocks. Right now, I'm enjoying the night."

They say their goodbyes and Stef heads inside. Dennis takes a deep breath after she's gone, feeling buoyed, then he turns and begins his walk home. The way he feels right now, he might walk all the way back, no matter how long it might take.

As he nears the end of a block, out the corner of his eye he sees a quick dash of movement coming from an alleyway to his left, from down the side of another apartment building. The suddenness gives him a jolt, makes his heart beat a little faster. He pauses and takes a step back, waiting to see what happens next. He thinks it could've just been a cat, or a dog, but it was too big to be either. More like a person. It could just be someone messing around, but it could also be someone dangerous. Dennis has been around enough junkies to know when to give them a wide berth.

But, watching, he sees that it's a woman, and he doesn't think she's tweaking, despite being barefoot and in her pyjamas. She's too clean. She's running too straight. She's not babbling incoherently. She doesn't look wild – she looks scared. Something about her, as she passes under a street-lamp and he catches a glimpse of her face, looks familiar.

Before he can place this familiarity, he hears an engine roar, and the screeching of tyres, and a car bursts out from the same alleyway where the woman first appeared. Dennis watches, frozen to the spot, as the car plows straight into her.

Dennis feels his breath catch in his throat. His eyes won't

blink. The moment has a sense of unreality, like it's something he's watching on a television.

The car mows her down. It drives over her. Dennis hears the rattle and thud of her body beneath the wheels. It's a sound he'll never forget. The car veers to the left, away from where Dennis is, away from the body, leaving her lying in the street.

Dennis thinks the car is driving away. A hit and run. He looks around. There's no one else nearby. No one has seen. Before he knows it, his legs are carrying him toward the fallen woman. As he gets closer, he sees that the car has stopped in the middle of the road up ahead, its brake lights glowing. And, from the same alleyway where the woman first fled, two figures appear. Dennis is about to call to them, to ask for help, to tell them what's happened, but he stops himself. Something about the men silences him. As they turn toward him, he realises what he saw, what prevented him from calling to them. They're both armed.

Both men spot Dennis at the same time. They pause, just briefly, scanning the rest of the area. Then, they start coming for Dennis. He notices how the man in the lead tries to conceal his gun.

"Hey – wait there, buddy," the lead man says.

Dennis looks to the woman on the ground. She's lying very still. One arm is clearly broken, and one leg is pointing the wrong way, but she's not screaming. She's not in pain. Dennis doesn't think she's breathing. There's nothing he can do for her. She's already dead. He looks back up at the two men coming his way, and sees how the car that killed the woman has its reverse lights on now.

He turns and runs.

"*Hey!*"

Dennis braces himself for a gunshot to ring out behind him, but none comes. He hears footsteps pounding the ground, following. It's hard to tell if it's both men or just one of them. Dennis doesn't look back to check. He runs faster than he ever has in his life, turning corners and going down alleyways, launching himself over chain-link fences and trash cans until he can't hear the man in pursuit anymore.

Now he looks back, and he sees no one behind him. His chest feels tight, constricting, and he's struggling to breathe. He turns down another alleyway and throws himself behind a dumpster, squatting low to the ground and peering down the back of it, through the gap between it and the building. He watches the opening of the alleyway, breathing hard, silently praying that he doesn't see anyone, that he's lost them and they've given up on finding him.

He sees the lead man's face in his head. Sees the cold look in his eyes as he approached Dennis, calling for him to stop. Dennis has no doubt that he was going to be their next victim, after the woman. The woman he's sure he recognised. He wishes he could remember why she looked so familiar to him, but he can't.

He didn't recognise the man, that's for certain. A complete stranger to him. Did the woman they killed know who he was? Probably. Why else would they kill her? Dennis didn't recognise either of the men on foot. He's never seen them before. He never saw the driver, but he wishes he had. He wishes he had because he needs to know who all of them are. He needs to remember their faces. They've run a young woman down in cold blood, killed her in the middle of the street, so brazen, and he's the only person who knows. They can't get away with this.

Then, he hears footsteps. They're coming fast, running.

They come from the direction of the alleyway's opening. A short moment later, the lead man comes into view. He pauses and looks around. Dennis notices how he's not breathing hard, how his face isn't twisted with exertion. This run was nothing to him. Dennis was only able to get away because his spike of adrenaline gave him a boost, added an urgency to his limbs that carried him to freedom.

Except he's not clear yet. He holds his breath and watches the man, hoping he doesn't investigate further.

The man's head turns on a swivel, looking around. He looks into the alleyway, eyes scanning, tilting his head this way and that. Dennis covers his mouth with his hand to prevent any unbidden sounds from escaping him.

The man raises something to his lips. To Dennis, it looks like he's speaking into his right cuff. His voice is low. Dennis can't hear what he's saying. He lowers the arm and looks around again, his eyes narrowed. Then, he turns and starts running back the way he came. Dennis hears his footsteps disappear. The way is clear.

Dennis can't stand. His legs won't let him. He's fine with that right now. He stays right where he is.

8

Next morning at the construction site, the first thing Tom notices is that there's no sign of Dennis. Tom thinks to himself that perhaps things last night went *very* well between him and Stef after he walked her home. He doesn't think on it too hard and he gets to work. After a couple of hours, however, the foreman comes to see him.

"Rollins!" Neal calls loudly to be heard over the sound of Tom breaking blocks of concrete with a sledgehammer.

Tom turns at the sound of his name. He balances the sledgehammer on its head and leans against it.

"You're close with Dennis, right?" Neal says.

Tom nods.

"You know where he is today?"

Tom doesn't tell him everything he knows. Instead, he asks, "He hasn't called in sick?"

The foreman shakes his head. "Hasn't called, hasn't messaged, nothing. Just seems unlike him, y'know? Whole time he's been here, never heard a peep out of him and he's been so eager to please. He's a good worker, too. I like the kid." He looks around the site as if expecting Dennis to suddenly appear. His eyes settle back on Tom. "Just wondering if you'd heard from him."

"No, I haven't," Tom says, his brow furrowing, wondering if he should be concerned. "I'll call him, let you know if I get through."

"You do that," Neal says. "I hope it's nothing serious. Actually, no, scratch that. I hope it *is* something serious, like a stomach bug or something and he ain't been able to get to the phone for sitting on the toilet. Otherwise..."

Neal doesn't need to finish his thought. Tom understands. Three strikes and you're out. Not calling in sick is strike one. The foreman walks away.

But Tom has deeper concerns than a sickness, concerns that he isn't going to share with anyone. He worries Dennis has relapsed. He just saw him last night, just a handful of hours ago, but he knows that anything can happen in a short period of time.

Tom leaves the sledgehammer behind and goes to a private corner to call Dennis, away from prying ears. There's no answer. It doesn't even ring. Dennis's phone is either off, or the battery has died. Tom sends him a message, telling Dennis to call him back as soon as he sees it.

Next, he calls Melissa. "Tom," she says, answering, her voice bright, still riding high on last night's success. "This is a pleasant surprise. You don't usually call me from work."

"I know this is a long shot, but have you heard from Dennis?"

"From Dennis?" From her reaction, Tom can already tell that she hasn't. "No – why, is something wrong?"

"He hasn't turned up to work today. Hasn't called in

either. I've tried to contact him but I can't get through. Phone is off or something. Have you spoken to Stef?"

"Yeah, I've heard from her."

"What did she say?"

"Just that they'd had a good time and they'd made plans to meet up again."

"So he's not with her."

"No, she's at work. Tom, what are you thinking?"

"Nothing, right now."

"But you're worried?"

"Yeah."

"Concerned he might have slipped up?"

"It's a possibility."

"But it doesn't make any sense. He's been doing so well. He really got along with Stef. We could both see they liked each other."

"Sometimes none of these things matter. People relapse. It happens all the time, for the smallest of reasons."

"What are you going to do?"

"I'm gonna give him until the end of the work day to get in touch with me, and then I'm gonna go look for him."

"Where?"

"I'll start at his apartment and I'll take it from there. Hopefully it's nothing major, he's just ill. But then I'll speak to every drug dealer and visit every crack den in this city if I have to."

"But it can't be that, right? He seemed so serious about his sobriety. In the bar he would never even *look* at the drinks. I could see he wasn't tempted. He's been doing so well. And then last night, he really hit it off with Stef. He's got so much going for him right now, surely he wouldn't throw it all away like this."

"We'll find out," Tom says. "Don't say anything to Stef."

"I won't," Melissa says. "Keep me updated."

Tom returns to work. It's a long day. He tries not to keep checking his phone. Whenever he does, the screen is blank. Dennis hasn't responded to his message or tried to call him back.

When five o'clock finally arrives, Tom goes straight to his car and drives over to Dennis's building. Someone is coming out as he arrives, and they recognise Tom from visiting Dennis so they hold the door for him. Tom nods his thanks then marches inside and hurries up to Dennis's floor, taking the steps two at a time. He pounds on Dennis's door with the side of his fist. There's no answer. Tom tries the handle. It's locked. It'll be easy enough to pick, but Tom hasn't brought any tools with him and he doesn't have the time to waste. He takes a step back, making sure the corridor is clear, then prepares to raise his boot and kick the door open.

He stops himself and takes a deep breath. He calms. He's getting ahead of himself. The long day and the lack of response has him tightly wound. He's concerned about Dennis, but he's about to get carried away. Before he kicks the door down, he needs to check the possibility that Dennis is inside.

He steps closer and knocks again, lighter this time. "Dennis," he calls, his mouth close to the door. "Are you in there?"

There's a brief pause, a hesitation, and then Dennis calls back, "Tom?"

Tom feels relieved, but at the same time angry. He hides the anger from his voice. "Yeah, Dennis, it's me. Let me in."

"Are – are you alone?"

Tom frowns at this. "Yeah, I'm alone."

"Okay, give me a second."

As Dennis approaches the door, Tom thinks about how he sounds. He doesn't sound high, or like he's coming down. His speech isn't slurred. He seems alert. He sounds like himself. It doesn't take him long to get to the door and unlock it. He opens it just enough for Tom to step through, Dennis waving him inside.

Tom enters. The apartment is in darkness. The curtains are all drawn tight. The television is off. Everything is off.

Dennis pokes his head out of the open door, looks left and right down the corridor, then snatches his head back inside and relocks the door.

"What's going on?" Tom says. He notices that Dennis is still wearing the same clothes as last night. His hair is wild and he looks dishevelled, as if he hasn't slept.

"Did anyone follow you inside?" Dennis says.

"Follow me?" Tom says. "No." He knows no one didn't. He wasn't expecting to be followed, but he always checks for these things.

"Did you see anyone outside? Anyone, like, I dunno, watching the building or something?"

"No, I didn't see anyone like that. What's going on?"

It's clear that something has Dennis spooked. He crosses the room and goes to the window, peering out through the curtains to the street below.

"Dennis," Tom says. "Speak to me."

Dennis turns from the window. He presses his hands to his temples like he has a headache. "I saw something, Tom," he says. "Last night, after I walked Stef back to her place."

"What?"

Dennis tells him. About the hit and run. About the armed men chasing him through the streets. "I managed to get away, but then I didn't know what to do. I must've lost my phone somewhere – I was running so fast it must have flown outta my pocket. I never even noticed until I got here. And then, when I got here, I started to wonder if this was the worst place I could have come. Because they saw me – I saw them and they saw me. They could maybe work out who I am, where I live. But then I was already here, and I didn't want to risk heading back out and being seen if they were already here, and I didn't have any way to get in touch with anyone, so I just locked myself in."

Tom has listened closely. This isn't his first time dealing with someone in trouble. He needs all the information they can give, and he needs to get it clear in his head. "Has anyone been by while you were here?" he says. "Knocked on the door, tried the lock, anything like that?"

"No one until you," Dennis says.

"Okay. And you said you knew the woman?"

"No, I didn't *know* her," Dennis says. "I *recognised* her. I just can't think why. But she was familiar. *Very* familiar. Like maybe I've seen her around a lot, or even on TV or something – an actress, maybe."

"And you think there were three guys who killed her? Two chasing, one in the car?"

"I guess there could have been four of them," Dennis says after thinking for a moment. "I never saw inside the car. Not very well, anyway."

"But you saw the two men who chased her out of the alleyway?"

"Yeah."

"And you'd recognise them if you saw them again?"

"I can't forget them."

"All right. Have a shower. Change your clothes. We're going to the police station, tell them what you saw. Someone might have reported it already. What you saw could help catch whoever did this."

Dennis looks like he doesn't want to leave the apartment. "Go to the police station?" he says.

"I'll go with you," Tom says.

"But these people could be looking for me."

"I won't let them get you."

"But –"

"Dennis," Tom says firmly. "I'll keep you safe. This isn't my first time."

"What do you mean by that?"

"You know I was in the Army, right? That's not where the story ends." Tom tells him of what came after. Of his time with the CIA, running black ops missions. Of how he left that life behind and has helped people since. "And I can help you," he says. "You trust me, don't you?"

"Y-yeah," Dennis says. He looks shellshocked. "Does Melissa know all of that?"

"She knows enough. Now go take a shower, and let's help the cops do their job."

9

J ames doesn't speak, but Scarlett has plenty to say for both of them.

"Someone *saw*?" she says, her voice rising. "What do you mean, someone *saw*?"

Lee has had a busy day. After they had to give up the search for the man who saw them, he, Graham, and Rich got out of Newark. The body of Tessa Maberry was in the trunk of the car when Lee returned from his failed pursuit. Rich and Graham had dealt with that while Lee searched for the witness. The son of a bitch managed to give him the slip. In the moment, he'd had to let him go. They needed to get rid of the body. They took the old Ford to an isolated spot and doused it with gasoline. They made sure to pour it liberally over Tessa's body, and they started the fire from the trunk, dropping a lit box of matches into the shallow pool of gasoline coating her.

They watched it burn from a distance, making sure the evidence of both the body and the vehicle were destroyed. Satisfied, they finally left the scene. Lee has spent the rest of the day trying to find out who the man was, and to track him down. He has all of his people looking for him, and has them reaching out to their various contacts, telling them in turn to keep their ears to the ground. They hang around in the neighbourhood where he was spotted, looking out for anyone who might fit his description. They've sent Lee pictures of men who look similar, but none have been the guy. Lee had hoped to come to this meeting with the Penneys bearing good news. Able to tell them of last night's problem, but how he had already resolved it. Unfortunately, that isn't to be.

"We're looking for him," he says. "I have everyone out searching."

"And who are they searching *for*?" Scarlett says. "You said you don't have a name. You don't have his face –"

"We'll get his face," Lee says. "Like I said, I have people working on it."

"You don't have it yet, and it's been nearly a full day." Scarlett stares at him, eyes fiery. She shakes her head. "This is careless, Giles. This isn't acceptable."

James sits at the kitchen island behind them, chewing on his lips and the inside of his cheeks, looking jittery and nervous. There's a tumbler of whisky in his hand, and he turns it and turns it on the countertop. Lee sees how his leg jiggles and how he occasionally swallows. He hasn't touched the whisky. He's too upset at what he's hearing. Too concerned about what it means for them, how it could affect them.

"I know," Lee says. "And I apologise. But it'll be fixed, and soon."

"And if he goes to the police?"

Lee isn't concerned about this. "What if he does? That's the best thing he can do for us. We'll have him."

"Not if he doesn't go to one of ours."

"He was in the same neighbourhood where Tessa lived – chances are he's going to go to the nearest precinct. Everything there passes through Doug. We'll hear about it."

Scarlett exhales, her nostrils flaring. Her tongue flickers out over her lips. She's calming herself, Lee can see. "Tell me about Tessa. Tell me what happened."

"She's dead," Lee says. "As intended." He fills her in on the details. He started off the meeting by telling them about the problem with the man who witnessed them. Get the bad news out of the way first. Follow through with the good to dull the frustration.

"And you're sure her body is disposed of?"

"Certain," Lee says. "We watched it burn. We got rid of what little was left. Scattered her ashes and buried her bone fragments out in the middle of nowhere. She'll never be found. There's hardly any of her left to *be* found."

"That's one thing we don't have to worry about at least," Scarlett says, looking back toward her husband.

James perks up as she faces him. He nods eagerly. "Yes," he says. "Very good." He finally takes a drink of his whisky.

"But the man," Scarlett says, "the man who saw you – dealing with Tessa doesn't absolve you of that. I'm not happy, Giles." She takes a step back. "But Tessa being gone is good. Very good. The rest of her unwashed pals will fall apart now, I have no doubt."

James speaks up suddenly. He's reaching into his pocket for his cell phone. "I'm getting a call," he says, holding it up to Scarlett, like he needs to prove it's true. "It's business. I'd best take it."

"Go to your office," Scarlett says. "Answer it in there."

James nods dutifully, then hurries out of the kitchen and down the hall to his office. He answers the call on his way.

When he's gone, Scarlett turns back to Lee. She steps closer to him, but she's slow about it, taking her time. Swaying her hips. Wetting her lips again. She stands very close to him. She's shorter than Lee. He can feel her breath on his chin as she looks up to his face. "I meant what I said, Lee," she says. "I'm very, *very* unhappy about what's happened. You don't want me to be unhappy, now, do you?"

"I live to keep you pleased," Lee says, leaning closer, breathing in her sweet breath.

"If you can't make me happy fast, I might just have to cut you off. And I know you don't want that."

"That's the last thing I want."

She places a hand on his chest, letting it linger there above his heart. "You know that I'll reward you *very* well – but *only* once you've fixed this mess."

"You always do," Lee says. "And I will. When have I ever let you down before?"

"I'd hate for this to be the first time. And in such a major way." Her hand rises from his chest, a finger tracing the line of his jaw.

They hear James returning from his office. Scarlett takes her hand back, but slowly. She doesn't step back, doesn't create space between herself and Lee. Lee notices how James's eyes narrow as he comes back into the kitchen, but he doesn't say anything.

"Giles is just leaving," Scarlett says, her eyes never leaving Lee's. "There's a lot he needs to do."

10

Tom and Dennis are in a small room in the police station. Dennis is talking to a composite artist, describing the two men that he saw. Another cop, a detective, has already taken his statement about what he saw last night.

Tom sits back, lets Dennis give his descriptions, wishing he had been there to see the men too, and wishing he'd been there to help the woman they killed.

The artist does the composites by hand. Tom knows that a lot of places do them on computer now. He's heard some places prefer doing them by hand. It provides a more accurate representation of the person. This must be one of those places. The artist is not alone. The detective who took Dennis's statement is also present. He stands behind the artist, watching over his shoulder while he works. When the artist finishes, he turns the work around. "Did he look like this?" he says. "Let me know if there's anything needs changed. Pay close attention to the eyes and the mouth."

"Shit, that's him," Dennis says. "He was the lead man – the one who chased me."

Tom commits the drawing to memory. The man's face is chiselled, his dark hair cut short. His eyes, even in the drawing, are intense. His face is clean-shaven.

The artist puts the drawing to one side. He starts work on the second man's composite. Tom notices how the detective is staring at the completed drawing. Tom observes, but he doesn't look directly at the detective. Doesn't let him know that he's being watched.

The detective tries to look casual. A moment later, he slips out of the office. Tom notes this. There was something about the way that the detective was studying the drawing. If it was recognition, the detective managed to keep his face blank and hide it.

Ten minutes go by before the detective returns. He's not alone. He's brought another man with him, also in plain clothes – presumably another detective. Tom glances up, but he keeps his expression plain, barely interested in the new arrivals. He manages to get a look at the badge dangling from the new detective's neck. Sergeant Doug Posey. He looks to be in his late forties, balding, with the hair around the side and back of his head shaved short. He peers down at the composite drawings over the artist's shoulder.

Again, much like the first detective, Sergeant Posey mostly keeps his face impassive. Tom notices, however, how his eyes narrow, just a little, when he sees the drawing of the first man. There's recognition there. Tom looks away before the sergeant can look back up and catch his eye. He doesn't want either of them to notice that he's seen, that he's registered their reactions.

He has a bad feeling now. While he remains casual in his

chair, sitting up straight but appearing relaxed, in reality he's tense. He's watching the detective and the sergeant out the corner of his eye. He's listening to the footsteps out in the hall, making sure no one stops outside, gathering nearby, as if waiting for them to leave. His muscles are ready to pounce from the chair should anyone try anything.

The sergeant hangs around. The drawing of the second man is finished and shown to Dennis. Dennis nods. Tom commits it to memory, same as the last one.

It's the sergeant who speaks next. "Dennis, I'm Detective Sergeant Doug Posey. We'd like to thank you for coming in today and bringing this to our attention. Your report has been filed and I can assure you we'll be looking into this young lady and these men you've provided us the descriptions of."

"Has anyone else said anything about her?" Dennis says. "Said that they saw what happened to her, or maybe reported her missing?"

"I'm afraid not," Doug says. "But if this happened just last night, as you say, then her friends or family may not have noticed she's missing yet. You'd be surprised at how long these things can take sometimes, before a parent or a friend realises they haven't heard from a loved one, and by then it's often too late for us to find any leads."

"But this will help, right?" Dennis says. "These pictures. My story. It'll help, those are leads, right?"

"Of course," Doug says. "Your coming here today is greatly appreciated." Doug offers his hand to shake. Dennis does. Doug turns it toward Tom. "I'm sorry, I didn't catch your name."

Tom stands and shakes the hand. He doesn't want to give his name to the sergeant, but he's already given it to the detective and the artist. At this point, it doesn't matter. "Tom," he says.

The sergeant doesn't ask for a surname. He turns back to Dennis. "We'll get right on this. And I assume if we have any further questions, you have no problem with us getting in touch?"

"Uh, no, I don't, but I like I told the detective, I lost my phone when I was chased."

"We have his address and his work details," the detective says.

"Very good," Doug says. He smiles, briefly, at Dennis and Tom, and then he leaves the office.

The detective motions toward the door. "Let me show you both out."

Tom doesn't speak until they're out in the parking lot. "Do you think that'll really help?" Dennis says when they reach the Toyota.

Tom remains silent until they're inside the car. He sees cops coming in and out of the station, and a couple of them holding a conversation nearby. They occasionally glance toward the vehicle. There are cameras nearby, too. Bullet cameras, small dark orbs that will cover the entire parking lot.

Tom starts the engine and pulls out of the parking lot. He notices how Dennis is looking at him curiously, confused as to why he isn't answering.

"I don't trust them," Tom says when they're finally out of the lot and on the road.

"Who?" Dennis says. "The cops?"

"Maybe not all of them," Tom says. "The artist didn't give anything away. But the detective, and the sergeant. They know something."

"They *know* something? What are you talking about?"

"They recognised those men you described. They recognised both of them. That's why the detective went to get the sergeant in the first place. Why else do you think the sergeant came to the room?"

Dennis thinks about this, but he doesn't have an answer.

"Do you think a police sergeant comes to speak to every witness and tell them they're going to do all they can?" Tom says. "He wanted to see the pictures for himself, to be sure. He wanted to see *you*. He wanted to see me, too. That's why he was asking the questions about wanting to be able to get in touch with you."

Dennis can't speak for a moment. He's ingesting all this information, and he's struggling to process it. "You – you think there's some kind of conspiracy happening, and the cops are in on it?"

"I don't know for sure," Tom says. "It would help if you could remember why you recognised the woman, and if we knew who she was. What I *do* know is that I don't trust the detective or the sergeant. We're going to your place and you're going to pack a bag. You're coming to stay with me."

"Are you really that worried?"

"It's better to be safe than sorry," Tom says. "And going forward, I'm not letting you out of my sight."

11

After Dennis packs his bag, Tom takes a detour to The Corner Spot. He wants to tell Melissa what Dennis saw, and how things went at the police station. It's getting late and the bar is getting quiet. Melissa is able to take a break and join them in a booth. Tom sits with his back to the wall and a clear view of the room, and especially the door.

"Holy shit, you saw a girl get *killed*?" Melissa says.

Dennis nods, clearly shaken, the memory of it still making him ill no matter how many times he's told the story by now. "Don't tell Stef," he says. "I don't want her to be spooked. And would you let her know I lost my phone? Don't tell her how. Just say it got broke on the construction site or something."

"I'll do that," Melissa says.

Dennis pauses before adding, "But make sure she knows I'm not trying to blow her off. I really do want to see her again. I guess we should maybe just wait a while..."

Melissa places a hand on his arm. "Dennis, relax. You're babbling right now. I'll talk to her. And don't worry, I'll make sure she knows you're not trying to ghost her."

"Dennis is going to be staying with me for the time being," Tom says.

"How long do you think that might be?" Melissa says.

"I don't know. We're gonna have to play everything by ear for now. But in my experience, if someone is going to come looking for you, looking to make trouble, you always find out about it sooner rather than later."

"But if these are crooked cops, I mean, what can you do?"

"I'll think of something," Tom says. "The main thing to figure out right now is the *why*."

Behind the bar, on the television, the late news is playing. Tom notices how Dennis does a double-take and stares at the screen, eyes narrowed. Something has caught his attention. "Wait a minute," he says. He starts to stand.

"What is it?" Tom says, following him.

They go to the counter. Dennis's eyes never leave the television, like he's waiting for something to happen, or to reappear. He leans forward, eyes fixed on the screen. "Melissa, can you turn it up please?" he says.

Melissa does. They all watch the television, Tom and Melissa's attention occasionally flickering toward Dennis, watching him and his reactions, waiting for a clue as to what he saw.

The news is at Monmouth Beach. The reporter is talking to one of the protestors camped out there. The protestor is a young female with rainbow streaks of colour dyed through her hair. She looks concerned about something. "Tessa usually checks in with us every day," she says. "We've been by her home and she's not there. We can't get in touch with her. This isn't like her."

"And you think something might have happened to her?" the reporter asks.

The protestor chews her lip, clearly choosing her words, careful about how she answers. "None of us have seen her for over twenty-four hours now, and we've filed a missing person report."

Then, on the screen, an image of Tessa Maberry comes up. Dennis becomes animated. He points at the screen. "That's her! That's who I saw!"

"You're sure?" Tom says.

"Yes – one hundred percent," Dennis says. "That's why I recognised her – the *news*. I'd seen her on the news. They keep reporting on that marina at Monmouth Beach and the protestors there. That's why she looked so familiar – they would always talk to her."

"They said they've just filed a missing person report," Melissa points out. "Should you all get back in touch with the cops?"

Dennis is about to respond, but Tom cuts him off. "No," he says. "They didn't say when they'd filed it. The cops could already have had that information while we were at the station. This doesn't make me suddenly trust them. This is worse. They recognised the men who killed her. Something doesn't add up." Tom falls silent momentarily, scratching his neck while he thinks. "It's a concerning situation. The last thing we want to do right now is go back to the cops."

"So what *do* we do?" Dennis says.

"I'm going to look into it," Tom says. "See what I can find. But for now, we act normal. Tomorrow, we go to work. Life goes on. We stick to our routines. We don't do anything that lets them know we're suspicious." Tom stares at the TV screen, at the image of Tessa Maberry still there. "If you saw something you weren't supposed to, that makes you a loose end. They could be coming for you, Dennis. You don't go anywhere without me."

12

Detective Sergeant Doug Posey has got in touch with Lee. He told him it was urgent.

Lee drives to meet him. They meet at a quiet spot down by the Bay. Doug is already there when Lee arrives. He pulls up next to him and puts the passenger window down. It's late and most of the workers have left the docks. Off to their right is a cargo ship waiting to be loaded, the cranes dangling in place above it, unmanned. It's quiet.

"Do you have something for me?" Lee says.

"Yeah, I do," Doug says, looking pleased with himself. "We got the guy you're looking for. The one who saw what happened to Tessa Maberry."

This *is* good news. Lee wants to smile, but he doesn't get ahead of himself. He keeps his face still for now. "You've *got* him? In a cell?"

"Well, no. But we know who he is, and we have his details."

"Then you don't *have* him, Doug. Words are important. Choose them carefully."

"Sorry, I just thought you'd be pleased –"

"Tell me what happened."

Doug tells him. One of the detectives, also unofficially on the Penney Pharma payroll, took a statement from a man called Dennis Kurtley. He spoke with a composite artist. At the time, the detective didn't know that Lee had put the word around to be on high alert for this man. All he knew was, the composite drawing was starting to look a hell of a lot like Lee Giles. That's when he came to get Doug.

"The artist isn't on the payroll, is that right?" Lee says.

"That's right. He has no idea who you are."

"And why didn't the detective know that we were looking for a man telling this story already? I wanted the word spread, Doug."

Doug's mouth works a little. He looks like a brainless goldfish, but then he stammers out an excuse. "He'd only just started his shift," he says. "I hadn't had a chance to talk to him yet. I keep everything low-key, just like you want."

"This Dennis," Lee says. "Do you have a picture of him? For confirmation."

Doug nods and hands over an image taken from the station's security cameras. Lee studies it. He recognises Dennis Kurtley. The man who got away. His attention, however, is drawn by the man sitting next to him. Muscular guy, average height, his arms folded. It's clear he's there with Dennis. Dennis must have told him what happened. Lee wonders how many people he could have already spoken to. "Who's that?"

"He came to the station with Dennis," Doug says.

Lee looks at him. "Name?"

"Tom Rollins."

"Did he see anything?"

"No, he was just there with Dennis is all. Accompanying him."

"Dennis is a grown man."

"I don't know what to tell you. He wouldn't speak to anyone without this Rollins present."

"But he doesn't know anything? Only what Dennis has told him?"

"I think so," Doug says. "That sounds right."

Lee stares at the picture, committing Rollins's face to memory too, just in case. He could be another problem that needs dealt with. He would've seen the composite drawings, too. He'll know Lee's face. Lee doesn't like it. "What else do you have on Dennis?"

"He didn't have a phone number," Doug says. "Says he lost his cell when he was chased."

Lee doesn't remember seeing him dropping it during his pursuit, but he hadn't been able to keep him in view for most of it.

"We have his address. And his place of work."

"Has anyone been by?"

"His home? Yeah, I've sent a couple of our cops by his apartment building, but they said it didn't look like he was home. They tried the intercom too, but no answer."

Lee considers this, wondering if he could be hiding out somewhere else. "What about Rollins? Did you get his details?"

"No, but it would've been suspicious to take them."

Lee stares at the sergeant. "What, you can't make up an excuse?"

"Low-key, remember? You always tell me, low-key. I'm trying to keep this guy's nose *out* of things."

"It's too late for that," Lee says. "It became too late the

second Dennis told him what he'd seen. It didn't cross your mind that Dennis could be hiding out with him?"

Doug stares back. He's a cop. A detective sergeant. He's not used to being spoken to like this. "I didn't take his details," he says. "The detective did."

"I don't need excuses," Lee says. He'll talk to the detective sergeant however he pleases, and Doug needs to remember that. He needs to remember exactly where his monthly bonus comes from, and who controls it. "I need you to do your job – the job that we pay the generous stipend for you to do. Do you want to lose that, Doug? Because in this story you've told me, I've heard a lot of carelessness, and I don't like it. Maybe you need a couple of dry months to remind you of what's expected from you."

Doug keeps his mouth shut. He doesn't look humbled, but he understands the threat, and the need to behave. "I'm sorry," he says eventually. "You're right. This is on me. It won't happen again."

"I'm glad to hear that." Lee looks across the dark water, thinking. "Where does he work?" he asks without turning.

"He works construction," Doug says. He tells him where the site is. "I think Rollins works there, too. The detective said they both came in together, and Dennis mentioned that they'd come straight from work."

"Good." Lee nods along, still thinking. Finally, he turns back to Doug. Doug is watching him expectantly. "I have an idea. It's going to need your assistance."

13

Next day, Tom and Dennis return to work. Dennis makes an excuse to the foreman, tells him he was ill and how he'd lost his phone, and he's sorry he didn't turn up or find a way to get in touch. Neal didn't make a big deal out of it. He's a good guy. Just told Dennis he won't hold it against him so long as he doesn't make a habit of it.

Tom stays close to Dennis through the day. It's clear to him that Dennis is unnerved, paranoid. He's not sure how obvious it might be to anyone else, but no one else knows what's going on, or what Dennis has seen. They probably don't notice the way Dennis repeatedly pauses in his work, looking toward the parking lot or toward the road running down the side of the site.

There's nothing to see, though. Nothing to be concerned about.

Until the end of the day.

A police cruiser pulls onto the site close to quitting time. Dennis comes to Tom as soon as he spots it. "Do you think they're here for me?"

Tom looks toward the cruiser. There are two cops inside. They're not looking around the site. They're getting out of the cruiser. Neal is on his way to see them. He's frowning, wondering what they want. Tom watches. The two cops talk to him for a moment. It doesn't last long. The foreman points in Tom and Dennis's direction. The cops are smiling at Neal. One of them pats his arm, like they're reassuring him no one is in any trouble.

"What do we do?" Dennis says.

The cops are coming their way. "Just stick by me," Tom says. "And trust anything I say." He heads, slowly, toward a workbench. There are tools upon it. Tom puts down the hammer he's carrying. He waits by the table, his back to it, and Dennis alongside him. The cops get close enough to talk. Tom doesn't recognise either of them. One of them is young, clean-shaven, and the other is older, with a moustache.

"Dennis Kurtley?" the one on the left, the older cop with the moustache, says. He's looking at Dennis.

"Yes, sir," Dennis says.

The younger cop doesn't speak, but Tom notices how he's watching both of them through his aviators, sizing them up. Tom pretends he doesn't see.

"We need you to come down to the station with us, Mr. Kurtley," the older cop says. "It shouldn't take long. We just have some new information we'd like you to corroborate."

Tom pays attention to both of their demeanours when he asks, "Is this about Tessa Maberry?"

Both cops stiffen. There's a sudden tension that thickens the air between them all. The older cop brushes at the side of his moustache and tries to keep his tone casual. He exchanges a brief glance with the younger cop. "That's what we're trying to find out," he says.

The younger cop finally speaks. He addresses Tom. "Can I check your name, sir?"

"Why?" Tom says.

The younger cop is taken aback, but he tries to hide it behind his shades. "Excuse me?"

"Why do you need my name?" Tom gave his name at the station. These cops should know it, he thinks, especially if they're potentially crooked. The younger cop is acting tough. He could be making out like he doesn't know who Tom is as a way to demean him.

Or maybe they know exactly who Tom is, and they don't want any trouble with him. They see Dennis as an easy target, and they want to leave Tom out of it.

The older cop holds up a hand to his partner. "We're just here to collect Mr. Kurtley," he says. "Will you accompany us to the cruiser, sir?"

While they're distracted, Tom reaches behind himself and takes a screwdriver from the workbench. He slips it into his pocket without the cops seeing.

"Uh..." Dennis looks at Tom.

"We can follow you there in my car," Tom says. In the distance, by the cabin, he can see how Neal is watching them.

The older cop talks to Dennis as if Tom hasn't said anything. "We can bring you back here after. It's no problem."

"We'll follow," Tom says.

"I'd rather travel with my friend," Dennis says, motioning to Tom.

"I don't like your tone," the younger cop says to Tom. "I don't like your entire general attitude."

"The feeling's mutual," Tom says.

"Sir, are you obstructing our duty here?"

"Not at all. I'm helping you along. Saving you a return trip."

"That's enough now," the older cop says. "Mr. Kurtley, if you want your friend to accompany you, that's fine, but the two of you are going to accompany us in the cruiser."

"I don't know anything about Tessa," Tom says. "What good am I to you?" Tom thinks they know exactly who he is. They know that he accompanied Dennis to the station the first time. They must already know his name. He's been curious to see if they slip up and use it.

"You're being purposefully obstructive to our investigation," the younger cop says. "You can either accompany Mr. Kurtley at his request, or we can take you in forcefully."

"Am I in trouble?" Tom says. He doesn't back down to the younger cop. Doesn't back down to either of them.

"If you keep this up you will be," the younger cop says.

"I'm not looking for any trouble," Tom says. "I'm just here trying to do my job and you've rolled up with an attitude. I'm just looking out for my friend here."

"He's not in any trouble," the older cop says. "We just need his help."

"Then we'll follow you," Tom says, continuing to push buttons.

The younger cop is bristling now. "Do I need to put you in cuffs, Rollins?"

There it is. As he suspected, they know exactly who he is.

The older cop grimaces, his jaw clenching. He knows

what his younger partner has done. Tom sees how he tenses, like he expects Tom to attempt something physical.

"That won't be necessary," Tom says, smiling at both cops. "Like I said, I'm not looking for any trouble." He nods to Dennis. "Let's go and help these men out, shall we?"

14

Tom and Dennis sit in the back of the police cruiser. It's not an ideal situation, but he couldn't lash out at a pair of cops just because he's suspicious of them. And not because one of them was an asshole, either. He needs to be sure.

Tom and Dennis don't speak. They're not in cuffs. They haven't been patted down. There's no reason why they should have been. They're not under arrest. Tom can feel the screwdriver in his back pocket. He's sitting on it. He wants to move it around to the front, within easier reach. He doesn't do it yet. Doesn't want them to notice his movements and become suspicious. If they're lucky, he won't need it. The cops say they're taking them to the station, and maybe they are. They'll know soon enough. If the screwdriver is noticed, it's easily explained. They've brought Tom straight from work. He can easily say he forgot he had it on him.

The cops don't speak either. The older cop is driving. The younger cop sits in the passenger seat, and Tom thinks he's watching them in the rear-view mirror, eyes concealed by his shades. A partition separates Tom and Dennis from the front. There's a Benelli M4 shotgun between the cops. They'll also have their standard-issue Glock 19s in their holsters, Tom knows. And all he has is a screwdriver.

Tom notices that the radio is off. They're not receiving any kind of dispatch calls. He thinks they've purposefully turned it off. It makes it seem like they're not on duty.

Tom watches the road. They're not heading toward the station. He's not surprised. He leans closer to the partition. "This is an interesting route you're taking," he says. While he speaks, distracting the attention of the cops, he moves the screwdriver from his back pocket to his front.

Neither of them answers him. They remain silent, looking straight ahead. They don't look at him. The younger cop isn't watching in the mirror anymore.

"I've been to the station," Tom says. "This isn't the way."

Again, they don't answer.

Tom sits back. Out the corner of his eye, he sees how nervous Dennis looks. His right knee is bouncing. His hands are clasped tightly together, his knuckles and fingers turning pale. There's nothing they can do right now, especially with the metal partition between them and the cops. They have to wait. Tom looks out of the window. He keeps the route in mind.

They drive for an hour. No one speaks the whole time. The cops take them out of the city. They take them into woodland, to a secluded spot. Tom keeps his hand close to the screwdriver.

They reach an opening, closed in on all sides by tall, thick trees. There are a couple of other vehicles already here. There's a small group of men present, too. The cruiser gets closer to them and then comes to a stop. There are four men.

Tom recognises two of them. One is from the composite drawing that Dennis did. The man who chased him. The man who oversaw the killing of Tessa Maberry. The other man he recognises is Detective Sergeant Doug Posey. Doug stands apart from the other three. His arms are folded and his mouth is twisted. He's not happy to be here. The other two, who flank the man from the drawing, are unknown to Tom. Neither of them is the other man who Dennis provided the composite of. Tom can't see any guns, but he has no doubt that they're all armed.

The older and the younger cop start to get out of the cruiser. Tom removes the screwdriver from his pocket, holding it in a reverse grip like a knife, keeping it close to himself and out of view.

The front doors of the cruiser remain open and Tom can hear the people outside speaking. "You got Rollins as well?" says the man who appears to be in charge. The man from Dennis's drawing. Tom wonders if he's police, too, or if the cops present are crooked and this man is part of something worse.

"Yes, sir, we got them both," the older cop says.

"Rollins is a mouthy asshole," the younger cop says.

"Well, that ain't gonna be a concern much longer," the leader says. "Get them out."

Tom sees how the younger cop makes a beeline for his door. He's a young guy with a clear chip on his shoulder, always got something to prove. He's wanting to show off, to handle the guy he's just labelled as mouthy. Perhaps to impress the clear leader of this party. His hand rests on the handle of his Glock, but he's cocky and his grip is loose. He thinks Tom is unarmed. Thinks they have the numbers advantage. Thinks he can afford to be careless.

The older cop heads toward Dennis's door. He moves slower. He's more experienced than his partner. His hand is on his Glock, too, but it's firmer, ready to draw. He's not taking any chances. He's not trying to impress anyone.

But he's too slow, and he's going to reach Dennis's door too late, and so the whereabouts of his hands don't concerned Tom too much. The younger cop is already at his door. He's pulling it open. He's stepping in closer. He's grinning and he's starting to say something.

Tom doesn't hear what it is. He jabs the screwdriver deep into the meat of his thigh. The younger cop yelps and then stumbles back, staring down at the screwdriver sticking out of his leg.

Tom is already out of the back of the car, clamping his left arm around the throat of the younger cop, holding him close as a shield and knocking off his shades, while his right hand shoots down toward the holster, pulling the Glock free and raising it, covering the other men.

The others take a step back. Apart from the leader – he stands his ground, staring at Tom and his captive. The other men start reaching for their handguns, but the leader raises a hand, waving them down. The older cop has stopped where he is, away from Dennis's door. The younger cop is sucking air through his teeth, feeling the pain from the screwdriver running through his body. Tom can feel his pained convulsions where he holds him.

"Dennis, get out of the car," Tom says. "Come out on my side."

Dennis scurries over and stands behind Tom.

Tom turns to the older cop. "Throw over the keys and your cuffs."

The older cop looks toward Detective Sergeant Doug

Posey. Doug's jaw is working hard, his teeth grinding together. "Just do it," he says. "Do as he says."

"Put them on the roof and slide them over," Tom says. "Dennis, grab them both."

The older cop does as he says. Tom keeps an eye on the leader. The man doesn't move. He's still as a statue. Ice-cold. He speaks. "You're making a mistake."

"The only mistake would be waiting for you to take us out into the woods to dig our own graves," Tom says. "This feels like the right thing in the circumstances."

"And what now?" the leader says. "What's your grand plan, or did you think beyond this moment?"

Tom ignores him. "Dennis, get into the front of the cruiser. You're going to drive us out of here. Give me the cuffs."

Dennis puts the cuffs into Tom's left hand, and then gets behind the steering wheel.

Tom motions with the gun to the older cop. "Back up," he says. "Get clear or get mown down." He looks at Doug and the leader. "Just like Tessa Maberry, right?"

Doug swallows. The leader remains stationary. All that moves are his eyes. He's like a lizard. Tom doesn't think he's a cop. He thinks he's something much more. He's had training. It's in his bearing and his demeanour.

"You can't get away," the leader says. "We found you both already. We'll find you again."

Tom starts pushing the younger cop toward the open rear door of the cruiser.

"You can't escape us," the leader says. "And look around you, Rollins. Look who's here." He smirks. "Where do you think you can go?"

Tom pauses by the rear door. "I feel rude," he says. "You

clearly know who I am, and yet I don't have any idea what your name is."

The leader snorts.

"Worth a try," Tom says. "I'll be seeing you around, mystery man." He pushes the younger cop into the car and gets in after him. "*Drive.*"

15

T he cruiser tears up the ground, spitting grass, stones, and dead branches out from the sides of the tyres as it quickly reverses. The driver pulls on the handbrake and spins the car around, then slams his foot down onto the pedal and they start to drive away.

Lee turns to his men. He's furious, but he's containing it. Now is not the time to lose control. "What are you standing around for? Let's go!"

The older cop who arrived with Dennis and Rollins hurries up to them, eyes wide like an owl's. He opens his mouth but before he can speak Lee strikes him in the side of the head, knocking him to the ground. "You didn't think to check them before you brought them here? You didn't cuff them?"

The older cop looks up from the ground, cradling his head where he was struck. "We got them from the construction site," he manages to say. "We were told not to make a scene."

"I'll put out an APB," Doug says. "They're in one of our

cars, for Christ's sake. I'll have the whole city come down on them."

"Don't you fucking dare," Lee says. "That's too much noise. Do you expect us to pay off the whole damn department? Don't be stupid. If that was an option we'd have already done it, but there's always a Serpico in the midst."

Lee's men have started up their car and are turning it around.

Lee is still staring at Doug. "Are there trackers in the cruiser?"

"Yeah – yes, there are."

Lee steps closer to him, cowing him. "Then get in your fucking car, take this old bitch with you," he points to the older cop, "and *get after them*. We'll follow."

16

Tom handcuffs the younger cop's hands behind his back and then forces him down into the footwell. The cop cries out whenever something knocks against the screwdriver. "If you stay down you'll survive this," Tom says. "Leave that screwdriver in until a paramedic can look at it."

Dennis gets them clear of the woods. Tom tells him to pull over and let him out of the back. Tom takes over driving. Dennis rides in the passenger seat. He tries to look back at the younger cop, but he's too low to see. They can hear him cursing and breathing hard. Tom races back toward Newark. He turns on the police radio.

"Oh shit, oh shit," Dennis says. He holds a hand to his chest, over his heart. "I've never done anything like that before in my life. Holy shit." He keeps swallowing. "What do we do now? Oh, fuck, it's the *cops*. The cops are after us. What's going *on*?"

"Dennis, I need you to calm down," Tom says, overtaking cars, glancing back in the mirror to see if he can spot either of the vehicles from the clearing in pursuit. He can't. Despite this, he doesn't slow. There's no sign of them yet, but they're sure to give chase. "I need to listen to the radio."

Dennis falls silent, though Tom can still hear him breathing hard. He runs his hands down his face and back through his hair. He looks in the side mirror and then back through the partition, trying to see the captured cop again. Finally, after a couple of minutes have passed in silence, he turns back to Tom. "What are you listening for?"

Tom thinks it should have been long enough. The detective sergeant was there, along with another cop. After Tom and Dennis took the cruiser, they should have gotten straight on their radios. "There's no APB," he says. "They haven't called anything in. We've stole a cruiser and we've kidnapped a cop, and they haven't tried to report it."

"What does that mean?"

"It means they're working off the books. It means not everyone in the department is crooked, and they're trying to keep this quiet."

"So, we can go to the station, right? We can tell them what's happening, and about the –"

Tom cuts him off. "Do you want to turn up to a police station with a stolen cop car and a stabbed and captive cop?"

Dennis falls silent. "When you put it like that..."

"Plus, we don't know who is and isn't crooked. We don't know if they're in the minority or the majority. We can't risk it."

"Then where are we going?"

"We're going back to the site," Tom says. "We're going to get my car. We need to get rid of this cruiser as fast as we can. It's probably got a tracker on it. They'll know exactly where we are. We get back to the site, get my car, and we keep moving."

They drive the rest of the way in silence, Tom alert not just for the pursuing vehicles, but also for other cruisers. The last thing they need is to be seen by a cop in their work clothes, driving a cop car. When they finally get back to Newark, Tom heads for the construction site. They still haven't heard anything on the radio. Tom has driven fast, but there's been no high-speed pursuit. He hasn't spotted either of the vehicles from the clearing behind them, neither getting up close nor keeping a safe distance. They've had plenty of time to give chase. Tom knows a lot of police cruisers have trackers, and he thinks this must be one of them. The others have been able to stay further back, out of view, not wanting to risk a chase or a gun battle on the way here.

The construction site is deserted, as Tom knew it would be. The entrance is locked, but he can see his car parked outside, in the lot. It's the only vehicle still there. Tom gets out of the cruiser, pulling his keys from his pocket, and motions for Dennis to get out with him. He doesn't want the cop in the rear footwell to hear them talking.

Tom hands the keys to Dennis. "Take my car and go to The Corner Spot," he says. "But don't go in. Park down an alleyway nearby and stay in the car. Wait for me there. You got that?"

"You're not coming?" Dennis says, taking the keys. "What are you going to do?"

"They're coming after this car," Tom says. He tells him about the probable tracker. "We won't have long, especially now that we've stopped. I'm going to buy us some time. Get out of here – we don't have time to waste. Stay in the alley and I'll find you there."

Tom gets back into the cruiser before Dennis can say anything further. Dennis finally turns and runs toward Tom's car to do as he's told. Tom calls into the back. "You'd better brace yourself." He spins the wheels and then plows the car forward, through the locked gate leading into the construction site.

"Ah, *fuck!*" he hears the injured cop cry out, the impact no doubt jostling the screwdriver in his leg.

Tom drives the cruiser up to the building and parks it around the back, inside, concealed from immediate view. He leaves the cop where he is. He grabs the M4 and gets out of the cruiser.

17

Tom throws the cruiser's keys away, toward some bushes that line this part of the site. He heads back around the building, but he's careful, moving slowly, keeping watch for approaching vehicles. He can't see anyone just yet, but he knows they must be coming.

Dennis is gone. He's glad he got clear before the others could show up. Tom didn't want them to follow him. He wants them to come here and only here, where he can disable them and buy himself and Dennis some more time and breathing room.

He sets up position behind a low wall being built at the front of the building. It's starting to take the shape of a window. Tom peers through this gap, keeping watch. He holds onto the M4 shotgun. He has the Glock still, too. Tom checks the Benelli's rounds. One in the chamber and five in the magazine. Six shots. Fully loaded. He checks the Glock, too. Fifteen in the magazine and one in the chamber. Between the two weapons, it should be more than enough for now.

He watches. He'd have a better view from a couple of floors up, like where he takes his lunch, but he doesn't want to get trapped up there when they invariably fire back. Doesn't want to risk injuring himself by having to jump down, either, or hurry through the under-construction stairwell. On the ground, behind cover, with an easy escape route in sight is his best option. When it's time to go, he's close enough to the chain-link fence to leap it and flee, hiding himself in the brush there and making his way toward the nearest neighbourhood, where he can take backroads and alleyways and remain out of view.

It doesn't take long for the two cars he saw at the clearing to come into view. They approach slowly, cautiously, no doubt searching for the cruiser, and knowing that there could be a potential ambush awaiting. They spot the busted gate and crawl through.

Tom ducks low behind the wall for now, waiting. It's late evening. The sun is nearing the horizon and spreading long shadows across the ground. From one of the cars, a large flashlight comes out of the passenger side window and starts scanning the site. Tom assumes this vehicle belongs to Detective Sergeant Doug Posey. He saw it at the clearing. He doubts a non-police vehicle would have a flashlight that size inside.

By this point, both cars have probably noticed that there are no vehicles in the lot. They're being careful though, as they should, in case someone has hung back and is watching them. They're making sure. They're not rushing in. Tom ducks back down as the flashlight scans over his position. When it's past, Tom waits a beat and then rises with the shotgun. He shoots out the flashlight. There's a cry of alarm.

Tom promptly reloads the chamber and shoots out the front tyres on the lead vehicle. It's getting too dark for him to see if it's Doug behind the steering wheel.

He crouches and leaves his position before they can figure out where he is. He hears the men shouting, calling to each other, trying to figure out where the shots came from. Tom moves through the building, heading in the direction of the chain-link fence, slipping into the room next to the one he previously occupied. He presses his back to the wall. He can see the two cars, but they can't see him. The lead car, Doug's car, is stationary, crippled by the shotgun blasts. The other car is hiding behind it, using it as cover. The two men inside Doug's car are ducking low. Tom can hear them shouting, begging the men in the car behind to help them, to do something.

Tom moves through the building in the opposite direction, staying low and out of sight. He can see the people in the rear car peering out, trying to find him. He can see how they have their handguns out, raised, ready to use them.

Tom gets to the far end of the building and slides down the wall, getting as close to the edge as he can. Cautiously, he looks out. They still don't see him. Tom fires again, blowing out the passenger side tyres on the rear vehicle.

As it sags, he's already moving. He thinks they must have worked out where he is by now. There's nowhere else for him to be hiding out. He hears gunshots coming his way, but they're wild and random. They can't see him. Tom slips down the centre of the building and fires the last shotgun round. He isn't aiming at anything specific. He just wants to spook them, to give them something to keep them distracted. While they're occupied, he drops the shotgun and pulls out the Glock, getting to the end of the building and dropping flat. He crawls down the slight hill, hearing them shooting into the building behind him still, not realising he's already gone. He climbs the fence and drops down the other side, and he makes his escape.

18

Lee thinks the shooter – either Rollins or Dennis – is gone. His men and the two cops have been returning fire for a couple of minutes, and nothing has happened. Nothing has been returned.

Pulling out his Glock, he tells his men to cover him, and then he gets out of the car. He crouches low at its side, staring at the building. He crosses into the darkness at the perimeter of the site and then makes his way closer to the building, circling round.

They can't afford to be here long, he knows. Someone must have heard the gunshots. This isn't an isolated area. They're going to have to dump the crippled vehicles and leave Doug to smooth things over, but first they need to make sure they can get out of here without taking a bullet in the back.

Lee reaches the building. It's still under construction. There are few walls. It's easy for him to see through. He pulls out his phone and calls his men, speaking in a low voice.

"Don't fire – I'm going in. Make sure Doug and his boy do the same."

"Is it clear?"

"Looks it."

Lee heads inside, Glock raised. He can see the cruiser. It looks empty. He makes his way through the building, room by room. He finds the discarded M4. The ground floor is clear. He looks at the stairwell. He doesn't think someone would head up that way, where there's no escape, but he needs to make sure the area is clear. He goes up. He's careful. There's only a few floors to investigate, and most of them are all open spaces. Rooms haven't been built yet. They're all clear.

He gets on his cell. "They're gone," he says. "The cruiser's back here. Send Doug up to me."

Lee makes his way back down the stairwell. By the time he reaches the bottom, Doug and the older cop are both at the cruiser. They've found the younger idiot, cuffed, with the screwdriver still sticking out of his leg, his trousers darkened with blood around the wound.

Doug stands with his fingers laced atop his head, looking stressed. He turns to Lee. "I'm gonna have a hell of a time explaining all of this."

"You'll think of something," Lee says, his tone cold. Doug picks up on it, but he's not surprised by it. He knows he's messed up. "Me and my men are getting out of here." Lee stares at Doug, like what he's about to add is his fault – which, as far as he's concerned, it is. "On foot."

"I know this has been a mess, Lee –"

Lee doesn't let him speak. "Find out what you can on Rollins and get back to me ASAP. Clear up what's happened here and think up a believable cover story. You and these two morons have a lot to make up for. Expect your payments to be light this month."

Doug purses his lips, but he nods.

"I expect to hear from you soon," Lee says, then he turns from the cops and walks away, waving to his men to follow.

19

As Tom nears The Corner Spot he gets rid of the Glock, unloading it and depositing the bullets down a storm drain, the empty magazine down another, and the pistol itself down a third. He spaces the dumpings out. He doesn't want to be walking around with a cop's gun, but nor does he want it to be easily found by someone who shouldn't get their hands on it.

He made sure he was clear, that no one was following, before he made his way to the Ironbound neighbourhood. He circled a couple of blocks and lay in wait down alleyways to make sure he didn't see any familiar faces. He didn't. He'd lost their pursuers.

It's dark now. His car is parked down an alleyway a block from The Corner Spot, as instructed. He can't see Dennis inside, concealed in the shadows. As he approaches, he spots movement. He raises both empty hands to show Dennis that it's him, and he's unarmed. Dennis gets out of the car.

"Are you all right?" he says. "What happened?"

"I'm fine," Tom says. "Have you seen anyone while you've been here?"

"I don't think so. No one suspicious, anyway. It's been quiet."

Tom nods, and then they head to The Corner Spot on foot. Melissa spots them as soon as they enter, as if she's been awaiting their arrival. She doesn't loudly greet them, like she ordinarily would. Perhaps she sees the looks on their faces, and understands that something is wrong.

Melissa isn't working alone. There's another bartender behind the counter with her, a man called Steve. Tom and Dennis go to her and she steps aside to meet them. "What's wrong?" she says. "You both look like hell."

"We need to talk to you," Tom says. "Privately. Can we go in the back?"

Melissa looks around. "Sure," she says. It's quiet in the bar. Tom sees that no one from the site is present, and he's glad. It's getting late. Most people who would have come here for a drink after work, or to socialise, have already gone home. "Let me just tell Steve."

Melissa takes them through into the back office. It's a small room, but big enough for the three of them. There's a desk, and a filing cabinet to the side of it. There's a clock on the wall telling the wrong time, the batteries in need of a change. There are papers piled up on the desk. Bills that the owner needs to work through. There are a couple of spare kegs in the corner, and some crates in another. The office is more like an extra stockroom. On the wall is a whiteboard with shift patterns, and around it are out-of-date beer company calendars and bottle labels that have been stuck up.

Tom tells Melissa what has happened. "There's something deeper going on, and I think it connects back to Tessa Maberry. I intend to find out what it is."

"Jesus Christ," she says.

"We came here to get you," Tom says.

"You need me to hide you out?"

"No – you're coming with us. You're in danger too."

"I am?"

"They know who I am," Tom says. "They won't stop at my name. They'll look into my history. Into friends and relationships. They'll come to talk to you, and like for me and Dennis tonight it won't be in an official capacity."

"What do we do?"

"Right now we need to get clear, and fast. We've gotten away from them and I've disabled their rides. That's bought us some time. But the first places they're going to come are here, and my apartment. We need to get clear fast. And we need to go to my apartment, too, before we disappear."

"What for?"

"Weapons," Tom says, thinking of his backpack with his Beretta and KA-BAR. "After that, we'll have to figure things out on the move. Go talk to Steve. Tell him you're going to have to leave early. We'll go get the car and pick you up at the front."

"What should I tell him?"

"Nothing. Just that you have to go." Tom tilts his head toward the office door, indicating to Dennis that it's time to leave. He glances back at Melissa. "I'm sorry you've been dragged into this."

"Nothing to be sorry for," she says. "You didn't ask for this and neither did Dennis." She reaches out, places a hand on his arm and squeezes. "But we're all in this together now, and whatever we're going against we'll get through it together."

"These people are dangerous. They're armed. They have connections."

"I'd gathered that already."

Tom leans in and kisses her. "I know you can handle yourself," he says. "I'm not afraid of that."

"Likewise," Melissa says. "And we'll both look out for Dennis."

"We'd best move," Tom says. "We don't have any time to waste."

20

L ee is waiting, along with his two men, to be collected by Graham when his phone starts to ring. It's Doug.

Lee and the others have gotten far away from the construction site and found an area where they can lie low, concealed under trees, awaiting their pickup. They didn't hear any sirens as they departed, and he assumed Doug was keeping this contained and under control. He'd like to think this is the case, but he's been very disappointed by the actions of the cops on their payroll so far this night. If one of his own men was making this many mistakes, after all of the training they'd received from him and from each other, he'd have kicked them off his team a long time ago. Depending on how much they knew, he'd be giving serious consideration to taking them to an isolated location and putting a bullet through their head.

Like what was supposed to happen tonight, with Dennis and Rollins. It was all supposed to be so simple. So straightforward. And instead, it's a colossal fuck-up and once again

Lee is thinking how he's going to explain this to James and Scarlett. Well, more so Scarlett. She won't be pleased, he knows. And if she's not pleased, it could mean she won't be coming out at midnight to visit him in the guesthouse for the foreseeable.

He remembers the first time she turned up at his door. Lee had been working for them six months. He'd seen how Scarlett looked at him, but he didn't think there was any kind of attraction there. She kept her nose stuck up at everyone she came across, like she herself was the old money and not some ex-waitress gold digger that got lucky with a weak husband. No, what he saw in her eyes back then – what he *thought* he saw in her eyes – was disdain. She saw him as just another part of the household help, and she was going to treat him as such.

But he also noticed how she always lay close to the guest-house on his days off, setting up her lounger and lying back on it while wearing the skimpiest bikini he'd ever seen in his life. Her long, tan body glistened with the coconut-scented oil she'd spread over it. From inside the guesthouse, observing her from the shadows where she couldn't see him, Lee imagined he could almost smell it. And then she turned over to do her back, lying on her stomach, and Lee saw how the bikini was practically non-existent from behind, and he had to grit his teeth and walk away, thinking how he'd have to go to the bar that night and find some easy woman he could relieve himself with.

This went on for six months. They rarely spoke to each other. Lee was there to do his job, and he stuck to it. If ever Scarlett referred to him, she did so by his surname, as if she was ex-military, too. She kept things formal.

Until the night she turned up.

It was just after midnight and Lee was still awake. Even when he wasn't working he found it hard to switch off, and he usually stayed up until one or two, frequently checking in with his men on duty to make sure everything was as it should be. He'd lie in the dark on his bed at the back of the guesthouse, the rear window open so he could hear the sea. It should have been soothing, but mostly it reminded him of his time with the SEALs. It reminded him of all the action he'd seen, and the friends he'd lost. It reminded him of how when his service ended, he was expected to make his own way in this world, with no support behind him. How all of his service had been taken for granted. Remembering made him angry. Reminded him of why he and his surviving friends had gone into private security in the first place. It was time for him to get what was owed him. A pushover like James Penney was the right way to go about it. A decade or so in his employ, and he could retire rich. In that respect, he and Scarlett had at least one thing in common.

When he heard the light knock at his door he sat up straight but didn't leave the bed. He turned his head, listening. He had a Glock nearby atop the bedside table, but he didn't reach for it just yet. He listened to the door, to see if anyone tried to break in. He'd last checked in with his men a half-hour before, and they'd said everything was clear. Nothing suspicious, and why should there have been? At that time, there was nothing to worry about.

No one tried to break in. No one tried to pick the lock. They just knocked again, a little harder this time, but clearly not wanting to be heard by the grounds of the household. If it was one of his men, they would have radioed him.

Lee got off the bed. He didn't think it was anything to be

worried about, but he took the Glock anyway, just in case. Better to be prepared.

He went through the guesthouse to the door. He stepped lightly, not wanting to alert whoever was there to his coming. A third knock came, insistent, still not risking banging on the door and rattling it in its frame.

Lee checked the spyhole and then opened the door, keeping the Glock low by his side, and saw Scarlett Penney give a start. She wore a silk slip that clung to her body, and was wrapped in a stole to protect her against the night's cool. Her legs and feet were bare, and her hair was tied up atop her head. Her face was devoid of make-up, but she didn't look like she'd been sleeping.

Lee frowned. "What is it?" he said. "Has something happened?"

"Everything's fine," she said, and Lee noticed how her voice was softer than he'd heard it before. Noticed how she looked him in the eye, and didn't turn her nose up. "Can I come in?"

Lee stepped aside. He kept the Glock out of her view, stashing it in the cabinet next to the door. When he turned, Scarlett kissed him. She pressed her body close to his. She let the stole fall to the ground.

Lee placed his hands on her hips and held her away, instantly suspicious, suspecting a trap or a test. "What are you doing?"

She smiled at him, coquettishly. "Don't be coy, Lee," she said, the first time she'd used his first name. "Do you think I don't see you looking? I know you try to hide. I know you try to stick to the shadows. But I see you. I see everything."

Lee remained cautious, his hands upon her hips. He felt the silken material of the slip sliding in his palms. He felt the firmness of her waist, the tension in her muscles while he held her back. She was pushing against him, still trying to get close, to continue what she'd started. She made his mouth dry, made his heartrate increase. "Where's James?" he said.

She scoffed. "He's asleep. I made sure of it. He's a heavy sleeper. You don't have anything to worry about."

"How do I know he didn't send you?"

She looked unimpressed then. "When have you ever heard him tell me to do *anything*?"

She had a point. She'd bark orders at her husband, and he'd meekly do everything she said as promptly and efficiently as he could. He lived to serve her. He worshipped the ground she walked on. Lee doubted he was the first man to cuckold James.

He relaxed his grip on Scarlett's waist and she held him tight, fiercely, hungrily. Lee took her in his arms, raised her from the ground, and carried her through to his bedroom.

It was no trap. No test. Scarlett was just used to getting what she wanted, and it turned out that now she wanted him.

The affair has proceeded in such a manner for as long as Lee has been in their employ. Scarlett comes to him at midnight, or she invites him into the house when James is out. She still teases him on his days off, sunbathing close to the guesthouse wearing hardly anything at all. She knows how it drives him wild. Knows how it makes him fuck her harder.

He wonders, sometimes, how much James knows. If he's aware of what's happening. If he's really asleep when Scarlett sneaks out, like she thinks he is. James has never said anything to Lee, but Lee sees the way he looks at him sometimes. The perpetual sadness in his eyes, like a man with a low-wage job who feels beaten down and pushed around by the world. Lee thinks James has to be the most pathetic multi-millionaire walking the face of the planet, and in his current position Lee has met many of them now, including some billionaires.

This is Scarlett's goal. Billionaire status. This is what she's pushing her husband toward. This is where the idea for the marina came from in the first place. This is why they went into business with the cartels, until the clampdown began.

Lee pushes thoughts of Scarlett and their animalistic escapades aside and prepares to answer his phone. As he does so, one of his men nudges him and points down the road. A familiar car approaches slowly. Graham has arrived.

Lee answers as they start to walk toward the car. "Doug."

"I'm sending you everything we've got on Tom Rollins," Doug says. Lee detects a hint of apprehension in his voice. "As well as details on all known associates, but I don't think they're going to help much. He's well-travelled. Most of the people he knows seem to be spread across the country, and I doubt you're going to want to travel to speak to them, especially not if we want to keep this whole thing contained to our locale. I've got guys out finding out who he knows in Newark, who he's friends with, if he's dating anyone. I'll get back to you with that info soon as I have it."

Lee reaches Graham's car. The two men with him get into the back. Lee stands by the front passenger door but doesn't get straight in. "What are you holding back, Doug?"

Doug sighs. "Just..." He trails off momentarily, like he's trying to find the right words. "Listen, man. You're not gonna like what you read."

21

Tom has changed the plates on his car, swapping them for another vehicle parked in Ironbound while they waited for Melissa to leave the bar.

The three of them are on their way to Monmouth Beach, to where they would see Tessa Maberry when she appeared on the news. It's late, and dark out. It's only an hour from Newark to there, and the journey is already halfway over.

"My dad used to fish out of Point Pleasant," Melissa says. She sits in the front with Tom. Dennis is in the back. Dennis's head keeps nodding, his eyes struggling to stay open. Tom watches him in the rearview mirror. The night's adrenaline is wearing off, and now his body is worn out. He needs to rest. "It's only a half-hour south of Monmouth Beach. Point Pleasant is a nice place – like its name suggests, huh?" She chuckles, but it's as much for the two men in the car with her as it is for herself. She's trying to keep their spirits up. "It's nice, but it's not quite as wealthy as Monmouth County and Monmouth Beach. When my dad would take me out on his boat, we'd sometimes go into Monmouth Beach's waters and he'd point out all these beachfront properties to me. They were *huge*. Mansions, some of them. I remember one time – and keep in mind that I was young – one time I asked him if we'd ever live in a house like that, and he just laughed. I didn't understand at the time why he was laughing. I asked him, and he just ruffled my hair and told me that was a good one. Now, twenty years later, working in a bar and just barely making ends meet, I get it. It *was* a good one."

Tom watches the mirrors. It's hard to make out vehicles behind them in the dark. He watches the headlights behind, and sees how most of them turn off, going in different directions. It's nighttime and it's quiet. For a spell, the road behind them is clear.

"A couple of times, when he'd let me pilot the boat," Melissa continues, "I'd get us as close in as we could go to the shore, just so I could see those houses better. They were even bigger up close. I could tell we weren't supposed to be there. It wasn't a place for us. We didn't belong."

"How often did you go out with your dad?" Tom says.

"Every weekend," she says. "That's how I remember how to sail. It's like riding a bike. It's not something you forget in a hurry. I always thought it was a good life skill to have, but I've never had to use it much these last seven years, apart from when we go out fishing. I always wished..." She pauses, like she's unsure if she's going to continue. "When I became a teen, I stopped going out so much with my dad. I wanted to spend my weekends with friends, or with boys. I've regretted that these last seven years."

Teddy Ross, Melissa's father, died seven years ago, Tom

knows. Dennis doesn't question it. He's still busy trying not to fall asleep. He's not listening.

"What do we do when we get there?" Melissa says.

"We know there's protestors out there, and we know they knew Tessa Maberry," Tom says. "They were organized by her. We're going to talk to them, see if they have any ideas why she was killed –"

"They don't know she was killed," Melissa says. "On the news, the woman they spoke to said she'd disappeared. Are we going to spook them like that?"

"This isn't my first time," Tom says. "Trust me, I know how to talk to them. If they have any ideas who was making a target of Tessa, that might explain to us why Dennis is now in their sights. It might lead us to some answers."

"It's already late. Are we going to talk to them tonight?" Melissa glances back at Dennis, who has started back awake for the dozenth time.

"Not tonight," Tom says. "We're strangers to them. We don't want to approach them out of the dark and spook them. We're going to find a place to hole up and get some rest. We'll continue in the morning."

Melissa looks around, checking where they are, eyeing the signs they pass. "I think there's a motel not far from here. Ten more minutes, tops. You'll have to take the next left, though."

Tom nods. When they finally near the next left, Tom puts the signal light on.

"How many cops do you think are after us?" Melissa says.

"It could be all of them, or it could just be the ones on the payroll."

"How many do you think are on the payroll?"

"I've seen four, and that's including the detective sergeant. But I have no way of knowing a full number. There could be more out in Monmouth, too."

Melissa hesitates, thinking. She doesn't speak again until they near the motel. The neon sign flashes that there's vacancies. Tom parks away from the road, down the side of the building, then turns off the engine and turns to Melissa, waiting for her to speak.

Dennis comes around with a sharp breath, forcing himself to sit up. "Are we there?" he says, peering out into the darkness. He starts rubbing his eyes until they're bleary and red.

"We're gonna get some sleep," Tom says. "We don't have far to go to Monmouth Beach now. We'll continue in the morning. Melissa, I can see there's something on your mind."

"I have a friend," she says. "She's a deputy. Vanessa Gilpin."

"Where does she cover?" Tom says.

"Bedfordshire County," Melissa says. "It's just west of Monmouth County, to the north. We could reach out to her. Tell her what's happening. Tell her about the corruption."

"How well do you know her?"

"Really well. We went to high school together."

"And you trust her?"

"Yeah. We keep in touch. We meet up a few times a year. Last time I spoke to her would've been a couple of months ago. Last time I saw her was a couple of months before that. Should I call her?"

"Don't call her," Tom says. "No phones. If we talk to her, we do it in person. We don't let her know we're coming."

"I said I trust her."

"I know you did, but I've never met her. And what about the rest of the sheriff's department in Bedfordshire County? We need to be sure about the rest of *them*, too. But that's a job for tomorrow. Now, we need to eat and rest." Tom starts to get out of the car. "I'll go and book us a room."

22

D oug was right. Lee doesn't like what he's read.

It's clear that Tom Rollins is a dangerous man. The police reports that Doug has managed to fish out from around the country, along with various news reports, don't give the full story. He's listed as ex-Army, but there's a long period of time between when he was discharged and when he resurfaced as a nomad do-gooder that indicates to Lee that Rollins didn't entirely leave the service of his country. Plus, since then, he's survived a lot of dangerous scrapes, and that kind of survival doesn't come with luck. It comes with training. He wasn't just a grunt. He was something more, something secretive.

Lee is at the Penney mansion in Monmouth Beach, but he's sitting outside, in the car Graham drove him here in. The other three men are gone. Lee is alone. He's staring at his phone, reading through, over and over, what Doug has sent him. He sent more information, too, not just on Rollins. He sent what little is known of Dennis Kurtley. He sent information on a woman called Melissa Ross. Rollins's girlfriend. The information on this latter came later, once Doug's men had gotten back to him after they'd finished asking around in The Corner Spot, a bar Rollins and Dennis are known to frequent.

Melissa is already gone. Doug had sent men straight to her apartment. It was empty. Lee wasn't surprised to hear this. Again, Rollins has had training. He's prepared for this kind of trouble.

It's not ideal. It's not ideal at all. Rollins is clearly a dangerous man. Lee has seen him firsthand. This doesn't sweat Lee, though. *He's* a dangerous man, too. He's well-trained. He's prepared. The problem is going to be the chase. The problem, as ever, is *time*.

He puts his phone away and starts moving, getting out of the car. It's late and the house is mostly in darkness, and if he's lucky both Penneys will be in bed, asleep, and he won't have to explain this latest disaster to them.

He could go straight to the guesthouse, get to sleep himself and hope that when he wakes up there may be some updates and some good news, but he's not going to run away like a coward. He's never run away from anything in his life. So instead, he goes up to the house and lets himself in, stepping lightly in case they're asleep. He comes across Rich in the surveillance room. There's no surveillance inside the house. Scarlett insisted on this, for privacy. All of the cameras are outside, watching the grounds and the road. On the screen, Lee can see the handful of activists camped out in front of the house, but he already saw them on his way in with Graham and the others.

"Where are they?" he says.

"Living room," Rich says. "I think they're waiting for

you." He looks Lee over and chews his lip. "I assume it didn't go well?"

Lee doesn't answer. He leaves the surveillance room and heads to the living room at the rear of the house. Only a few lamps light his way. In the living room, all of the lights are off. There's a fire roaring in the fireplace, providing more than enough illumination. Scarlett and James are sitting together on the sofa, facing out of the wall-wide window toward the sea. They haven't heard Lee's arrival. He clears his throat to announce himself.

They both turn to him. "Lee," James says, getting to his feet. "How –"

"We have a problem," Lee says. "And that problem's name is Tom Rollins."

James frowns. He takes a seat on a nearby chair.

Scarlett stands. "Should that name mean anything to us, Giles?"

They're both dressed for bed, and Lee wonders if they've been waiting up for him, waiting to hear that their problems are all over and the future is bright and clear. James is in silk pyjamas with his initials embroidered above his heart. Scarlett wears a thin kimono, and it's hard to tell if there's anything underneath.

Lee tells them what he knows about Rollins, as well as what he witnessed tonight, and then tells them of his suspicions that he could be ex-special forces, or a government freelancer.

"Is this – is this going to be a *big* issue?" James says.

"I intend to nip it in the bud," Lee says.

"But you have to find him first," Scarlett says, like reading his mind. "*Again.*"

Lee can see the disappointed expression on her face.

She's angered, too. There's a flash of that disdain he saw so much when he first became head of security.

Scarlett perches herself on the edge of the sofa, holding her kimono around herself. "You said there's a woman with them now?"

"Melissa Ross," Lee says. "Rollins's girlfriend, it seems."

"What do you know about her?"

"Not a great deal. She lives in Newark and works in a bar called The Corner Spot. She was raised by her father but he died seven years ago, so that's no good to us. Dennis himself is an orphan, and a former crack addict."

Scarlett's eyebrows rise at this.

"Managed to get himself clean over the last year or two. Has started his life anew. Anyone he may have known from that time will be of no use to us. They won't know anything. He's severed all ties."

"And what about Rollins? Does he have any other friends? Any family? Anyone else you can lean on?"

"A few friends and some family, but none in New Jersey, other than the people we already know about. Doug is going to question the workers at the construction site, but he heard there was a fight in The Corner Spot a few weeks back between Rollins and some of his colleagues, so he may not be on the closest of terms with any of them. And concerning family, he's from New Mexico. He doesn't have much, but none of them are close enough to us. And his other known associates are spread far and wide."

"This Rollins," James says, fixating on what Lee told him about the man. "How worried should we be? In case you can't find him, I mean."

"It won't come to that," Lee says. "He's on the run. They all are. I intend to run them to ground."

"I trust you," James says, nodding, looking like he's trying to convince himself. "You'll get them, I know you will. You'll get this all cleared up. You've never let me down before."

Scarlett doesn't look so sure, though her expression can be hard to read.

"I have my people working to track them down," Lee says. "We won't rest until we find them."

"Mm," Scarlett says. She stares at Lee for a moment, then turns to her husband. "James, I think it's time for you to go to bed."

James's face drops lower than it already was. "I –"

"It's getting late, James," Scarlett says, her tone firm, brooking no discussion. "Go up to bed. You have to be up early in the morning."

James hesitates. He looks between his wife and his head of security. Lee notices how he's deflated. Lee can see the look in his eyes, and in this moment he knows. He knows, without any doubt, that James *knows*. "Are you – are you coming up, too?" he says, his voice strained and weak.

"Soon," Scarlett says without looking at him. She's watching Lee. She smirks a little. Lee thinks she's enjoying this. "I need to discuss some further business with Giles. Don't wait up for me."

Again, James hesitates, but he says nothing further. He pushes himself out of the chair, his shoulders slumped, and he walks slowly from the room, occasionally pausing as if he might be about to grow a spine, but he doesn't. He never says or does anything. He leaves, and they hear him dragging himself up the stairs and to their bedroom.

Scarlett's eyes have never left Lee. "I'm very, *very* disappointed in you," she says. It sounds like she's being playful, but her tone is serious.

Lee nods back toward the empty doorway James exited through. "That was brazen," he says.

She shrugs. She doesn't care. "Does that concern you?"

Lee doesn't answer.

She grins. She's still sitting on the arm of the sofa. She leans back a little. Her legs part. Lee swallows. She's naked under the kimono. She lets it slip from her shoulder, and down her chest.

"Come here," she says.

Lee does. She reaches out to him. The kimono hangs loose. She reaches for his trousers and undoes his belt, his button, and his zip. She spreads her legs wider and pulls him closer, and Lee fucks her there on the arm of the sofa.

Scarlett, at least, is quiet. She doesn't cry out or scream. Instead, she bites his shoulder. Her brazenness has its limits.

When they're through, they sit together on the sofa, slipping down on it, almost lying. "I hope you enjoyed that," Scarlett says. "Because it wasn't for you."

"Oh?" Lee says.

"No. It was for me." She sits up, covering herself back up with the kimono. She turns to him. Her face is deadly serious. "If it was anything for you, it was motivation. Until this is all resolved, you won't be getting any of this again. You're cut off." She stands, preparing to leave. "I'd rather fuck my husband than the man whose negligence could cost us everything."

With that, she leaves him alone in the dark.

Lee watches her go and balls his fists. He pulls his trousers back up. His negligence? *His* negligence? He's the only person in this whole damn situation who's doing things right.

He breathes deeply, compartmentalising. It's a setback, that's all. He's dealt with setbacks before, and he's still here. Still living, still breathing. Rollins might seem tough, but Lee isn't scared of him, just as he isn't scared of Scarlett's threat. This'll be over before any of them knows it. Lee will see to it.

23

The motel room has two single beds and an adjoining bathroom. They were able to order a pizza, then they each took turns in the shower.

After eating and washing, Dennis passed out almost as soon as his head hit the pillow. Tom showed Melissa how to keep watch at the window, what to look out for, and told her to wake him if she saw anything concerning. She never did. She woke Tom four hours ago and Tom has been on watch since. He's let Dennis sleep. He's still in a deep sleep.

Tom sits by the window, the curtains open just a crack, enough for him to see out of. Enough for him to see a vehicle that concerns him. His Beretta and KA-BAR are both close by, ready should they be needed.

It's morning now. The sun is rising. It's getting lighter, and warmer. Dennis wakes first. "Oh, man," he says, shuffling forward so he's sitting at the foot of the bed. "I was out like a light last night. How long have you been up?"

"A few hours," Tom says without turning, keeping his

eyes on the vehicle. The man inside shouldn't be able to see into the room.

Dennis picks up on Tom's demeanour. "Is something wrong?"

"Maybe," Tom says. "Wake Melissa for me."

Tom waits while Dennis does as he says.

"What time is it?" he hears Melissa ask.

"It's just after eight," Tom says, again without turning. "Both of you, stay there. Don't come closer."

"What is it?" Melissa says.

"A couple of hours ago, a car pulled into the parking lot," Tom says. "It's a tan, ten-year-old Mazda with a few dents and scrapes. The guy got out once. He walked around the building, out of view, and I didn't see where he went. I assume it must've been to the main office. Despite that, he returned to his vehicle and he's sat there ever since."

"What's he doing?" Dennis says.

"I think he's watching our room," Tom says.

"Shit," Melissa says. "Is it just him?"

"Just him. Alone in the car."

"Do you think he's with the others?"

"I don't know," Tom says. "Something about him and his vehicle doesn't look right, though. It's an old car, clearly second-hand, and it's obviously well-used. The car the three men came after us in last night – not Doug's car, the other one – it was in good condition. Just a couple of years old. Not a mark on it until I hit it with the shotgun. And the three men, they were smartly dressed. They didn't look like thugs. The guy I saw, when he went around the building, he looked dishevelled. Jeans. An untucked shirt. He doesn't look like them, and neither does his car."

"You don't think he's with them?"

"I'm not saying that exactly," Tom says. "He could have been hired by them to find us. He could be a freelancer. Whoever he is, I don't trust him. Here's what we're going to do. In a moment, I'm going to stand up and open these curtains wide and I'm going to make like I've never seen him at all. And then, all three of us, we're going to leave this motel together and go back to our car, and none of us is going to so much as glance at that Mazda. That clear?"

Dennis nods.

"It's clear," Melissa says. "But what are we going to do? Just let him follow us?"

"No," Tom says. "We're going to set off, and if he *does* follow us, we're going to find out who he is and what he wants."

24

It's morning, Scarlett and James are getting dressed, and Scarlett can tell that her husband wants to say something to her. He's been moping all morning. He's been moping since last night, when she came to bed and knew that he was pretending to be asleep, lying with his back to her and refusing to turn.

Scarlett sits at her vanity table, applying her makeup. She keeps one eye on her husband in the reflection. He's finished dressing. Today, he wears a charcoal-grey suit. He shuffles his feet as he goes to his dresser and puts on his cuff-links. He's ready. He could leave if he wanted to, get on with his day, but he doesn't. He remains where he is and hesitates, his eyebrows knitting as he avoids looking at his wife.

Scarlett sighs and puts down her foundation. "*What*?" she says, still watching him in the mirror.

James gives a start, like he had no idea she was looking at him. He clears his throat. "Last night," he begins, but does not continue.

"What about it?" Scarlett says, impatient.

James swallows. He looks toward the door like he wishes he'd just left when he had the chance. He stammers, but doesn't form a sentence.

Scarlett rolls her eyes and turns around to face him fully. He withers under her stare.

"I'm – I'm sorry," he says.

"No," Scarlett says. "You had something to say. Spit it out. I'm waiting."

"I just – I was just going to say – to *ask* – would you..." James stops and settles himself. "I was just going to ask, please, if you wouldn't be so obvious. Like you were last night, I mean."

Scarlett says nothing. She stares at him. Her stomach turns at the sight of him. He disgusts her. She doesn't try to hide this fact.

She could have had her pick of wealthy men, she knows. She picked James. Picked him because she knew he'd be easy. Knew he'd be grateful to have a younger woman way out of his league. Knew she could twist him around her little finger, and keep him there, under her control.

Scarlett wasn't born into wealth. This life was alien to her for a long time. She grew up in a motel, her mother a pill-popping part-time cleaner who fled to a new motel whenever the rent was due. As a child, this way of living was normal to Scarlett. As she grew, she realised it was anything but. The kids she went to school with didn't live like that. They had homes. They didn't have a mother like hers, either.

Over time, Scarlett came to hate her mother. Hated the life she was forcing upon her daughter. Hated the mess she'd make of herself. Hated when she was strung out, desperate for her next fix, and hated the kind of men she'd bring home to help her get that fix, like she'd forgotten she had a daughter waiting there for her.

Scarlett also hated how hungry her mother would let her get. There was no love in her upbringing. No affection. The only love her mother felt was for her pills.

In her teens, Scarlett swore she wouldn't grow to be like her mother. She wouldn't live the same life she'd been brought up in. She saw how other people lived, saw their homes, and she resolved to be rich. She deserved it. She'd already been through Hell. It was long past time for her to get to Heaven. What everyone else had, she would get more. She would get everything. And she would get it no matter what she had to do.

Enter James. Scarlett was in her early thirties and working as a waitress when they met. She'd never given up on her goals, but she was starting to get desperate. She hit the gym regularly and watched what she ate, but was starting to wonder if it was all worthwhile. She was living in a motel at the time. Every night, she looked at familiar walls and ceilings like those that had shaped her youth, and she felt like a failure. She felt like her mother.

By that point, Scarlett had spent most of her working life hopping from restaurant to restaurant, until finally she'd got a job in a high-end location. The kind of place where the people she was waiting for – people with money – would come to dine. The night James arrived, he was with two other couples. The maître d', whom she had gotten close to and was friendly with for just such an occasion, had told her how the table was a group of whales. The maître d' had worked in Atlantic City and carried a lot of the gambling slang over with him. A table of whales was a wealthy group who were liable to tip well if they were impressed by the service. He singled out James Penney particularly, and explained how he was in line to inherit a pharmaceutical company from his father. The maître d' had read this in the news. He always kept abreast of local happenings, wanting to be prepared in case VIPs entered the restaurant. Scarlett saw her opportunity. She nudged the waitress heading their way off course and took over her section without asking. She zeroed in on James. She saw he was the only one not wearing a wedding ring. She made sure to smile at him a little longer than she smiled at everyone else. She flirted with him. She was shameless. The other wives gave her filthy looks, but she didn't care. James's attention was firmly on her. He was enraptured.

At the end of the night, when it was time to pay, James searched her out. He paid the bill, and slipped her a generous tip and, along with it, his number. She waited three days and then she called him. He was hers.

Looking back, it's amazing that he was ever able to bring himself to do something so bold.

James is sweating. She can see beads of it running down the side of his face. He wipes his brow with the back of his hand. "Would you, please, not be so dismissive of me, especially in front of Lee. He works for me."

"He works for *us*," Scarlett says. She stands. James flinches. He takes a step back, though she doesn't approach him yet. "Look at me, James," she says.

He forces himself to do as she says.

"I had important business to discuss with Giles," she says. "I didn't dismiss you. I asked you for privacy."

James frowns. This isn't how he remembers it.

Scarlett steps close to him now. She makes herself smile. She notices how James's shoulders rise and tense, and her smile becomes genuine. She reaches out and strokes his cheek. "Come on, now, James. You know I'd never *dismiss* you. I needed to make it clear to Giles how important it is that he fixes the mess he's made. You understand, don't you? You're not tough like I am, James. You're a good man. *I'm* the tough one, because one of us has to be. You've always needed that from me, haven't you? If I wasn't, where would we be?"

James looks unsure, but he knows she's right. She puts a finger under his chin and turns his face to hers.

"James," she says. "You know that, don't you? Without me, where would you be? The company would be folded. You would have ruined your family's legacy. Penney Pharma wouldn't exist anymore. You would have lost it. But I didn't let that happen, did I? So when I say you need to trust me, what do you need to do?"

"I need to trust you," James says.

"That's right," Scarlett says. She kisses him lightly on the lips, though doing so sends a shiver of nausea through her. They part and she runs both hands down the sides of his face, smiling at him. "Everything will be fine soon. Things will all be how they should be."

James takes a deep breath. "Okay," he says. "You're right."

She nods. "I know I am."

She lets go of him and steps away, returning to her vanity table, turning her back on him once again. She resumes applying her makeup. James still doesn't leave. He looks like he has more to say.

"What is it?" Scarlett says.

"There's a meeting later," he says. "I don't know if you remember. With Awais."

"I remember," Scarlett says.

"Okay. Good. We're going out on the yacht, if you want to join us."

Scarlett grins to herself. "Do you *want* me to join you?"

James nods, and then, because he doesn't know if she's watching him or not, says, "Yes. Yes, I think I'd like you to be there."

"Bikini, or smart casual?"

James swallows. "Bikini," he says.

Scarlett nods. She thought as much. "I'll see you there," she says. "Now, you'd best run along or you're going to be late to the office." She blows him a kiss in the mirror.

James makes a half-hearted effort to catch the kiss, and makes a show of storing it in his pocket. His smile is weak. Finally, he leaves her alone.

25

Tom doesn't head for Monmouth Beach. The tan Mazda is following them from the motel. He takes a diversion, turning off his intended route, luring the follower away.

The man keeps his distance. Tries to always keep a couple of vehicles between them. When Tom and the others first left the motel, he didn't pull out directly after them. He let some space build up. Tom was watching for him, though. Spotted him as soon as he came into view. That tan colour is hard to miss.

Melissa and Dennis are more nervous than he is. They've never been in a situation like this before. Tom is more accustomed to them.

"How far are you going to go?" Dennis says.

"Until we can find somewhere to get the drop on him," Tom says. "And until we can be sure he's on his own."

"Do you see anyone else?" Melissa says.

Tom has instructed them both to remain facing forward. To not turn in their seats or lean closer to the mirrors.

Nothing that could alert the man following them. Right now, they have the element of surprise on their side. They're aware of him, but he doesn't know about this.

"Not yet," Tom says. "It looks like he's alone. It'll be best for us to deal with him ASAP before anyone else can turn up." Tom adds, thinking out loud, "He *has* had plenty of time to call in reinforcements, though." Tom watches the signs they pass, trying to look for somewhere suitable to make their move. There's a gas station a couple of miles down the road. He checks the gauge. They're half full.

"I'm gonna pull in up ahead," he says. "I want to see what he does. If there's an opportunity to deal with him there, I'll take it. Otherwise, the two of you remain in the car and you both stay casual. I'll leave the Beretta with you, Melissa, in case he tries something while I'm inside paying."

They reach the gas station and Tom gets out to fill the tank. He keeps his movements casual, not giving anything away. To anyone else it'll look like he's watching the amount going up on the screen, but out of the corner of his eye he keeps watch on the road. The Mazda has not appeared. It hasn't passed them by. There was no parking back the way they came. The man must have pulled over to the side of the road.

Tom goes in to pay. He grabs some jerky and water, too. Supplies to keep them going. All the while, he watches out the window. The gas station isn't busy. Another car pulls in to the pumps, but it's not the Mazda. Tom watches the driver regardless as he gets out. He doesn't pay any attention to Tom's car, nor the people inside.

Tom gets back to the Toyota, passing the supplies to Melissa. "I didn't see him," he says. "He must've held back." He resumes driving. He looks behind them in the mirror, down the road as he pulls out. The Mazda is nowhere to be seen, but the road is lined by trees. It could have concealed itself behind them.

Tom drives, continuing to watch the mirrors. A Ford appears, and then another Toyota. Tom maintains his pace. A moment later, he spots the tan Mazda behind the Toyota.

"There he is," Tom says. "He's sticking with us."

They drive on for another twenty minutes. Tom continues to check the signs that they pass. Finally, he spots one for a public restroom. "I'm going to try and corner him there," he says.

"Where?" Dennis says.

"The restroom?" Melissa says.

Tom nods. "I'll pull in and park up. I'll need to see the area first before I can decide what we do next."

Tom turns off for the restroom. He spots the Ford behind him continuing on. Ahead, the restroom, a small white building, is in an open space, surrounded by trees, concealed from the road. This is good. Ideal, even. There are a couple of picnic benches either side of it, on the grass. The road loops through the rest area, the entrance where they came in and the exit a little further down. "All right," Tom says, speaking quickly. "After I park, we all get out and head into the restroom. I'll slip around the back and lie in wait for him, but this only works so long as he pulls in after us. He might've seen the sign back there and know where we're going, and he'll hold back like he did at the gas station. If he doesn't, I'll go through the trees, see if I can find and ambush him that way." He holds out his hand for the Beretta. Melissa gives it back to him.

Tom parks the car. In the mirror, he sees the Mazda at

the entrance to the rest area. It noses forward, checking how it looks, and then it reverses out of view.

"He's not following us in," Tom says. "Stick to the original plan, in case he's watching. I'll get around the back of him."

They all get out of the car. Melissa and Dennis head into the restroom. Tom slips down the back of it. There are some discarded beer cans here, a few syringes and used condoms. Tom ignores them and goes into the trees, keeping low and working his way through the bushes, then makes his way around to the trees that line the road. As he gets closer, he can start to see through them. He can see vehicles passing by on the road. He spots the tan Mazda. It hasn't reversed back far. With the exit being further down, the driver likely thinks he didn't have to put himself too far out.

Tom moves through the trees, toward the rear of the vehicle. He can see the driver. The driver is looking down the road, watching the exit, waiting for them to reappear. The car is idling. Tom pulls out his Beretta. He makes his way to the back of the car, to the rear door on the passenger side. He assumes it'll be open. It's an old car, unlikely to lock itself instantly when the driver sets off. Few drivers lock themselves in when they're driving, especially not when travelling along an open, high-speed area like they have been.

Tom gets into the car. The driver jumps in his seat, startled by the door opening and closing. Tom presses the Beretta into the side of his head. "Pull into the rest area," he says. "And don't try anything stupid. We're going to talk as a courtesy, but I have no qualms with putting a bullet through you right now."

26

The man's name is Eric Braun, and he's a private detective.

The first thing Tom noticed about him once he got him out of the car was his blackened eye, his bruised face, and the way he was subtly nursing his ribs, all things easily disguised by the dark this morning when Tom first spotted him.

"I'm not stalking you," Eric says, keeping his hands in view while they sit at one of the picnic tables. "I was trying to find you all. To speak to you."

"Show me your ID," Tom says. He sits directly opposite Eric, holding the Beretta on him under the table. Melissa and Dennis are standing next to the table, watching the man who's followed them from the motel.

"I'm reaching into my pocket," Eric says. "Stay cool."

"Doesn't he look cool?" Melissa says. "He's stone-cold."

Eric reaches into his pocket and brings out his wallet. He slides it across the table toward Tom. Tom checks the driving license first, confirming Eric's name. Next, he pulls out his private detective license.

"Are you part of an agency, or do you work solo?" Tom says.

"Solo," Eric says. "And most recently, I was hired by Tessa Maberry."

Out the corner of his eye, Tom sees how Melissa and Dennis exchange glances. His focus remains on Eric. He slides the wallet back to him. "Why did she hire you?"

"We'd worked together before," Eric says. "She knew I'd deliver. Except, I guess this time I didn't." He indicates the fading black eye.

"What happened?"

"Tessa wanted me to look into Penney Pharma. How much do you know about Tessa? Do you know how she operated?"

"We don't know much at all, other than who she was and what she was attempting at Monmouth Beach."

"*Was?*" Eric says.

Tom thinks Eric must have some kind of an idea what's happened to Tessa, but officially she's been declared missing. "Keep telling us your story," he says, not wanting to get sidetracked right now, still not completely certain they can trust this man.

"All right," Eric says, reluctantly. "Well, Tessa, she's incredible. She'd leave no stone unturned, man. If she was going after an organisation, she looked into *everything*. She was like a force of nature. So with Penney Pharma, she wanted me to look into their business practises, into how they manufactured their drugs, what they were putting into them. I don't know where she'd heard it from, maybe friends in the government – she had friends everywhere – but she told me she'd heard rumblings that they were conning the FDA, and about them working with Mexican cartels. She wanted me to find out why."

"Who's Penney Pharma?" Tom says.

Eric looks surprised. "You don't know about Penney Pharma?"

Tom looks at him.

"All right, all right," Eric says. "They make an opioid called Sentit B. It's taken from the Latin *sentit bonum*. It means 'feel good'. Cute, huh? They make a drug twice as strong as codeine, and they call it *feel good*." He snorts, then looks them all over. He tilts his head. "Who do you think is coming after you right now?"

"Why would we suspect a pharmaceutical company?"

"Because of Tessa," Eric says. "Because of who she was going up against. She was going up against *them*."

"We haven't gotten that far into our investigation yet. We've only just started. In fact, you've cost us some time. So why don't you cut to the chase? How do you know about us, and tell us what happened to your face."

Again, Eric points to his black eye and bruised face. "This is courtesy of Penney Pharma's head of security, and personal bodyguard to James and Scarlett Penney. James is the head of Penney Pharma, by the way. Scarlett is his wife, but you could probably guess that. Their bodyguard, man, he's a mean piece of work. Ex-Navy SEAL. Knows his shit. And he throws a hell of a punch, believe me."

Tom perks up at this. "Ex-Navy SEAL?"

Eric nods. "You met him?"

"Do you have a picture?"

"Matter of fact, I do. It's in my car. Glove compartment."

"I'll get it," Melissa says.

"There's a gun there," Eric says. "So don't be surprised."

Melissa goes to the car and comes back with a folded headshot. She has the gun, too. It's a Smith & Wesson 629. Tom can see that it's loaded. "Keep that out of view," he says, taking the picture from her.

Tom straightens out the picture and sees a familiar face. Close by, he hears Dennis say, "Oh, shit."

"You *have* met him," Eric says.

"Last night," Tom says. He makes sure Melissa gets a good look at the face, too. "And Dennis first met him two nights ago. What's his name?"

"Lee Giles. He and some of his goons found out about me snooping around, and they laid a beating on me. Tried to scare me off – and truth be told, they were successful. At least, they were until I heard about Tessa disappearing."

Tom grunts. "Like I said, we had the pleasure of making his acquaintance last night. He wasn't looking for conversation and a handshake."

"And you got away unharmed? I'm jealous."

"They were looking to put us both in the ground. Still are."

"That doesn't surprise me."

"How'd you find out about us?"

"I have connections," Eric says. "Friends on the force. People I trust."

"Do you know that some of them are corrupt?"

"I guess I'm not surprised. Not my guys, though. They told me about Dennis. How he came in to say he'd seen Tessa had been run over. They came to me, because they couldn't understand why this information wasn't being released. They knew I'd done work for her. They didn't know anything about my looking into Penney Pharma. They just didn't like how Dennis's story was being suppressed. They told me about you, too, Rollins. Last night, I came looking for you all at The Corner Spot. I've followed you since then. I saw you switch the plates on your car."

"You gave yourself away at the motel," Tom says.

"Like I said, I wasn't stalking you. I *wanted* to talk to you. I just wasn't sure how to go about it. When I realised you were all running, I figured you'd be spooked and paranoid. I couldn't just walk up on you. I know your backstory, Rollins. I did my research. You think I was gonna take a risk like that?"

"Why were you looking for us?"

"For answers," Eric says. "To talk to Dennis. To verify what he saw."

"He saw Lee Giles and his men kill Tessa Maberry," Tom says. "They ran her down, like your cop friends told you Dennis said, and then they got rid of her body. Now, what are you going to do with that information?"

Eric looks like he's taken a shot to the gut. Absently, he rubs at his injured ribs. "Ah, man," he says. The verification of this news, despite likely suspecting it to be the case already, has hit him hard. "Ah, shit."

Tom watches him. Eric's mouth twists. It's clear that he liked Tessa. Admired her.

Eric is silent for a while. He looks to the side, into the trees. He bites into his bottom lip, and Tom thinks it's to keep it from trembling. He blinks a few times and sniffs hard before he finally turns back to Tom.

"Well, shit," he says. "I guess I'm gonna have to bring these assholes to justice."

Tom considers everything Eric has said. Everything he's told them. He thinks he's been telling the truth about who he is, what has happened to him, and what brought him to them. His reactions have been genuine. He's not playing a role in order to lure them out. Tom believes he's who he says he is. "You don't have to do it alone."

Eric looks at him. "You didn't know Tessa," he says. "You don't owe her anything."

"Perhaps not, but the people who killed her are trying to kill us, and we take that kind of thing personally. If nothing else, we owe them for *that*."

Eric smirks. "You gonna trust me enough to give me my gun back?"

"Not just yet," Tom says. "Don't push it. And going forward, you're leaving your car here. You'll be travelling with us."

"Why?"

"Because we're allies now, and we're travelling together. And because while I believe what you're saying, that doesn't mean I trust you."

"All right. Fair enough. Then I guess we're on the same team." Eric holds out a hand to shake. Tom takes it. "You mind not pointing the Beretta at me now?"

"It's already lowered," Tom says. "But I'm a quick draw, so don't do anything stupid."

"Wouldn't dream of it. Where were you all heading? You have a plan?"

"We're going to Monmouth Beach," Tom says.

Eric frowns. "You realise you're going in the wrong direction?"

"Courtesy of you," Tom says.

"Ah. When did you say you made me?"

"As soon as you pulled into the motel's parking lot.

Speaking of, if you followed us from Newark, what took you so long to get to the motel?"

"I saw you all check in, figured you weren't going anywhere for a while. I went to get something to eat, then grabbed a few hours' sleep in the backseat. I got to the motel early and made sure your car was still there, then flashed the license at the receptionist to see what room you all were in."

Tom nods. "Our plan was to speak to the protestors who worked with Tessa. The people who knew her. See if they had any answers as to why she was killed. To find out who's coming after us. It sounds like you've answered the latter for us. Do you have an answer for the former?"

Eric shakes his head. "I'm afraid not. That's something I was going to have to find out, too. But listen, I know that a lot of the other activists and protestors out there, especially the ones higher up who knew Tessa best, they're not out at the beach. They've gone into hiding, afraid they're gonna disappear the same way that Tessa did."

"You're in touch with them?"

"I am. I know where some of them are. I can take you to them." He thinks for a moment. "Carla Mann. She'll be the best person for us to speak to. When Tessa wasn't present, everyone answered to her."

"Where is she now?"

"She's hiding out with a few others in a squat in Leeport."

Tom begins to stand. "Then that's where we'll go."

27

Tom doesn't go straight to Leeport. He wants to go by Monmouth Beach first, to see the site of the protestors and the spot of the proposed marina they're preventing from being built.

Eric sits up front with him. Melissa sits directly behind Eric. Tom spoke with her to one side before they set off. "I think he's with us, but keep an eye on him," he said. "He tries anything, I'm counting on you to subdue him."

"I'll choke him out," Melissa said, patting her left forearm. She's taken self-defence classes for working at the bar. She knows how to get behind a man and wedge the bone on the inside of her forearm, close to her wrist, up into his carotid artery, to apply pressure and hold it there until he passes out. "You can count on me."

Thus far on their journey, Eric has behaved himself. He sits still. He's not jittery. At no point does he try to reach for his cell phone, to send secret messages or give away their location. He doesn't complain about Melissa still being in control of his firearm. He seems content to prove himself to them.

"Tell us more about Penney Pharma," Tom says. "About James and Scarlett."

"Well, their offices are down in Atlantic City," Eric says. "That's where Lee Giles caught me snooping around, after hours." He pauses for a moment, thinking. "Have you heard of the Sackler family?"

"The name sounds familiar," Tom says.

"They manufactured OxyContin," Melissa says. "Took the main blame for the opioid crisis. They were sued for billions."

"*Ding, ding, ding,*" Eric says. "That's correct. They persuaded the medical establishment that strong opioids should be more widely pushed, and that fears of them being addictive were overblown. Well, we know now that was a whole crock of bullshit. They were taken to court, and while they were on trial – and it was a big trial – they were called the most evil family in America. They were told they were addicted to money. You hear the story of the Sacklers and of OxyContin and you think, oh boy, that's a cautionary tale, right? Well, the Penneys seem to hold them in high regard. They see this story as aspirational – just without the court case. Currently, the Penneys are multi-millionaires, but there's no doubt that they've got their eyes set on reaching billionaire status."

"And how are they going about that?"

"Up until a few years ago, Sentit B wasn't selling too good. Like, it sold okay, but it wasn't one of the main brands. And then, all of a sudden, it explodes in popularity. It was something more than just a good advertising push, or hiring the right kind of reps to get it into the hospitals. No, it was becoming people's opioid of choice. Suddenly, it's the painkiller everyone wants. And I'm not just talking in hospitals. I'm talking on the streets. Pill poppers, junkies – they were buying it up, getting blissed out in dens and on street corners."

Tom turns his head so Dennis can hear him. "Did you ever hear of Sentit B?"

"I must've missed it," Dennis says. "But I had my drug of choice, and I didn't like to stray from it. A lot of people I ran with, they didn't always know what they were taking, though. They just swallowed whatever they could get their hands on."

Eric looks intrigued by this sidebar, but he doesn't ask for clarification. There's not much to question, and he can probably read between the lines. "To all intents and purposes, there's no reason for Sentit B's sudden popularity. Nothing changed. According to the FDA, the recipe remained the same. Tessa wanted me to find out if that was true."

"You said earlier that Tessa thought they were conning the FDA," Tom says, "Could they have been paid off?"

"Maybe, but I managed to speak to a couple of them, and they were just as confused as everyone else about this sudden surge. I think they were legit."

"Is there a way around the FDA?"

Eric snorts. "Probably. But they can only test what's manufactured in the plant, right?"

"You mentioned something earlier about cartels."

"I did, but it's just a rumour, and I don't have as much information as I'd like to either verify or deny it. What I *can* say is that after the recent border clampdown, the Penneys suddenly announced their intention to build a marina in Monmouth Beach."

"Where does the marina fit into all of this?"

"The official story is that they want somewhere closer to their home to moor their yacht. And for friends or others with similar seafaring craft to park up. They say it'll increase tourism in the area from wealthy visitors. But realistically, there must be more to it. Tessa thought so. She was protesting the environmental impact, but she suspected there was more going on behind the scenes. Maybe the Penneys have decided to partake in smuggling? Or if the cartels can't cross the border with the same ease as before, maybe they could sail up – but who knows? It's all theory."

"You really admired her, didn't you?" Melissa says.

"I did," Eric says. "I'd never met anyone like her before. She had such a *vision*. Such a moral sense of right and wrong. It's so rare. When you're used to dealing with cheating spouses and investigating corporate embezzlement, you start to only ever see the worst in people. But all I ever saw in Tessa was the good." He pauses a moment, his head inclining toward the window. In a quiet voice, he adds, "I'm not sure what it was she ever saw in me."

They reach Monmouth Beach. Eric directs Tom to the protestors at the proposed marina site. There aren't as many of them as there were on the news. The half a dozen that remain stay the course, marching and chanting on the sidewalk, waving banners. There's a police presence parked over the road, observing them.

The beachfront houses nearby, overlooking the beach and the sea, are large and impressive. There are expensive cars parked in the driveways. Tom slows without stopping, looking the area over. He can't see the beach from the road. There's a manmade embankment of stone and boulder, a breaker, presumably to protect the road and homes should the waves ever get too high and wild. In places there are wooden steps and walkways that grant access down to the beach.

"Do you want to see where the Penneys live?" Eric says. "It's not far from here."

Tom nods. "We should check it out."

They continue on down the road until Eric says to stop. Tom doesn't really need the directions. Again, there are a handful of protestors outside the gated driveway. The home itself – a mansion – is at the end of the rising driveway, over-looking the sea, and potentially the rest of Monmouth Beach. Again, Tom doesn't stop. He watches as he passes by, spotting a bodyguard at the top of the drive, likely making a sweep of the grounds. Tom wonders if James and Scarlett Penney are home. He knows their faces. Melissa looked them up on her phone. Scarlett is a beautiful woman. James, however, despite his forced smile and his apparent wealth, appears a broken man, the weight of the world bearing down on his narrow shoulders, and not the inheritor of a multi-million pharmaceutical company.

Tom wonders, too, if Lee Giles is in there. The guard at the top of the driveway is too far to make out his features, but Tom doesn't think that's him. The man doesn't have Lee's bearing. Chances are, Lee is probably far from the grounds, far from here, searching for them.

"That's a big house," Dennis says. "Jesus Christ, how do people get that kind of money?"

"Sometimes legally, sometimes not," Eric says. "But in James Penney's case, his father made it."

"Is his father still alive?" Melissa says.

"He's an old man – a *very* old man – but yes. He's retired. Lives down in Florida."

"How old are you talking?"

"Early nineties."

Melissa whistles.

Tom has passed the house by. He looks for somewhere to turn around. "And Tessa wanted you to find evidence to cripple the Penneys with lawsuits, like what happened to the Sacklers?"

"One of her many fronts of assault, yes. Tessa was determined that just because they had money, they couldn't just do what they wanted. She wasn't going to let them build that marina, no matter what they really wanted it for."

Clear of the Penney mansion, Tom swings the car around in an empty driveway. "Call Carla," he says. "Tell her we're on our way. It won't take us long to reach Leeport."

Eric takes out his cell phone. "She's gonna be wary of new people," he says. "But I'll get through to her. She'll listen to me. She knows Tessa trusted me, and that's why she trusts me too. It's why I know where she's hiding out." He pauses a moment, thumbing through his contacts. He looks up before he calls her. "I'm not gonna tell her about Tessa just yet. I'm gonna have to break that to her in person. That's gonna be a little gentler than over the phone."

"Do what you think's best," Tom says. "We'll leave that to you."

28

Lee stares out to the sea. The sound of its gentle waves does not soothe him. It reminds him of missions overseas in years gone by. It reminds him of gunfire, explosions, bloodshed. Of killing, and nearly dying.

It doesn't upset him. These are, however, happy memories. The times in his life when he felt most alive.

He got a flash of that last night, with Rollins. Having to chase him, and then the confrontation at the construction site. Coming under shotgun fire, their vehicles being disabled. Having to sneak up to the building, knowing even in that moment that Rollins was clearly a capable opponent and could have been scoping him out, unseen. It bought back something Lee hasn't felt in years.

Lee should be out there now, searching for Rollins and his two compatriots. But he has to stay here. There's a meeting on the yacht soon, and James wants Lee present.

His men are out there, looking, and he's put out the word to all of their contacts, and the cops on the payroll are searching, too. Even without the meeting, it'd be best he stays here and mans the fort, waits for anything worthwhile to come through to him, and *then* he can strike.

Billy comes to find him. "Sir, I've got news."

Lee turns to him, tearing himself away from the sea. Billy is an ex-cop. He used to work with Detective Sergeant Doug Posey. He's the man who told Lee that Doug would be a worthy asset. "Good news, I hope," Lee says.

Billy smiles, and Lee turns toward him fully. A good sign. "Yes, sir."

"Then don't keep me in suspense. Tell me. Is it about Rollins?"

"Yes – but it's also about Eric Braun."

"Eric Braun? The private eye?"

"One and the same."

"The beating wasn't enough for him?"

"It would seem not."

"What's that asshole doing now?"

"We've been keeping tabs on him, like you said. He behaved himself for a while, after the beating, but then last night he went for a drive."

"Christ, please tell me there's a tracker on his car."

"Of course," Billy says, and Lee is relieved. He's talking to one of his own men. A professional. "He went by a few points of interest. The apartments of Tom Rollins, Dennis Kurtley, and Melissa Ross, as well as The Corner Spot bar. Soon after that, he left Newark."

"And?"

"And we've kept tabs on him. At first he was coming this way, but then he took a sudden detour this morning. I sent a team to follow him, see what he's doing. They kept their distance. Easy enough to do with the tracker on him. He pulled into a rest area, and he stayed there for a while. I told our team to get closer, see what was happening. Well, he'd caught up to Rollins and the others."

Lee feels a flare of excitement in his gut.

"He's travelling with them now. Left his shitty little Mazda behind at the rest area, so the tracker's no good to us anymore. But we've got eyes on them."

"Where've they been?"

"They passed right by us not so long ago."

"*What*?"

"Figured you wouldn't want to do anything right in front of the house. We let them get clear. We don't want to be making any noise here."

Lee calms. He nods. "Right," he says. "That's right. That's good."

"I sent a couple extra teams out to trail them. What you told us about this Rollins, I thought we should be careful."

"How many, total?"

"Three. I've got them floating in and out, keeping the targets in sight, the way I taught them. I told them to be aware of Rollins. He's no doubt looking out for anyone following them."

Lee places a hand on Billy's shoulder. "That's good, Billy. You've done good. Where are they now?"

"Not far. Heading south, away from here. I came to update you. With them clear of here but still so close, I thought now was the best time to come and tell you. I would've come sooner but it's been a busy time keeping eyes and ears on the operation."

"Tell the teams not to engage," Lee says. "I want regular updates on where they go. If we're going to confront them, I want more numbers, and more weaponry. This is a dangerous motherfucker we're dealing with – and make this clear, Billy: he's *mine*. You got that?"

"Yes, sir."

Lee checks the time. "I have to be on the yacht for the meeting with Awais in an hour. I'll probably be there a few hours. If anything happens, don't hesitate to call me. Otherwise, I'll be hitting the road as soon as it's over and joining the others, and I'll be bringing a team with me." He thinks for a moment. "If they *have* to engage, then so be it. We don't want them getting away again. Tell them I want them kept alive if it comes to that. We need to know how much they know, and who else they might have spoken to."

"I'll do that now, sir."

Lee watches him hurry off. When he's gone, he turns back to the sea. They're so close, but he has to wait. He has to go out on the yacht. But he can trust his men. They won't let him down. He takes a deep breath, inhaling the salt air deeply into his lungs. It tastes like the past. It feels like home.

29

Leeport isn't far from Monmouth Beach. Just over a five-minute drive, but the difference in neighbourhoods is jarring. There are no mansions here. This is not a place where the wealthy come to live or play. This is not a place where millionaires will want to moor their yachts.

"Next right," Eric says. "We're not far."

Tom sees a mother and daughter sitting on their stoop, watching the car go by.

"Straight down this road," Eric says. "Okay, a left, and then the second left."

Tom follows Eric's directions. As he makes the second left turn, he sees a building on the corner scorched and blackened from a fire. The roof has caved in and the windows are all smashed. There's graffiti on the outside walls. There's no way of telling how long ago it happened, but Tom doesn't think it was a recent occurrence.

"All right, it's down here," Eric says. "Park up. I'll have to go in first, let them know everything's cool."

Tom finds a place to park the car where there is no broken glass from shattered bottles on the road. To their right is a large patch of overgrown grass. Some of the other buildings here have broken windows and look abandoned, but some of them look lived in, too. Eric gets out of the car and Tom watches him as he approaches one of the houses with boarded windows on the end of the block directly ahead. He knocks on the door and it opens a crack, like someone has been waiting on the other side for him, observing his approach. Tom can't see who opens the door. Beyond it, the inside of the house is in darkness. The door opens a little wider, just enough for Eric to step through, and then it's closed behind him.

It's a quiet neighbourhood. Tom doesn't see anyone around, and there's no vehicles passing by. He keeps an eye on the mirrors, making sure no one tries to sneak up on them.

"How long do we give him?" Melissa says. In the backseat, she and Dennis lean forward together, watching.

Tom has kept the engine running. "Five minutes," Tom says. "Maybe ten. He's already spoken to her on the phone. They shouldn't need to talk much longer."

"You still don't trust him?" Dennis says.

"I have no reason to," Tom says. "None of us do. When he talks about Tessa and about Penney Pharma, I believe what he says. But that either means he's telling the truth, or he's a very good liar. I'd like to believe it's the former, but we have to remain vigilant."

They wait, and they watch. Minutes go by.

Tom's phone rings. It's Eric. "All right, we're cool," he says. "Come on in."

Tom hangs up the call and turns off the engine. "Melissa,

keep hold of the gun and keep it ready. Dennis, go between us. Be ready for anything in there, both of you. If I start shooting, the two of you start running."

They get out of the car and go toward the house – the squat. Tom looks it over as they approach, checking the windows that aren't boarded over. He sees someone upstairs keeping lookout, watching them approach, but he's not trying to hide himself.

As they get closer, the door opens. Again, just a crack, just enough for them to pass through, single-file. Tom doesn't like it, and he has no intention of obliging. When he's in front of it, he pushes the door wide, catching the guy on the other side by surprise, almost knocking him off balance.

"Shit, dude," he says, a young Korean guy dressed in baggy clothes.

"Go through there," Tom says, tilting his head into the house. "With the others."

The young Korean guy looks confused, but he does as he's told. Tom follows him, keeping his hand close to his Beretta.

"Rollins, I told you," Eric says. "It's cool."

They enter the living room. Tom looks it over. It's lit by candles. Eric is standing with a young blonde woman. Her hair is cut short and there's a streak of purple running through it on the left side. She looks Tom over as he nears, her blue eyes concerned. She must be Carla Mann.

Other than her and Eric, there are four other people in the room. The young Korean guy, a Black guy, and two women. There's also the man upstairs. "How many other people are here?" Tom says.

"Glen's upstairs," Carla says. "He's on lookout. That's everyone."

"Rollins, look at them," Eric says. "They're just kids. This isn't an ambush. They're terrified."

Tom looks at them, and he knows that Eric is right. These young people are all huddled together, keeping the house in darkness, fearing for their lives. There's no sign of any weapons, other than some pipes and pieces of wood.

"I apologise for barging in," Tom says. "But we have to be careful."

Carla nods. "I understand," she says. "It sounds like we're all living the same lives right now."

"How long have you all been here?"

"Not long. Just since Tessa disappeared. We worked closest with her, and she always told us that if anything ever happened to her – if she got hurt or if she disappeared, anything that kept her away from us – then we should run and we should hide. We go up against rich and powerful people, and she always said that if she went missing, that likely meant she was dead." Carla bites her lip. "She said that would mean we were probably next."

"Carla," Eric says, gently. "I'm afraid... I'm afraid we've got some bad news for you. For all of you."

Eric doesn't have to say what it is. Carla knows. Her lip trembles and tears fill her eyes. They stream down her face. She cries openly. She doesn't try to stop it. Tom glances around the room and sees how the others are upset, too. The Korean guy bites his lip, trying to be strong about it. The others comfort each other.

Eric reaches out a tentative hand and pats Carla on the shoulder, trying to comfort her. She steps closer to him, into him, and Eric has to put his arms around her. He looks at Tom, helpless. He strokes Carla's hair and says, "I'm sorry. I'm so very sorry."

A moment passes. Tom sees how Dennis observes the scene despondently. He can see how much Tessa meant to all of these people. Can see how much her absence is affecting them.

Carla pulls away from Eric. She wipes the wet from her cheeks and the tears from her eyes. "I'm sorry," she says.

"Don't be," Eric says. "You've got nothing to be sorry for."

"What happened to her? Do you know that?"

"I know," Dennis says, speaking up. "I saw it happen."

They all turn to him. Dennis tells them what he saw. The men that ran her down. He tells them about Lee Giles.

"We're familiar with Lee Giles," Carla says. Her voice is bitter. She takes a deep, shuddering breath and looks to the ceiling. "That son of a bitch. He did it. He actually did it."

"This was expected from him?" Tom says.

"He had his men follow us around, find out our addresses. When we first got to Monmouth Beach, he was paying off cops to come and break us up, to bust our heads. Tessa said he was the one we needed to watch out for. If there was going to be any dirty work done, he was going to be the one to do it. If we ever saw him coming, we needed to run."

"You said the cops were busting heads when you first turned up? We went by there earlier and it didn't look like that was still the case."

Carla shook her head. "No, man. It didn't last for long. That was Tessa – she started speaking to the community, explaining to them what this marina could cost them. She won them over. The residents started complaining to the cops about police brutality. They were videoing them on their phones. After that, the cops backed off. But now she's gone, and everything she was working on, everything she was putting in place to stop the building of the marina, it's all falling to pieces."

"Why would they kill her for that?" Tom says. "It doesn't add up. It's an extreme reaction just for a place to put their yacht. Is that really worth killing someone for?"

"Tessa always thought there was something more going on," Carla says. "That's what she was trying to figure out, too. She always thought it maybe had something to do with Sentit B, but she didn't know what."

"Where is Sentit B manufactured?" Tom says. He directs the question to both Carla and Eric, assuming one of them might know.

"A factory in North Carolina," Eric says.

Tom thinks on this. "When they beat you in Atlantic City, what were you trying to do?"

"I've already told you."

"Tell me again."

"I was trying to get into the building. I was trying to get into their files, see if I could find anything worthwhile. Anything that would raise a few eyebrows."

"But they caught you."

"Almost instantly."

"The building is well secured?"

"Twenty-four-seven security," Eric says. "Cameras. The works."

"And you tried to get in in person?"

"I was gonna charm my way past security," Eric says, defensive. "It wouldn't be the first time."

Tom continues to think. "I know someone who might be able to help us," he says finally. "She's in Texas, but she doesn't need to come here. She could get inside remotely. If there's anything in that building to find, in their systems, she'll get it."

"Who?" Eric says.

"A friend," Tom says. "I'll call her." He looks at Carla. "If we find the information we need, if we can find proof that Penney Pharma murdered Tessa, we'll take it to law enforcement. We'll take it higher if we have to. You should stay hidden until then, but when the time comes, we're going to need you to come out into the open, to testify."

Carla is nodding. "Anything to make these bastards pay."

Tom turns, pulling out his cell. He's facing Melissa and Dennis. "Wait here. I have a call to make."

30

It doesn't take Tom long to get through to Cindy Vaughan.

"Well, look who it is," she says. "You miss me already?"

"Always," Tom says, feeling himself smile though she can't see it. "And what do you mean, *already*? It's been a year."

"But doesn't the time fly when you're not being chased by a bunch of wealthy snuff moviemakers?"

"It certainly does." Tom is outside of the squat, looking down the road. He doesn't see anyone else around. While inside, he'd assumed that if anyone had approached, then the man upstairs on watch would have alerted them. "Speaking of, have you heard anything from Chris and Louise?"

Almost a year ago, Tom assisted Cindy in helping Chris Parton to find his missing sister. Louise. Turned out she'd been kidnapped by a group of deviants making snuff movies.

Tom and Cindy almost became their star attractions instead. All four of them are carrying scars from that time.

"I have," Cindy says. "And they're doing well. We keep in touch. They ask about you whenever we talk. I tell them you're off being you, and you wouldn't have it any other way. You wouldn't recognise them anymore. They're both in therapy, and it's really helping them out. Oh, and Louise has gone back to school. She's going to be a teacher."

"That's good to hear. Tell them I said hello."

"I will do. Now let's get down to business. I assume this isn't a personal call?"

"Unfortunately not." Tom gives her a quick rundown of recent events. "We need someone to get into the Penney Pharma files. See if there's anything there we can use against them. When I heard it was an impossible situation with tight security, naturally I thought of you."

Cindy laughs. "I'm flattered. Sure, I'll get on it right away, but it's probably gonna take some time. If they're as security-conscious as you say, then they're probably gonna have firewalls and spyware, and likely a devoted team dedicated to keeping people like me out."

"I have faith in you. Otherwise I wouldn't call."

"That's all I ever need. I'll call you back as soon as I can. Stay safe, Tom."

"Always. You too."

Tom hangs up the call and goes back inside the squat. Eric is talking to Carla, his hands on her shoulders. He looks like he's reassuring her about something. Tom catches the tail end of what he's saying. He's promising to take down Tessa's killers.

"Cindy's working on it now," Tom says, drawing all eyes to him. "She said it might take a while."

"What do we do in the meantime?" Dennis says. "Hang out here?"

"No," Tom says. He nods toward Melissa. "We go to Bedfordshire County. We speak to your deputy friend."

31

The yacht's name is *Feel Good*. It's a Benetti, thirty-seven meters long, carbon fibre, in the Motopan-filo range. It has five cabins, as well as smaller bunk rooms for the cabin and crew while on longer journeys, and can sleep up to ten guests.

Right now, there are eleven people on board. Lee has brought Graham and Rich with him. James and Scarlett are here, naturally. There's the captain, who has piloted them into the Atlantic, seven miles from the shore, and is currently watching over the yacht while it idles. There are two smiling waiters in the lounge area, standing close by the spread of food that has been provided. And finally, there is Awais Choudhury, accompanied by two bodyguards.

James and Awais are talking business. James has taken him out on the yacht for two reasons. The first is purely ostentation. The second is more practical. It's to point out where the prospective marina is going to be built. One day very soon, Awais's people will be sailing this way, docking in the marina.

"We should break ground any day now," James is telling the Indian businessman.

"I understand you were having issues getting started," Awais says. His two bodyguards stay close to him. Lee, likewise, does the same for James. The two heavies don't worry him. They're muscular guys under their suits, clearly, but they're too pretty. Their hair is too well cut and their beards are too finely sculpted. There are no scars on their faces. Neither of them has ever suffered a broken nose. They're all show. Whenever one of them glances Lee's way he smiles at them, and they promptly turn away. They're armed, though. He can see that they're both carrying handguns under their suit jackets. For this reason he makes sure to keep them under observation at all times.

Graham and Rich are spread out on the boat, patrolling. Lee isn't expecting any trouble, but he doesn't want to be careless. Again, he doesn't know Rollins's whole background. Doesn't know what he's fully capable of, and what he's been trained in. Doesn't know how much he knows, either. Does he know about the yacht? Would he attempt to board it? It's better not to find out the hard way.

James, to his credit, doesn't hesitate over Awais's question. "That's resolved now," he says. "Just a few other minor things to get out of the way and then we're all good to go."

"I'm glad to hear it," Awais says. "The factory is ready and waiting. We merely await your say and production can begin."

James nods, looking across the water toward the spot that will soon be his marina. "And you'll be bringing it in personally, on your own ship?"

"Perhaps not every time," Awais says. "But certainly on the first occasion. I understand part of the subterfuge concerning this marina means that we'll need to look the part."

"It's a long way for you to sail."

"The boat shall remain moored in open water. The product will be delivered by helicopter. Once unloaded, we'll set sail. It's all about appearances, isn't that so?"

"How many boats do you have?"

Awais smiles. "Three," he says. "More than enough, should there be any unforeseen circumstances."

Scarlett makes her presence known. She's been at the rear of the boat, sunbathing in a yellow bikini. She saunters into view and enters the lounge, picking at the fruit on the table. Her eyes are concealed behind large, round sunglasses. She comes out onto the deck while sliding a piece of kiwi into her mouth, and smiles as she approaches her husband and wraps her arms around his shoulders from behind.

"I'm afraid I've been so rude," she says. "But I needed to take advantage of this glorious weather. This must be Mr. Choudhury, correct?" She steps aside from her husband and offers a hand.

Lee can see the strain on Awais's face and in his neck as he battles not to look Scarlett up and down. He takes her hand and bows down to kiss the back of it. "Mrs. Penney," he says. "It's a great pleasure to finally meet you."

"The pleasure's all mine," she says, draping an arm across James's shoulders.

"I was just explaining to Awais here where the marina is going to be," James says.

Scarlett shields her eyes and looks toward the shore. "It's going to look magnificent when it's complete," she says. "And it's going to make all of us so very, *very* wealthy."

Awais laughs a little at this. "Indeed," he says. "I look forward to our having a very lucrative partnership."

"Oh, I have no doubt," Scarlett says. "What part of India are you from, Mr. Choudhury?"

"Please, call me Awais," he says. His eyes have never left her since she appeared. "And I'm from Mumbai."

"And is that where the new factory is?"

"Just outside the city, yes."

"Are you in America for long, Mr. Choudhury – I mean, Awais?"

He smiles. "A few days more. I was rather hoping to see work beginning on the marina."

"I'll endeavour to see it started before you leave," James says.

Awais nods, but he has eyes only for Scarlett.

"I've never been to India," she says.

"Oh, you simply must come," Awais says. "Perhaps when the marina is complete, and the factory is fully operational, you and your husband will grace us with a visit?"

Scarlett squeezes James's shoulder. "How does that sound to you, James?"

"It sounds – it sounds like a wonderful idea," James says.

"Then it's a date," Scarlett says. "We'll have our people talk. Arrange something more concrete."

"I'll look forward to it," Awais says.

Scarlett peers over her shoulder, back toward Lee. Her smile drops a little, though it doesn't fade entirely. She knows he's looking. She wants him to see.

Lee sees her, but he's steadfast. He's unflappable. He keeps his attention on Awais's bodyguards. He checks the other boats on the water, none of them passing close by.

"Well, we've talked business," James says. "Would you like to eat?"

"That sounds most pleasant," Awais says. He holds out an arm toward the lounge. "Please, after Mrs. Penney."

This is always the part of Lee's job he likes least. The tedium of business meetings. Of rich men wagging their dicks. The dance of manners. The overly polite platitudes. The passive-aggressive comments back and forth, and the snide glances and self-serving smirks. The fawning and the flattering. The obsequiousness and the ostentation. James isn't particularly good at it, but Scarlett is a pro. That's why James brings her. That's why he makes sure she wears a bikini. It's all a power game, even when the two men are already in business together.

They make their way into the lounge and, dutifully, Lee follows. A couple more hours, and this whole game will be over. They'll be back on land, and he can finally make plans for getting his hands on Rollins.

32

L ee's cell phone is ringing as he gets back to land. They moor the yacht within view of the Penney mansion and take a speedboat back to shore. The call is coming from Billy. He indicates to Graham and Rich that he has a call to take, then steps to the side to answer it while the Penneys walk Awais and his bodyguards up the beach toward their home.

"What's the situation?"

"The targets are currently on the move," Billy says. "We're not sure where they're heading to right now, but we have eyes on them. I've got information I thought might be of interest to you, though. Are you still on the boat?"

"Just got off."

"Are you free to talk? It's not an emergency, so I didn't want to interrupt you out there."

"Just tell me."

"Well, our intrepid travellers went down to Leeport and stopped off at a squat. After they left, one of our guys managed to get in for a closer look without being seen. Seems it's a hideout for some of Tessa's people – six of them to be precise. Rollins and the others have been talking to them."

"That's interesting," Lee says, thinking how Dennis must have told them what he saw.

"I thought it was important to maintain the pursuit," Billy says. "I told two of the teams to continue the chase on Rollins and the others, and the third I told to stay behind in Leeport and keep watch over the squat. Do you want them to deal with the hideout now?"

"Keep it under observation," Lee says. "Make sure they don't go anywhere, but don't move in yet. We know where they are and we can deal with them later. Keep eyes on Rollins and the others and keep me updated. Things are wrapping up here. I'll put a team together and we'll get on the road. You've done well, Billy. Keep it going."

"Yes, sir," Billy says.

"How far are they?"

"Close enough for you to catch up to. It looks like they're heading out of Monmouth County."

Lee frowns. "To where?"

"Potentially Bedfordshire County, but that's an early guess judging on direction. I should be able to give you a more solid answer soon."

"I'll be en route within ten minutes."

"I'll let the teams know you're coming."

Lee hangs up. He jogs up the beach, following the others up to the house. He won't update the Penneys just yet. He's had to break bad news to them a couple of times already, all because he got ahead of himself. This time, he'll be patient.

He'll inform them when it's over. When Rollins and the others are dead, and all of their problems are resolved.

It shouldn't be long now. They won't see him coming.

33

"How long do you think it'll be before your friend gets back to you?" Eric says.

"Cindy will go as fast as she can," Tom says. He's driving them to Bedfordshire County. They're close to leaving Monmouth County. "We just have to be patient. I know her, and she won't stop until she gets answers, even if that means she's going without sleep. If we hear from her tomorrow morning or even the morning after, then we can be assured that she's been up all night – that she's been working at it since I got off the phone with her."

"You speak highly of her," Eric says.

"I'd trust Cindy with my life," Tom says. "I *have*."

"Should I try and get in touch with Vanessa?" Melissa says from the back. "We're not far out now."

"No," Tom says. "Don't contact her. I know you don't want to think about it, but if she *is* working with the other cops, if she's on the Penney Pharma payroll, we don't want to let her know we're coming. We don't want to give them any kind of idea where we are or where we're going."

"What if she's not home?"

"Then we wait."

Tom glances at the mirrors. Something has caught his eye a few times now. A couple of somethings, in fact. Two vehicles. He keeps seeing them. Never together. A black Ford and a white Toyota. Right now, it's the black Ford. The white Toyota turned off ten minutes ago, and the Ford promptly took its place, rejoining the road from a junction they passed by. The last time he saw the Ford was almost a half-hour ago. It's definitely the same one – Tom has committed the plates to memory. Likewise for the Toyota. He's been watching out for them.

"We're going to take a detour," Tom says. He starts signalling for the next junction.

"Why, what's happening?" Melissa says.

"Eyes forward," Tom says. "Same routine as when Eric was following us. I think we're being trailed."

Eric glances at the mirror on his side. "I haven't seen anything," he says. "Which vehicle?"

"Black Ford," Tom says, and reels off the license plate. He pulls down the off-ramp. It takes them onto a quiet road that runs parallel to the highway.

"I see it," Eric says. "Can you make out how many inside?"

"At least two, both in the front. There could be more in the back, but they're keeping their distance. Makes it hard to be sure. There's also a white Toyota. Again, at least two occupants."

"I don't see the Toyota."

"It turned off. They're flowing in and out."

"Like cops," Eric says. "Do you think they might *be* cops?"

"No way to tell just yet," Tom says. "But they've been

following us for a while now. They could've pulled us over at any time."

"Why didn't you say anything sooner?"

"Needed to be sure," Tom says. "Whoever they are, they're careful and they're smart. They're doing their best not to be seen, and they almost accomplished that. If there'd been maybe one or two more vehicles with them, they might have accomplished that."

Even on the quieter road, the Ford has managed to keep two cars between them. Tom spots a turn-off to the right up ahead, onto a quieter back road. He doesn't see any other vehicles on it. The two cars behind aren't signalling for it. Tom waits until the last moment, then turns down it without signalling.

The Ford doesn't follow. It continues straight on, and Tom and the others are momentarily alone.

"You've lost them," Eric says.

"For now," Tom says.

The empty road is long and takes them away from the highway. It remains clear behind them, and up ahead. There are plenty of trees up ahead, and they soon disappear in them.

"What do you think they'll do?" Melissa says.

"They might double back and try to follow us down here," Tom says. "But this road looks like it might loop around up ahead and I think we might be able to find our way back onto the highway. If we can get there fast enough we should be able to put some distance between ourselves and them, and then continue on to Bedfordshire without them following."

They emerge from the trees and the road is clear on

either side now, offering a view of a small town up ahead with a gas station and a small store.

"There's a Toyota," Dennis says, leaning forward and pointing so Tom can see.

Tom spots it. It's coming from an adjoining road and heading fast toward the town. They seem to spot Tom's own Toyota at the same time Tom spots them, and they begin to slow.

"Shit," Eric says. "Is that the same one?"

Tom nods.

"How are we gonna get rid of them?"

Tom drives straight through the town, as if he hasn't noticed the Toyota. They pass close enough by the junction and the white car for Tom to steal a look. He doesn't see any uniforms or badges. He continues down the road through the town. A glance at the mirror shows the Toyota turn down past the gas station and pursue. They keep their distance. There are no other vehicles to put between them.

Tom can see a turn-off to the left up ahead, but he doesn't take it. He doesn't head for the highway yet. The Toyota will just follow. Instead, he'll get them clear of the town, and then it's best for them to continue on this road, where it's quiet. "We're gonna have to deal with them," he says. "Melissa, give Eric his gun."

Melissa passes it forward, between the front seats. Eric takes it and quickly looks it over, holding it low. "Shit, man, what if they *are* cops?"

"They've picked their side."

He feels Eric staring at the side of his face. "You serious?" He glances back at Melissa and Dennis. "Is he serious?"

Neither of them answers.

"Aim for their tyres," Tom says. "It's just the Toyota right now – we lure it somewhere quiet, and we cripple it."

"Like you did at the construction site," Dennis says.

"Exactly. But Eric, if you see a face you recognise as one of Lee's men, maybe even one of the guys that kicked your ass, don't be afraid to aim a little higher, and to let me know to do the same. Do you know this area?"

"Not well," Eric says."

"Melissa? How about you?"

"No," she says. "If I come down this way, I stick to the highway."

"All right. Eric, does your minor knowledge extend to knowing if there's anywhere good we can lure them?"

Eric thinks for a moment, looking ahead. "There's some woods down the road a way," he says. "But I've never been in them. It *could* be a good spot for an ambush."

"How far down the road are we talking?"

"Five, maybe six miles? Something like that."

In the mirror, Tom sees fast movement. The return of the black Ford, trying to catch up to the Toyota. But there's another vehicle now, one that Tom hasn't seen before. Another Ford, but bigger than the other. An Explorer. It's following the smaller black Ford, and sticking close. Backup.

"The Toyota has company," Tom says. "And they're coming up fast. They're not trying to hide it anymore."

"Then neither should we," Eric says.

Tom nods. He puts his foot down and drives for the woods.

34

The woods are close. They're in view now. Behind, the three vehicles in pursuit are maintaining their distance, but they're keeping pace. They're looking for a good place to strike. They've probably spotted the woods, too.

"No sirens," Tom says. "They're probably not cops. Do you recognise any of the vehicles? Maybe the Explorer?"

"No," Eric says. "The Penneys get driven around in a Cadillac Escalade, but they've probably got a whole fleet of vehicles they can call on. They've got the money for it."

The woods are drawing closer. As they do, Tom notices how the three behind speed up again. The road ahead remains clear, and it's the same behind their three pursuers. They're the only four vehicles on the road.

"Melissa, Dennis," he says. "When I stop the car, get low. Stay down. If anything happens to me and Eric, start running. Don't let them catch you. If they catch you, there's only one way that ends. Same as it did for Tessa."

They both understand.

Tom presses down on the accelerator, pushing the car for all it's worth. They reach the woods. "Brace yourselves." He slams on the brakes as he spots a way through the trees. The Toyota behind slams on its own and loses control, skidding around them. Tom pulls on the handbrake and turns into the opening he's seen. The car does a three-sixty and comes to a stop, its rear pointing into the trees, away from the road. Tom slams it into reverse and pulls back into cover. "*Go!*" he says, stomping on the brake and pulling out his Beretta.

He and Eric throw their doors open and use them for cover as they open fire upon the two Fords.

They blow out the front tyres of the black Ford and it loses control. It careens out of view, down the road where the trees obscure it, but out of the corner of his eye, through the few gaps there are, he sees it start to roll.

The Explorer manages to hit its brakes and start reversing. Tom pursues, motioning for Eric to cover the Toyota.

Tom gets near the road and sees an MP5 emerge from the front passenger window. Tom ducks behind a tree as the MP5 opens up, chunks of wood flying and scattering. Tom gets low and fires toward the passenger, putting two bullets through the windshield. The MP5's fire goes wild, the shooter hit.

Tom looks back toward the Toyota. He hears gunfire as Eric shoots upon it, but Tom is aware that Eric only has six bullets before he needs to reload. He's already counted five. He sees the windows of the Toyota shatter. From here he can see there were only two men in the vehicle. Further down the road, he sees the black Ford on its roof. There's no sign of the men inside. They're either stunned from the crash or, with luck, dead.

Both front doors of the Toyota fly open and the men

emerge, armed with Sig Sauer Rattlers. Eric manages to hit the passenger with the final bullet in his 629, then he ducks into cover and reaches toward his back pocket to reload. Tom doesn't know how quick Eric is at reloading, but he doubts he's fast enough to hit the driver. Tom fires twice, putting him down before he's able to do anything with the Rattler.

He turns his attention back to the Explorer. It's still backing up, but now it stops, slamming the brakes with a screech. The back doors open. There are more men in the Explorer, and they're all armed with automatic rifles.

Tom breaks cover, firing upon them as he goes. He sees Eric, reloaded, hurrying up to take his place behind the tree, firing the 629. Tom gets to the Toyota. He dives forward and snatches the fallen Rattler from the dead passenger, then takes cover around the side of the Toyota.

Gunshots come his way, and toward Eric. They hit the road and nearby trees, and puncture holes in the Toyota. Tom drops to his stomach and returns fire, wiping out one man's ankles, almost severing them from his body, then peppering bullets along his torso when he's prone on the ground. Tom rises to a knee, sighting the other men who emerged from the rear. As he does so, he hears the roar of the Explorer. It's coming straight at him.

Tom dives to the side, over the bonnet of the Toyota. The Explorer scrapes along the car, rocking it, and drives over the top of the dead man on the road. It doesn't stop. It keeps going, fast, fleeing down the road, around the Ford on its roof.

There's one man left who got out of the back of the Explorer. He's been left behind. He fires between Eric and Tom, hitting the tree and the Toyota. On the ground after diving over the car, Tom can see him. He fires the Rattler in his general direction, to spook him, not taking aim, wanting to give Eric an opening. The man panics and turns his fire upon the Toyota. Eric understands. He shoots the man twice, then runs over and fires again to make sure the job's done.

Tom rises with the Rattler, making sure the area is clear. The men in the black Ford still haven't emerged. They're either dead, unconscious, or trapped. Whichever it is, they're not a threat. The Explorer is gone.

Eric is breathing hard. "Thanks for the distraction," he says. He wipes his mouth and forehead with the back of his hand and adds, "Did you see who was driving the Explorer?"

Tom checks the Rattler's magazine. It's almost out. He discards it. He shakes his head at Eric's question.

"It was Lee," Eric says. "Lee Giles."

Tom looks down the road. The Explorer isn't coming back.

"Well, we've given him something to think about," Tom says. They hurry back to the car, to Melissa and Dennis.

"Jesus, are you okay?" Melissa says.

"We're good," Tom says. He pulls out of the clearing and gets back onto the road. He doesn't follow the Explorer. He goes the other way, back toward the town and, beyond it, the highway.

35

Lee's heart is pounding. He can taste sweat on his top lip. He looks in the mirror and sees that he's not being followed, though Rollins must have finished with the man he left behind by now. If they're not following him, they must be carrying on their journey, to wherever they were going when he and the two teams intercepted.

Rollins must have spotted them. He knew they were coming, hence all of his sudden detours. And once he lay his ambush, it was clear he knew how to handle himself, as Lee suspected he would. Twice now he's seen him in action. Twice now Rollins has gotten away from him, and this time he's killed seven of his men. One of them lolls in the passenger seat next to Lee still.

He pulls to the side of the road when he's sure no one is following, then reaches over to push the door open. He kicks the corpse out to the side of the road and resumes driving, pulling out his cell phone. He calls Billy.

"It went to shit," he says when Billy answers.

"What happened?" Billy says.

"They saw us coming. Devolved into a shootout. I'm the only one left."

"The only one?" Billy sounds shocked. "Holy fuck. Was it Rollins and Eric?"

"The details can wait. Just listen to me – Rollins is too dangerous. I've trained you all as best I can, but it might not be enough. We need backup. I'm going to send you the number for Josh Moore once we're off this call. We served together in the SEALs, and we worked together in private security afterward. Last time I spoke to him he was doing mercenary work in Syria. Call him and tell him I need him, Cooper, and Silverstone. Tell him I require immediate fire support. They can name their reward – they know who we work for, and they know payment will be prompt. If they need any more encouragement, tell them *The only easy day was yesterday*. They'll enjoy the challenge. Did you get all that?"

"I did. If they're coming from Syria, it could take them some time to get here –"

"If I'm calling them for help, they'll get here as fast as they can, don't worry about that. They know I'd do the same for them."

"Yes, sir."

Lee checks the mirror again. He's clear of the shootout, and of all the dead bodies. He keeps going, spotting an on-ramp up ahead to merge with the freeway. He heads for it. "Some questions are going to come our way," Lee says. "We need a backstory in place for the men who were with me here, just in case. Their bodies are going to be found, if they haven't been already. We don't have any of them on the books, so we should be fine, but we need to be prepared if any cops decide to dig deeper and come asking. Contact Doug, make him aware, tell him to be prepared to deal with that for us."

"Got it."

"One last thing," Lee says, knowing he's already given Billy a lot of information. "We've lost Rollins and the rest. We're going to have to find them again. The team at the squat, make sure they're aware of what's happening. I need to get turned around and then I'll be on my way to them. The occupants spoke to Rollins. They might have some idea where they're going."

"I'll let them know."

"Have you got all that, Billy? This is important."

"I got it, sir."

"They're in order of importance. Josh first. We need them to get in motion. Then the rest."

"Yes, sir."

"You haven't let me down yet, Billy – this isn't the time to start."

"You can count on me."

36

Tom and the others are on their way to Bedfordshire County, certain now that they're no longer being followed. They make their way to Deputy Vanessa Gilpin's home. Melissa is giving directions. Tom follows them, and keeps an eye on the vehicles behind them, mentally noting what he sees, and if any of them appear more than once. So far, he hasn't seen anything, but he's not going to let anyone get the drop on him again.

Eric has reloaded his gun. He keeps it out, but it's low and concealed. He watches the mirror on his side, too.

"I hope you've got plenty of bullets for that thing," Tom says. "We could see a lot more firefights before this thing is through."

"I've got a couple dozen more," Eric says. "You wanna know what's crazy? I never used to carry so many. A full chamber and maybe a few spares, but after I had the run-in with Lee Giles and his men, that's when I started taking my security more seriously. Before that, this thing was just for show. I'd never had to use it, other than at the range."

"You should maybe think about getting something with a magazine. Something that holds more, instead of having to carry loose bullets around with you."

"It's on my to-do list, but things have been hectic lately."

"Do you know how many people Lee Giles has on his team?"

"I don't have solid numbers, but at minimum a few dozen. I think he expanded it recently, when everything with Tessa started. Became more security-conscious than they already were."

They hear Melissa do a low whistle at the numbers. "Maybe me and Dennis should be equipped, too," she says.

"If we'd had more time after the shootout," Tom says, "I would've gone through the bodies, see if there were a couple of handguns for each of you. I didn't think we should risk hanging around, though."

"Maybe Vanessa can hook us up," Melissa says.

"I'm not sure how I feel about having a gun," Dennis says. "I've never used one before. I'm not sure how comfortable I'd be with one, or how useful I'd be, either."

"It's not about having to use it," Eric says, turning to see Dennis. "Sometimes it's just about letting the other guy know you have it. That can make him hesitate, second-guess himself."

Tom isn't sure he agrees with that. If you have a gun, you should be prepared to use it. If you wave it around trying to scare people, they're going to know that. They're going to know that you're scared shitless. They might be willing to call your bluff. He doesn't say anything, though. He understands what Eric is trying to say to Dennis.

"Well, if we get a chance, maybe the three of you could

show me what to do," Dennis says. "If I have to carry one, I should at least be prepared, right?"

"Right," Tom says. He glances at the mirrors again.

Eric does the same. "Still looks clear to me."

"Yeah," Tom says. "I think we –" Tom stops. A thought occurs to him. "You need to call Carla," he says to Eric.

"What?" Eric says. "Why?"

"Because we don't know how long they were following us for. We don't know where it started. We don't know what they saw."

"Shit," Eric says, realising what he's saying. He pulls out his phone. While it rings, he says, "But we checked that area out. And they have the lookout."

Tom is aware of this. When he stepped outside to call Cindy, he didn't see anyone or anything that put him on edge. But their pursuit had to have started somewhere. "They were careful. They hid themselves from us for who knows how long? We can't run any risks. You need to tell Carla and the others to get out of there."

Eric turns away and starts talking. Carla has answered. They converse briefly. Eric tells her what happened, and that there's a risk she and the others have been found. "You got somewhere else you can go?"

Tom can faintly hear Carla's response. "Yeah, yeah we do. We've got a few places."

"Tell them to let us know when they get there," Tom says. "So we know they're safe."

Eric does so. The call ends. "Okay," he says. "They're spooked, but that ain't a bad thing right now. It'll put some pep in their step."

Tom sees a sign welcoming them to Bedfordshire County. "Melissa, how far out are we?"

"Not long now," she says. "Fifteen minutes, if that."

Tom stares ahead. He thinks about Carla and the others in the squat. It feels like he and his group are being pulled in all directions. There's a lot of ground to cover. They need to end this fast. Too many people are in danger. They need Vanessa to be clean. They need the whole sheriff's department to be clean. They need allies.

37

L ee is pulling back into Leeport and struggling to maintain the speed limit, but he knows the last thing he needs right now is to get pulled over for speeding, especially with a couple of bullet holes through the windshield and blood on the passenger seat. He gets a call. It's Saunders, one of the men left to watch the squat, along with Roden.

"What is it?" Lee says, knowing that this could be another dose of bad news he could do without.

"People inside seemed to get spooked all of a sudden," Saunders says. "Packed up their bags and looked like they were about to leave. We cut them off, kept them inside the house."

"You're with them?" Lee says.

"They're bound and gagged. We've taken their phones from them, and a couple of those fancy watches, just in case they're the kind that could help them contact anyone."

Lee breathes a sigh of relief. "Okay, that's good. I'll be with you soon, ETA five minutes."

"Come straight on in," Saunders says. "I'm sure they're looking forward to seeing you."

Lee wonders why the activists were starting to run. He assumes Rollins must have got in touch with them, told them what happened. He mustn't have been aware of how long they were being followed for, otherwise he would have told them to get out and go somewhere else right after he met them.

Lee pulls onto the street and parks the Explorer close to Saunders and Roden's vehicle. He quickly looks the area over. It's a shithole, and it's quiet. He heads to the squat and goes straight inside.

Saunders and Roden are standing over the bound and gagged captives, their Glocks out to make sure they behave. Lee strides between them, looking down at the six. "Is one of them in charge?"

Roden points toward a woman with short blonde hair, a purple streak running through it. "We think it's her," he says. "We used to see her out at the marina site. She was always going around with Maberry."

Lee smiles down at her. He recognises her from the files he and his men compiled. He grunts, remembering. "Carla Mann," he says, and her eyes widen. "What, you think we didn't have files on all of you?" He looks around, motioning to a nearby chair. "Sit her in that."

Saunders and Roden each take an arm and haul her to the chair. They sit her down. Lee grabs a wooden chair from the corner of the room and parks it in front of her. He indicates for Saunders and Roden to keep watch over the others.

"You and I are going to talk," he says to Carla.

She stares at him, biting down on the gag that keeps her

silent. She's trying to be defiant, but Lee can see that she's scared.

"And we're going to talk civilly," Lee says. "There won't be any shouting or screaming. We're going to use our indoor voices. Is that understood?"

Carla gives no sign that she does or does not.

Lee stares at her, still smiling slightly. He takes his time. He doesn't have any to waste, but he doesn't want her to know this. He reaches behind himself, under his jacket, and removes his SRK from its sheath. He holds it up in front of her face. "How much do you all know about me?" he says. She stares at the knife. "Do you know I was a SEAL? You probably do. Tessa was thorough, too, wasn't she? We know she kept files. This right here." He shakes the knife a little. "Is a keepsake from those SEAL days. Do you know what it's called? A Cold Steel SRK. I assume the acronym means nothing to you. Survival Rescue Knife." He snorts. "No one is coming to rescue you here, Carla. And your chances of survival are minimal. Because if you don't talk to me, I'm going to take this knife, and I'm going to start cutting pieces off these people here with you. You're going to watch me do it. You're going to watch me with the knowledge that your silence is compliant in their bloodshed."

Carla isn't blinking. All defiance is gone. She knows he means what he says.

Lee grabs the nearest body to him. A young Korean. Lee sits him up in front of himself and presses the tip of the SRK next to his right eye.

Carla makes a muffled cry through the gag, her body leaning forward, pleading.

"You're going to behave?" Lee says.

She nods.

Lee pulls the gag from her mouth, but he keeps the Korean guy seated in front of himself, between them.

Carla stretches her mouth, working her jaw like it cramped with the gag in it. She doesn't scream. She whispers to the Korean. "It'll be okay," she says, but she sounds like she's trying to persuade herself as much as promise him. "It'll all be okay."

"Well, that depends, doesn't it?" Lee says. He starts tapping the flat of the blade high on the guy's cheek. "You've spoken with Rollins. And Eric Braun, and Dennis Kurtley, and Melissa Ross. This isn't a question. We know this. What did they want?"

Carla is still looking at the Korean.

"No," Lee says. "Don't look at him. Look at me. Don't make me repeat myself." He presses down the tip of the SRK. A drop of blood blooms on the guy's cheek. It starts to roll down his face. He winces, closing his eye in fear that Lee might move it higher.

"Stop! *Please*," Carla says. "They – they told us what you did to Tessa. That's what they wanted. They wanted us to know."

This doesn't surprise Lee. He does, however, doubt that this is the only reason they came here. Carla is trying to hold out on him. "Did they tell you if they've passed this information on to anyone else?"

"No," Carla says. "They can't trust anyone. They said you've paid off the cops."

Lee smiles. "And did they tell you anything else? Ask you anything?"

"They asked about you, about Penney Pharma – about anything we knew about you. But we don't know anything –

we just know about the marina. We're just trying to stop the marina."

"Tessa was trying to do much more than just that, though, wasn't she?"

Carla doesn't say anything to this.

"Is there anything else you think I should know?" Lee says. "Anything else they said to you?"

Carla shakes her head. She does it fast. Her lips are pursed. Lee doesn't believe her.

"I'm not so sure about that," Lee says. "Think about it real hard." He straightens out the blade and presses the tip deep into the side of the guy's face. He cuts it down the side, stopping just above the gag which is tight against his jaw. The guy screams into his gag and his body twists side to side. Lee has cut him deep. Probably severed some nerves. Looking down, already he can see that his features are looking misshapen. Maybe it's just the pain he's in.

Carla almost screams, but she stops herself. She keeps her mouth shut. Lee looks at her and raises his eyebrows, waiting.

"I – I don't know, there was someone Rollins said he was going to talk to, but he went outside to call her."

"Talk to her about what?"

"To look into Penney Pharma – I don't know any more than that, I swear. I didn't hear her name, and I don't know what he asked her to do."

"Are they going to meet her now?"

She hesitates. "I don't know," she says. "Maybe…"

"You're lying to me again, Carla." Lee reaches down, toward where the Korean guy's hands are bound behind him. He straightens out one of his fingers. He's going to cut the tip off it.

"No – no, wait! *Wait!*"

Lee looks at her.

Carla closes her eyes. "They're going to Bedfordshire County," she says.

Lee lets go of the finger and sits back up. "What's in Bedfordshire County? Is the woman Rollins spoke to there?"

"Melissa has a friend – a deputy. A different woman. They're going..." She has to swallow and force herself to continue. "They're going to talk to her. To tell her what you did to Tessa."

"I'm glad you saw sense, Carla. Things could have gotten very nasty for a moment there. Is there anything else you need to tell us?"

Carla's head hangs, defeated. She shakes it no. He's broken her. He's confident he's gotten all the information he's going to get out of her.

"Are you certain?"

"I've told you everything," Carla says without looking up.

"That's good." From behind, Lee slips the SRK between the Korean guy's ribs, into his heart. His back arches as if he can escape it, but there's nowhere for him to go. Lee pulls the knife out as Carla looks up, realising what he's done. Lee is standing before she can react. He takes a handful of her hair and yanks her head back. He cuts her throat.

The other four captives have seen what's happening. They're panicking. They're trying to make noise through their gags, and rocking on the ground as if they can crawl away without the use of their arms and legs. Lee wipes the blood off his blade on Carla's jacket sleeve. He turns to Saunders and Roden. "Deal with the rest of them," he says. "Keep it quiet." He holds up his knife to illustrate his meaning. They understand, and they get to work.

Lee leaves them to it. He exits the squat.

38

Tom parks the car at the end of Vanessa Gilpin's
street and they watch her house from afar. The
driveway is empty, and there's no cars parked in
front, either. It's a pleasant and quiet neighbourhood of
single-storey homes. It's early evening now, and people have
returned from their day at work. Most of the other driveways
are occupied, and they can see activity inside the homes,
preparing dinner or settling down to watch television. There
have been a couple of joggers pass by the car, as well as a few
dog walkers.

Vanessa's house remains inactive. There are no lights
inside, and no signs of movement. "She's not in," Melissa
says. "She could be working the night shift."

They've been here over an hour. They've waited long
enough that if Vanessa were out running an errand, she
likely would have been back by now. There's no sign of her.

"We need to get off the street," Tom says, as another dog
walker passes them by. No one has checked them out or
seemed suspicious, but he doesn't want to push their luck.

He starts the engine and circles the block to get the vehicle out of view. He parks it outside of the neighbourhood, at the side of the road away from the houses. He kills the engine. They don't get out of the car yet. "I'd like to know for sure that Vanessa is at work," Tom says.

"I've got this," Eric says, pulling out his cell phone.

"What are you going to do?" Melissa says.

"Trust me, I do this all the time." He searches the number for the Bedfordshire County Sheriff's Department, then puts *67 before he hits dial to disguise his own number. Tom can hear the tone for the sheriff's department. It rings four times before it's answered.

"Oh, hello there," Eric says, deepening his voice and softening his New Jersey accent. "A couple of weeks ago I called in a domestic disturbance and I spoke to Deputy Gilpin. I have some further information and I was hoping to speak to her directly. Is she there?"

The woman on the other end responds in the affirmative. "She's on shift tonight. Let me just see if she's still in the station. What's your name, please?"

"It's Joe," Eric says. "Joe Campbell."

"Please hold, Mr. Campbell."

A holding tone comes on the line. Eric hangs up. "She's working," he says.

"Then it probably is the night shift," Tom says. "And we're likely not going to see her until the morning."

"So what do we do until then?" Dennis says.

"We get into her house," Tom says.

"What?" Melissa says.

"We go inside and we search it," Tom says. "If she has anything to do with Penney Pharma, if she works with them, it's unlikely there's going to be anything obvious lying around that would give her away, but that doesn't mean we don't check. We have to be thorough."

"I'm not comfortable searching her home," Melissa says.

"Then don't," Eric says. "*We'll* do it. Rollins is right. It's necessary."

Tom looks at Melissa. She's concerned, but she nods. "You're right," she says. "I get it. But I can't help. I don't want any part of that." She chews her lip, then asks, "How do we get in?"

"Through the back door," Tom says.

"You any good at picking locks?" Eric says.

"I can hold my own." The road they're parked on is quiet. Only one vehicle has passed them since they pulled over. "But I'll need to see the lock first. If it's not straightforward, then I might have to owe Vanessa a new window."

Eric grins.

"Me and Melissa will go first and get the door open. We'll call you once it's done. It's a small neighbourhood and Vanessa could be friendly with her neighbours. We don't want them to see a group of us go to her home when they know she's out. We go in groups of two, and we make sure no one sees us slip down the side and go around the back."

"Got it," Eric says.

Tom and Melissa get out of the car and head down Vanessa's street. They take their time, presenting as just a couple out for an evening stroll. Out the corner of his eye, Tom is scanning the homes they pass, and especially the ones directly next to and opposite Vanessa's own. There's no one out on the street right now, and he doesn't see anyone hanging around their windows.

"We're clear," Tom says as they draw parallel with Vanessa's home. It's still in darkness, and the driveway remains empty. He and Melissa head down the side of her house. At the end of the alleyway Tom holds up an arm to keep Melissa back, then peers out to check the backs of the neighbours' houses, as well as the house directly opposite her, their rear doors and windows facing each other. There's a fence between them, obscuring most of the view. It's clear on all sides. There are no lights casting their glow back here. Tom goes to the door and inspects the lock. It's a basic tumbler. He'd almost expected something more serious from a deputy, but from what he's seen of Bedfordshire County it looks a quiet, peaceful place. They probably don't have to deal with many break-ins, and thus don't fear them.

"Do you have a couple of bobby pins?" Tom says, still crouching. They keep their voices low.

"Maybe," Melissa says, checking her pockets. Her long hair is loose, nothing holding it together. Luckily, she finds three in her left pocket. She hands two of them over. "I don't know how long they've been there," she says. "They must've been through their fair share of wash cycles."

Tom prepares the bobby pins. He straightens one out. He twists the other into an L shape. He inserts them both into the lock.

After a couple of minutes of twisting and applying pressure, the lock turns. Tom pushes the door open. It leads into the kitchen. He doesn't step straight inside. He scans the room, making sure it's clear, and then makes his way through to the living room, indicating for Melissa to follow him at a safe distance. He sweeps the house quickly, making sure it's empty. It is. They remain in the dim light, not wanting to turn anything on and give themselves away. He calls Eric and tells him it's clear, and for he and Dennis to come along.

Melissa looks around. "This feels so wrong," she says.

"Melissa," Tom begins, but she starts shaking her head.

"No, I get it. I do. We have to be careful. We have to be sure."

"Do you know what time she'll get back from night shift?"

"I don't know for sure. Maybe eight or nine? But it could be earlier."

"Well, if we're going to be here for that long, at least we've got somewhere comfortable to hide out."

A few minutes pass and then Eric and Dennis arrive, coming through the unlocked back door.

"Anyone see you?" Tom says.

"I don't think so," Dennis says.

Eric shakes his head. "It's getting quiet out there."

Tom turns to Melissa and Dennis. "You two take a seat and keep watch through the front window. If anyone approaches, let us know." To Eric, he says, "I don't expect to find anything, but let's do this."

Eric nods. They begin their search.

39

Josh Moore, Shameik Cooper, and Val Silverstone do not fly directly into New Jersey. They parachute ten miles off the coast, under cover of darkness, and Lee picks them up in James Penney's Bowrider. He pulls them aboard and assists them in reeling in their equipment.

When they're all onboard, the four men pound fists and cry out, "Hooyah!"

Lee feels himself grinning, and an elation deep in his chest. There's a camaraderie here that he's been away from for too long. He takes them each by the hand and shakes them hard. "Damn, it's good to see you all again," he says.

Josh claps him on the arm. "And it's good to see you. We got your message, and I have to admit, Giles, it got our dicks hard. It sounds like you've got a challenge for us."

"Fuckin-A," Val says.

"Oh, I got a challenge," Lee says. "You think I would've called you all otherwise?"

"We just figured maybe you were getting soft out here," Shameik says. "We've heard stories about the Jersey Shore."

"You can see for yourself," Lee says. "Once we get through."

"Let's pause one second," Val says, suddenly seriously. "We were given the impression we could name our price."

"Mm," Josh says. "And truth be told, if we're working for a pharmaceutical company, we're gonna lay down a *steep* price."

"Fine," Lee says. He expected as much. "But wait until we're through before you start throwing any numbers around. I've seen Rollins up close, twice, and he's no joke. You're gonna maybe want to claim hazard pay on top of your standard rate."

"Ain't gonna be anything standard about our rate," Val says, laughing.

"Like I said, just name it," Lee says.

Josh takes a seat. "Get us to land, Giles," he says. "We've been in the water and it's cold."

Lee starts the Bowrider back up. He turns it toward land. Val stands close to him. "Do you have his whereabouts?"

Lee speaks loud enough for them all to hear. "Not right now, but I have a pretty good idea where he's going."

"Yeah?" Shamiek says. "How confident are you in that?"

"Not one hundred percent, but it's a strong lead. And where we're going, it could lead to some bloodshed. A *lot* of bloodshed, potentially."

"Nothing we've never seen before," Josh says.

"I'm talking about the law," Lee says.

"Oh yeah?" Josh says. "Well, we're not officially here. That's gonna be a you problem. You confident you can handle that?"

"They'll never know it was us," Lee says.

"So where are we going?" Shameik says.

"Little place...I doubt you've heard of it," Lee says. "West of here, in Bedfordshire County. Once we get back to land and the three of you have had a chance to get dried and eat, we're heading straight there."

40

I t's getting late, and they still haven't heard anything from Carla Mann.

It's pitch black in the house. They've raided Vanessa's cupboard and made a quick meal of tinned chili. Now, they sit and they rest, and they wait.

Apart from Tom. He isn't resting. He stays close to the window, on watch. They didn't find anything when they searched Vanessa's home, but he didn't expect to. They're going to have to talk to her to get the truth. Tom hopes, especially for Melissa's sake, that she's clean. That they can talk to her freely, and tell her what they know. That they can enlist her help.

He's growing concerned about Carla. He hasn't heard back from Cindy yet, either, but she said it could take a while. But for Carla, wherever they were going, they should be there by now. Every so often he glances at Eric for confirmation that she hasn't messaged him or tried to call, and every time Eric shakes his head.

Dennis is asleep on the sofa, his forehead creased. He's

not resting well. On the sofa opposite, Melissa is wide awake. She's uncomfortable being in her friend's home without her knowing. Eric sits next to her. He's looking at Tom. "I don't like it," he says. "We should've heard something by now. We should've heard from her *hours* ago."

Tom nods. He's aware.

"And what about your friend? Have you heard anything back from her?"

"She said it'll take time."

"We don't have a lot of that."

"Cindy will be going as fast as she can." Tom looks out of the window again. The street is silent. Some of the houses are in darkness, the occupants having gone to bed. In others, there are lights on inside, but their curtains and blinds are drawn. "I need to go back to Leeport," he says.

Nobody says anything. Eric and Melissa both know why. They know what he's thinking. They know what he's worried about.

"Call me if you hear from Carla," Tom says, preparing to leave. "Call me if Vanessa comes home, too."

"I'll come with you," Eric says.

Tom holds up a hand before he can stand. "You need to stay here with Melissa and Dennis. I'll be fine on my own. And I'll be fast."

Eric deliberates, but he stays where he is. "I hope you don't find anything out there," he says, his face grim and ashen.

Tom nods. "Me too."

Melissa stands. She puts an arm around him and kisses him on the side of the neck. "Be careful," she says.

Tom leaves the house out the back door and heads down the alley at the side. He pauses at the end, watching and listening. It's quiet here. No voices, no vehicles. The only engines he can hear are distant. He crosses lawns, where it's darkest, rather than heading out onto the sidewalk and walking along under the streetlights. He gets to his car and, with a bad feeling in the pit of his stomach, turns on the engine and heads back to Leeport.

41

James is pleased, buoyed by today's meeting with Awais, and by the updates that Lee Giles has been sending him.

Scarlett sits in a chair in their living room, one long leg crossed over the other, and sips from a glass of red wine as she watches him pace elatedly in front of the fireplace, rubbing his hands together.

"It's coming together now," he says. "I can feel it. All of our problems are going to go away. We'll all get what we want." He stops pacing and suddenly steps closer to her. He's beaming broadly. "We'll reach it, like you've always said – like you've always wanted. We'll hit that billionaire status." He motions to the house around them. "*This* will seem like a quaint bungalow compared to the places we're going."

Scarlett smirks for his benefit.

He drops to his knees in front of her and takes her left hand, the one not holding the wine. "It's all because of you," he says. "I couldn't have done this without you."

"I know," Scarlett says. She takes a drink.

"I know how they used to look at me," James says. "At *us*. How they used to talk about us. They said I was the weak son. They said you were just a waitress. But we're going to show them, aren't we? They're going to just *die* with envy."

"We can only hope," Scarlett says.

James giggles. He's like a schoolboy.

Scarlett looks at him. "I can't help but feel that you're maybe getting carried away prematurely," she says. "This isn't over yet. What *exactly* has Giles told you?"

James gets back to his feet. He takes a seat on the sofa opposite her. "That they're running Rollins and the others to ground," he says. "That they've been clearing things up along the way. That construction will begin on the marina in a matter of days, because nothing will be standing in our way anymore."

"Did he give any further details?"

"Just the broad facts."

"Hmm." Scarlett can't help but feel that Lee has been holding things back from them, potentially to cover up the failures of himself and his men.

"He's brought in others to help him," James says. "Old SEAL buddies, he says."

Scarlett arches an eyebrow. "Is that so? And how much do they cost?"

"I don't care about that," James says. "Once the marina is built, whatever they charge will be a drop in the ocean."

"Don't get ahead of yourself, James," she says. "You're too giddy right now. You need to reel it in. Act like a professional, like an *adult*, for God's sake."

James's jittery energy seems to dissipate almost instantly. He slumps a little, though he tries to sit up straighter. "No, you're right, you're right," he says.

"Tamper it," Scarlett says. "Don't celebrate until you have the good news. Does it really sound so promising to you if Giles has had to call in old friends to help him out?"

"He says it's just a precaution. Rollins is dangerous, and he doesn't want to put his less experienced men at risk. He says it's for the best."

"I'm sure he does. How many men has he called in?"

"Three."

Scarlett takes another drink, dreading to think the kind of numbers these three men are going to throw around once the job is done. This whole situation makes her stomach sour. The wine burns acidly at the back of her throat. She changes the subject. "Where is Awais staying?"

"I recommended a hotel to him in Atlantic City. Recommended him a casino he should visit, too." James's brow furrows suddenly. "Oh, that reminds me of something I was told at the office today."

Scarlett stares at him, waiting for him to explain.

"The online security team were getting strange readings. Like someone was trying to hack in. *That's* not what's unusual, they said. They deal with these things every day. *But,* they said it was a strong attack, not like anything they'd seen before."

Scarlett stares at him. "And? Were we hacked?"

"No, they managed to keep them out. They said what surprised them most was the suddenness of the attack, and how, despite its aggression, it didn't seem to be targeting anything of importance. It was almost like it wanted to be found." James shrugs. "It's all mumbo-jumbo to me. It all goes over my head."

He seems prepared to dismiss it and move on, like it was just something of minor interest it occurred to him to tell her about. She doesn't see it that way. "Maybe it was a distraction," Scarlett says.

James frowns. "A distraction? I don't know... I'll mention that to them tomorrow, see what they think. But I'm sure they know what they're doing. They would've covered all bases."

"If you say so," Scarlett says. "But I don't like it. Make sure they look into it properly. We don't want anything to bite us in the ass." She drains the remainder of her wine and gets to her feet. "I'm going to bed."

"Do you want me to join you?" James says, sounding hopeful.

"In an hour or so," Scarlett says, feeling gleeful as she sees his face drop. "Once I'm already asleep."

42

T om gets back to Leeport. He doesn't drive straight to the squat. He parks his car a block away and continues on foot. He makes his way toward it sticking to the shadows, avoiding streetlights and security lights, and he pauses once it's in view. He surveys the area. There are no visible lights on in the buildings here. No signs of life. The squat is in darkness.

Tom remains in the shadows. He lets the minutes go by while he watches. There's no activity inside. No one on watch. There's no one patrolling the area. No one in the nearby vehicles. It's clear. It's safe to approach.

He goes to the squat. The door is unlocked. Cautiously, Tom pushes it open.

The stink of blood hits him instantly, and Tom knows that things are not well. He pulls out his Beretta and steps into the squat.

He doesn't have to search far. The source of the blood is in the first room, the living area. Six dead bodies, all bound, most of them gagged. Tom checks the rest of the house, and once he's sure it's empty he looks the bodies over. Killed with knives, no bullet wounds. It was kept quiet.

Carla's body is slumped in a chair. Her throat has been cut. Her front is drenched with blood. It's not a fresh cut. The blood has dried and looks brown upon her clothes. On the ground, propped against another chair directly opposite her, is the young Korean guy. There's signs of torture on him. His face has been cut up before he was killed.

Tom drops into the chair opposite Carla. He breathes deep and stares at her, his jaw clenching. He looks down at the Korean guy, too. The smell of their blood is thick in his nose.

Eventually, he stands and straightens. He looks around the room, taking in the six bodies. Commits their faces to memory, along with Tessa's. Lee Giles and his men, and all of Penney Pharma, will pay for what they've done here and elsewhere. They'll pay for their crimes. Tom will see to it.

43

The sheriff's department in Bedfordshire County is a small building built far away from any of the county's small towns. A single road leads to it, and the building is surrounded by trees. It's an ideal location, Lee thinks. Isolated and concealed.

It's late, and it's quiet at the department. Lee watches the building through binoculars. He doesn't need night vision. The building is well-lit. There are outdoor security lights, along with a few streetlamps that line the road and illuminate the parking lot at the side of the building. The inside is lit up, too. They don't look busy. Cruisers have returned and set out intermittently throughout the night, but never in a hurry, and never transporting anyone. Lee has counted two deputies inside at all times, one of them manning the phones at the rear of the building, though they don't look like they're keeping them busy. He's counted at least three others patrolling in the cruisers. There's a lock-up inside, but he thinks it's empty. He wonders if there are more deputies active during the day.

Lee has mapped out what he's able to see of the department. He's been around the building, concealing himself within the trees, seeing as much of it as he can. It's a clear view through the windows. There are only blinds on one room at the back. He thinks this could be the sheriff's office. It's also the only room with the lights off.

Josh, Shameik, and Val are close behind him, checking over their equipment. They have M4A1s and Sig Sauer P226Rs, as well as flash and smoke grenades. Some of Lee's men are close by, too, a dozen of them, spread out throughout the woods, surrounding the building on all sides. Lee has come here in force. He isn't taking any chances. His men give Lee's SEAL buddies a wide berth, like they're intimidated by them. They should be. Like Lee, they haven't been SEALs for a long time, but it's not something that ever goes away. They've been working as private security and mercenaries ever since they left – if anything, they're more dangerous now than they were before.

Lee's radio crackles. It's Rich. "Doug's just arrived," he says.

Rich isn't close. He's down the road, awaiting Doug. Doug has been instructed where to pull over and meet with Rich and Graham. They don't want his car to be seen close to the sheriff's department.

Lee lowers the binoculars and gets on his radio. "Hide his vehicle and bring him to me."

"Is this the cop?" Josh says.

Lee turns to him. "Detective sergeant," he says. "But yes."

"And you trust him?"

"It's not about trust. He works for me. He's paid by Penney Pharma. He's in too deep now. He's seen and done things he can't afford to ever come out. He knows what he stands to lose."

It takes fifteen minutes for Doug to reach Lee, escorted by Rich and Graham. Doug looks around, peering through the woods at the men gathered, a startled expression on his face. "Jesus Christ, Lee," he says. "What's going on out here?"

Lee takes him to one side and explains what's happening, and what they're waiting for. "If we can't cut them off before they arrive, we're going to have to hit the building, and hit it hard."

Doug's eyes go wide. He looks toward the department building. "Are you insane?" he says. "This is a sheriff's department."

"Anyone you know work here?" Lee says.

"No, but –"

"You don't have any friends inside?"

"No –"

"Then it shouldn't be a problem for you. And it's not like I expect you to pick up a gun and join us. You're here as an eyewitness, Doug. You tell the version of events *we* want told. And look at it this way – if things *do* get messy, you get to be the hero of this story. No one will ever know the rest of us were here."

"*I'm* not supposed to be here," Doug says.

"I'm sure you'll think of something."

Doug is still staring at the building, watching it through the gaps in the trees and the branches. "How do you know they're coming here?"

"Reliable intel," Lee says. "They had to make a detour first, but my source didn't know where that was. Then they're going to come *here*. If they get here, you know what that means, don't you?"

Doug doesn't say anything.

"This isn't where they stop. They'll call in the FBI. They'll call in the press. And then everything comes out – about us, and about *you*. We may have to go to extreme lengths, but we're not going to let that happen."

"Who is your source?"

"That's not important right now," Lee says. "You don't have to worry about them. Just trust that they were reliable."

Doug looks like he isn't sure he wants to know more.

"Take a seat, Doug," Lee says. "Settle in. We could be here for a while."

Doug doesn't move from where he is. He bites his bottom lip and looks toward the building again.

"*Doug*," Lee says, more firmly now. He claps him on the shoulder to get his attention fully. "Take a seat. It's not a request."

Doug does as he's told, finding a space on the ground to prop himself under a tree. He swallows and runs his hands back through his hair, then clasps them together in front of his mouth. He almost looks like he's praying.

"Jesus Christ, Mr. Detective Sergeant," Josh says. "You heard what Giles said, didn't you?"

Doug glances his way, only his eyes moving.

"*Relax*. We could be here a while yet. Just think about how you're gonna be a hero real soon. They might even throw you a parade. Maybe give you a medal, a pay rise – a promotion. Just think about that. That'll carry you through."

Shameik and Val chuckle. Doug doesn't say anything to them. Lee resumes his position, keeping watch on the building through his binoculars.

44

Tom is driving back to Vanessa's home. He's not far out now. He didn't leave Leeport straight away. He got back to his car and he called Eric, told him what he'd found.

"Oh, *fuck*," Eric said, sounding nauseous. "Oh, holy shit. We led them right to them. We must've done."

Tom said nothing to this. He was already aware. If only he'd spotted the cars following them sooner, Carla and the others would still be alive.

"Christ, what have we done?" Eric said.

"This isn't on us," Tom said. "It's on Penney Pharma. It's on Lee Giles. What *is* on us is vengeance. We have a responsibility to make sure they didn't die in vain. That goes for Tessa, too."

Eric took a deep breath. When he spoke again, his voice was firmer. He'd steeled himself. "Yeah," he said. "Of course. You're right. We're gonna bring these bastards down. We're gonna make them pay."

"Yes, we are. So stay strong. We can mourn them after."

He's driven the rest of the way in silence. He replays what he saw in the squat, over and over. The blood. The wounds. The looks on their faces. The way they were tied and gagged. He doesn't succumb to the rage that bubbles within him at these images, but he wants it to be there. Wants it to be ever-present.

This war already had casualties. It already had reminders of why they're doing this – he needs to keep Dennis safe, and he needs to make it so Melissa can return to her old life. They needed to find out why Tessa Maberry was killed, and to bring the perpetrators to justice. And now there's Carla, and the five others. Tom never knew their names. He didn't need to know them in the moment, and he regrets that now. But he'll never forget their faces.

He's back in Bedfordshire County, not far from Vanessa's home. He parks in the same out-of-the-way place he did earlier. As he kills the engine and prepares to get out, his cell phone begins to ring. His jaw clenches, expecting bad news. As he pulls it out, he sees that it's Cindy. He relaxes, just a little. A glance at the time shows that it's early in the morning, though it's still dark. It'll be dawn soon.

"Cindy," Tom says.

"How are you doing out there?" Cindy says.

Tom doesn't give her details. "I'm okay," he says. "How are you?"

"Tired," she says, and laughs. "But also *wired*. I got through."

"Did you find anything worthwhile?"

"I think so. I assume you're free to talk?"

"Yeah."

"Okay, so, I won't bore you with explaining how I mounted a cyber-attack that I re-routed through servers in the Middle East and Europe, and used that diversion to get through their security and into their files."

"It would just be jargon that wouldn't make much sense to me."

Cindy laughs a little, but then she stops and says, "Tom, are you sure you're all right? You sound flat."

"It's been a long few days," Tom says. "I guess I'm probably drained. I can give you a full rundown once it's over, but for now we'd best stick to what you've found."

Cindy is silent for a moment. She's concerned for him. "Make sure you do," she says finally. "You know I worry about you, Tom. It's one thing to just assume you're out there getting yourself into trouble, it's another thing to *know* it's actively happening. Soon as you get clear, you call me."

"I will," Tom says. "I promise."

"All right. Well, here's what I've got for you. Two things stood out to me – I mean, I spotted evidence of all the usual kind of laundering and fraud and all that typical corporate bullshit, but that was expected, right? I figured you wanted more, something that could help you out with more immediacy. So, first of all, a few months ago, a large sum of money was sent to India. It took some looking but I eventually found out that the recipient was a businessman named Awais Choudhury. He owns a few factories over there, primarily in and around Mumbai. After he received this money from Penney Pharma, he started building a brand new factory. There's no prizes for guessing what they're going to be producing."

"Pharmaceuticals," Tom says.

"Exactly," Cindy says. "For export."

"What's the name of the factory? Does it have any obvious connection to Penney Pharma?"

"No – it's just got a generic name. Mumbai Pharmaceutical Productions."

"Is it active?"

"Not yet, but it's built. Could start any day now."

"Penney Pharma already have a factory in the US." Tom thinks. "So we don't know what they're making in Mumbai?"

"No, but it's got to be Sentit B. The funding sent to this factory coincides with the recent clampdowns at the border against the cartels. Which, by the way, I found offshore payments that were sent to the cartels in the past, but they cease around the same time as the aforementioned clampdowns.

"What clampdowns exactly?" Tom says, wanting to be sure he has all the details.

"The clampdowns on illicit fentanyl being smuggled into the country. Which ties into the second point of interest I found. Penney Pharma have been suppressing the death statistics of people who've overdosed on Sentit B. Those overdoses all had traces of fentanyl in their system."

"They're putting fentanyl into Sentit B?"

"That's what it looks like. It'll make it more potent, and more addictive – but it also makes it deadlier. They're basically presenting their product as high-end painkillers, but they're effectively selling street-level drugs."

Tom thinks, pondering what Cindy has told him. "The US factory must be a front," he says. "For the FDA. They're testing the product without fentanyl and giving it the go-ahead, and then Penney Pharma are smuggling the fentanyl-laced product into the country."

"Originally via Mexico," Cindy says. "And now it looks like it's coming from India."

"That's why they need the marina. It's nothing to do with yachts."

"And that's why they're willing to kill for it," Cindy says. "They're looking to flood the market, and they stand to make millions, probably even billions."

"They can't suppress that kind of information forever. If they flood the market there's going to be more deaths. The truth will come out."

"Yeah, but Tom, if you make billions, if and when the shit starts to hit the fan you can afford to disappear. Or else they won't need to – they'll just have to pay their court bills."

"Like the Sacklers," Tom says.

"Yeah, exactly, just like them. None of them went to jail. Why would the Penneys?"

Tom strokes his chin, looking down the road. "Thanks, Cindy," he says eventually. "I'm not sure we could have got this information without you."

"I'm always here when you need me," she says.

"You should get some rest."

"I'd try, but I'll be worrying about you. I know I won't be able to sleep. You need to call me as soon as you're safe. I'm serious."

"I don't know how long that's going to take."

"I'll be waiting."

"I'll try to make it fast. Goodbye, Cindy."

"Goodbye, Tom."

Tom lets Eric know that he's coming to the house so as not to surprise them, then makes his way back to Vanessa's. The sky is gradually beginning to lighten. Dawn is coming. Dennis is awake now. They all are. They're waiting for him. He tells them what Cindy has found out.

"Jesus," Melissa says. She runs her hands down her face. "These people are psychopaths."

"What can we even do?" Dennis says. "Is talking to a deputy going to be enough?"

"We don't stop at the sheriff's department," Eric says. "They're a gateway. They can keep you and Melissa safe while we get in touch with the FBI. We don't just give up."

"So long as the sheriff's department is clean," Tom says.

"We found nothing in the house that says Vanessa could be dirty," Melissa says.

"No, but I didn't think we would," Tom says. "And it's not just about Vanessa. It's about the whole department."

"She should be back soon, right?" Dennis says. "If she was on the night shift, that's gotta be over soon."

They sit in silence, staying away from the window as the day gets lighter. Tom stands close to the front door where he has a clear view of the road, leaning against the wall with his arms folded. He watches as cars leave the street, people heading off for their work day. No vehicles enter the street. The sun is up now. Tom can't remember the last time he slept, but he doesn't feel tired. He's too angry, and there's too much to do, for him to allow himself to feel tired.

"There's a car coming."

"A blue Honda?" Melissa says.

"Yes," Tom says.

"That's Vanessa."

45

Vanessa Gilpin is dressed in jeans and a white T-shirt. She wears a leather jacket over the top. Tom spots her through the window, careful that she doesn't see him. He catches a glimpse of a holster under her jacket. He steps behind the front door, out of view of her entrance.

Eric, Melissa, and Dennis have left the living room. They're hiding in the kitchen. Tom hears Vanessa's key enter the lock. She pushes the door open and steps inside. Before she can close the door, Tom grabs her from behind, kicking the door shut with his heel. He covers her mouth with his right hand to keep her from crying out, and clamps his left across the top of her chest to restrain her. He holds her firm enough that she knows there's strength there, and threat, but not so tight as to make her uncomfortable.

"I'm not here to hurt you," Tom says. Her blonde hair is tied back into a ponytail and it brushes at his cheeks and nose. "Please stay calm and I can let go of you." He quickly reaches inside her jacket and retrieves the Glock, tossing it onto the sofa.

Vanessa doesn't struggle. She's been captured, she knows it, and knows she isn't in a position to fight back without getting hurt or killed.

"Melissa," Tom calls. "Come on out."

Melissa appears from the kitchen where Vanessa can see her. She holds her hands out and she looks apologetic. Tom feels Vanessa straighten a little, no doubt confused.

"Vanessa, I'm so sorry," Melissa says. "We need to talk to you, and once we do I think you'll understand why we've had to sneak around like this."

"Eric, Dennis, come out, too," Tom says.

They do. Tom directs Vanessa toward a chair. "I'm going to let go of you," he says, lowering her into it. "Please don't scream, and don't try to run. We just want to talk to you." He lets go of her. She doesn't scream. Tom takes a step back.

Vanessa looks around at them all. She looks up at Tom, seeing him for the first time. "Do you understand I'm a deputy?" she says. "You've broken into my home and taken me captive–"

"We know you're a deputy," Tom says. "That's why we're here. You should talk to her." He tilts his head toward Melissa.

"The fact she's here is the only reason I'm complying right now," Vanessa says. She turns her attention to Melissa. "What's going on? Who are these people?"

Melissa looks like she isn't sure where to begin. "Uh, do you remember how the last time we spoke I told you I was seeing someone? Well, this is him."

"This is Tom?" Vanessa says. "I wish I could say it was a pleasure to finally meet you."

"Likewise," Tom says.

Melissa takes a seat on the sofa, perching on the edge of it, leaning forward, as close to Vanessa as she can get from across the room. "We need to talk to you," she says. "It's...it's serious. I mean, it has to be, right? You know I wouldn't just break into your house otherwise."

"How did you get in?"

"Picked the back door lock," Tom says.

"Jesus. Then I'm changing that ASAP."

"It was shockingly straightforward. But at least we didn't have to smash a window."

"Vanessa," Melissa says. "How much do you know about Penney Pharma?"

Vanessa frowns. "What? Not much. Why should I?"

"Do you remember hearing about Tessa Maberry? The activist who went missing a couple of days ago?"

"Yes."

Melissa bites her lip. "Okay, this is a lot, so you're just going to have to let me get it all out, okay? Just listen. Don't interrupt. Save all of your questions until I'm done." She proceeds to run down what they've been through over the last few days, starting with Dennis witnessing Tessa's hit-and-run murder. During the course of the telling, she explains who Dennis and Eric are too, as well as providing some extra background on Tom.

Eventually, she tells her of the murdered squatters, too, and of the information Cindy passed on to Tom not so long ago. "We know there are crooked cops in Newark and Monmouth Beach," she says. "But we can't be sure who is and who isn't. It's the same for the sheriff's department in Bedfordshire County. That's why we had to sneak around like this. For the record, Vanessa, I don't think you're crooked. I don't believe you would ever do something like that. I know you and I trust you."

Vanessa doesn't respond straight away. It's a lot of information for her to digest. Tom watches her face. She's stunned. She looks like she's been slapped, or has taken a swift punch to the gut and all the air has been driven out of her.

Eric clears his throat. "Melissa might believe you're clean," he says, "but we have to be sure."

"What do you mean?" Vanessa says.

"We want to trust you," Eric says. "We want to trust your whole department. Hell, at this point we *need* someone to trust, someone who can help us. But we can't be stupid about this. We need to know that you're clean."

"How can I prove that? I'm clean. What else can I say? I think the whole sheriff's department will be clean. This isn't that kind of place. There's nothing to cover up here, no one to pay off. We have some of the lowest crime rates in the state."

"That's all well and good, but we still need to be sure."

"I understand that, but what can I do?"

"I think she's telling the truth," Tom says. Out the corner of his eye, he sees how Melissa looks at him gratefully.

"Do you really believe that, or do you just hope it because your girlfriend does?" Eric says.

Tom ignores the jibe. "I've been watching her," he says. "This news is hitting her as hard as it hit us. But also, yes, what Melissa thinks of a person shouldn't be discounted. If she trusts Vanessa, so should the rest of us. Plus, I never took her phone from her. I did that on purpose. At no point has Vanessa tried to reach it. She's sat and she's listened."

"All right," Eric says. "But I'd feel a lot more comfortable if I could look through that phone."

Vanessa takes it from her pocket and holds it out to him. "I don't have anything to hide."

"I need you to unlock it." She does so, and then Eric goes through it. Tom goes to him and watches what he's doing. He searches her contact list, her call log, and her messages. He goes through her emails. He's thorough.

"I can see a banking app," Eric says. "I need you to unlock that, too. I need to be sure there haven't been any mysterious deposits."

"Eric, that's too much," Melissa says.

"No," Vanessa says. "I understand." She unlocks the app and gives the phone back. "Just keep an eye on him, Tom. Make sure he doesn't try to make any purchases while he has that access." She grins.

Tom watches. Eric goes back through her online statement. He goes far. It's all bills, food, and subscriptions. The only payments are from the sheriff's department. Eric goes back two years.

"All right," he says, handing the phone back. "I'm sorry I had to do that."

Vanessa puts her phone away. "I get it. I do. But we can all trust each other now, right?"

Tom takes her Glock from the sofa and hands it back to her. "I think so," he says.

She takes the gun and re-holsters it. "This is a major case," she says. "And we're a small department."

"What about the rest of the department?" Eric says. "Can you be sure they're clean, too?"

"Like I said, I don't know who would be trying to pay us off all the way out here. But even if they tried, I don't think anyone would take it. I know these people. I trust them with my life. They're good people."

"Who's the sheriff?" Tom says.

"Warren Hobbs," she says. "I've known Warren for years, and trust me, the last thing he'd ever take is a bribe. He likes the quiet life out here, away from the excitement of the cities, but he's also a good man. A family man. He wants his family to be proud of him. He'd never do anything to jeopardise that."

"Then we should talk to him. Tell him what we've told you."

"We should also check him out," Eric says. "The same way we have with Vanessa. We need to be certain."

"He's not working today," Vanessa says. "If I call him, if I tell him it's important, he'll come here, and then you can all meet him yourselves."

"Call him, but don't tell him it's important," Tom says. "We don't want to alarm him, and we don't want to alert anyone. Find another excuse to get him out here. Maybe tell him you saw something on the night shift last night that you'd feel more comfortable discussing with him in person."

"I can do that," she says.

"Just make sure he comes out here," Tom says.

Vanessa nods, a look on her face that says she's determined to prove herself. She pulls out her phone.

46

James calls Lee early in the morning.

"Lee, how are things going?" he says.

"Things are fine, Mr. Penney," Lee says. He's watching the station still. Night shift ended and day shift has begun. There are currently three deputies inside, and three out on patrol.

"It's not over yet?" James says.

"Not yet."

"Uh, I'm, uh, surprised it's taking so long, Lee."

"Things are currently in hand, and we all just need to be patient."

"Oh, I just –"

"This is a delicate situation, sir. I'm afraid we're going to require radio silence going forward."

"Oh. Yes, of course, I'm sorry, I –"

"I'll be in touch once we're through here, sir." Lee hangs up.

James isn't the only one getting antsy. His men are, too. Doug has been since the moment he arrived. Josh, Shameik, and Val, however, are not. They're cool. They're the only ones Lee feels like he can truly rely on.

Josh steps up next to Lee. "How confident are you?"

"It doesn't matter how confident I am," Lee says. "This is our one lead. We need to have faith in it."

"We've been here all night."

"The deputy they were going to talk to, she could have been on the night shift. I spotted a couple of female deputies. She could've been either of them."

"I assume you're keeping eyes elsewhere, too."

"Of course. I don't put all my eggs in one basket. But it's going to be like looking for a needle in a haystack. This is our best option. Are you having doubts, Moore?"

"Not me," Josh says, grinning. "I'm not so sure about the rest of your boys, especially the cop there."

Lee grunts. He knows Josh is right. He gets on his radio. "Stand tough, gentlemen. Anything could happen at any minute and I want everyone on high alert. Look alive."

He motions for Josh to keep watch on the department building while he goes to talk to Doug. He squats close to him on the ground. "I can see you're looking nervous, Doug."

"Are you surprised?" Doug says.

"No. So long as you can keep it professional."

"I'll do my best."

"That's not good enough."

"Fine," Doug says. "I won't let you down. It's not like I have to do anything, do I? I just need to stay out here, out the way, hidden."

"Exactly. If things get messy, Rollins takes the blame and you attest to that. You saw his rampage. Your other cops can say how they've witnessed his violent tendencies, too. And now you get to be the one that guns him down. How's the guy he stabbed in the leg, by the way?"

"He's on leave," Doug says, but he doesn't look like he really cares about this. There are more pressing matters. "Said he had an accident doing DIY. When are you going to turn on the jammers?"

"When our targets arrive," Lee says, patiently. "Have you been working on your cover story, why you're out here?"

"I'm trying, but there's a hell of a lot on my mind already."

"The story should be your priority."

Doug holds out his hands. "I'll say I was following a lead," he says.

"You'll need more than that. It needs to be believable. Say you were friends with one of the deputies – make sure it's one of the ones we kill – and he called you, told you they had Rollins, that they'd picked him up for speeding or whatever, and they were concerned about this guy. You were on your way when Rollins shot the place up. You managed to gun him down while he was attempting to escape."

"Okay," Doug says, nodding that he's got it. "Okay, yeah, that'll work."

Lee taps the side of Doug's head. "You keep going over it. Think on it so much that you start to believe it." He gets up and leaves Doug alone. He returns to stand next to Josh, watching the building. He doesn't say anything. Neither of them does. They wait.

47

Sheriff Warren Hobbs is Black, with a neatly trimmed beard and his hair shorn close to his skull. He's a thickset man, his gut straining against his plain grey T-shirt. He's in his late forties and over six foot in his boots. As he enters Vanessa's home, he looks over the gathering, eyes narrowed.

"Friends of yours, Vanessa?" he says.

"Yes, Sheriff," Vanessa says. "They are. And they have something to tell you."

"To tell me?" Warren says. He pauses and looks at her. "Then I have to assume what you told me on the phone was just a ruse to get me here, or do they play into it?"

"It was just to get you here. I couldn't tell you the real reason. You should take a seat."

"I almost feel like I should be relieved. You had me worried with all that talk about seeing things last night that you could only share in person."

"Maybe hear them out before you give in too much to that relief. You'll want to take a seat, trust me."

Warren zeroes in on Tom, standing nearby with his arms folded. "I think I'll stay standing, if it's all the same to you."

"These people need our help," Vanessa says. She tells him what she's been told. Warren listens, his mouth twisting as the story goes on. He strokes at his beard, then looks at Tom, Melissa, Eric, and Dennis in turn while Vanessa talks.

"Well, that's a hell of a conspiracy you're claiming to have stumbled on," he says when she's finished.

"It's not a claim," Tom says. "It's a fact."

Warren studies him. "Do I know you? You look real familiar to me."

Tom knows Warren could probably take his pick of reasons he might recognise him – San Francisco, New York, Texas, maybe even some occasions Tom isn't aware of. He doesn't say this. Instead, he shakes his head and says, "We've never met. I've never been here before yesterday."

Warren looks doubtful, but he shrugs it off. "Well, I guess the best thing we can do right now is take you all out to the station and we can look into this further –"

"Not so fast," Eric says. "Weren't you listening to your deputy's story? What's to say we can trust you?"

Warren stares at him with steely eyes. "Son, I'm the sheriff of Bedfordshire County. That might mean nothing to you, but it means everything to me. Are you accusing me of something?"

"I don't believe I stuttered," Eric says.

"Uh-huh. You're a private investigator, did I hear that right?"

Eric nods.

"You ever worn a real uniform?"

"No."

"Then you don't understand the responsibility that

comes with it. You don't understand what it means the wear the badge I wear."

"Warren..." Vanessa says.

"With all due respect," Eric says. "Cops have been coming after my friends here – and they wear uniforms, too."

Warren opens his mouth to reply, but Tom speaks before he can. "Vanessa trusts you," he says. "She says you're a good man. Vanessa also let us check her phone to be sure she was on the up and up. Are you willing to do the same?"

Warren doesn't answer. He doesn't move.

"We need help," Tom says. "But I'm afraid we're not going anywhere with you until we can be sure."

Warren purses his lips.

"I know you don't have anything to hide," Vanessa says. "Neither did I."

Warren grunts. He pulls out his cell phone. He unlocks it and tosses it to Eric. "You ain't gonna find anything," he says.

"I hope not," Eric says, beginning the search.

Warren turns away from him, looking at Melissa and then at Dennis. "You saw them run that young lady down?"

"I did, sir," Dennis says.

"And then they came after you?"

"Yes."

Warren turns to Tom then, his eyes narrowed. "And you say they've been chasing you ever since?"

Tom nods.

"I heard about a shooting over the county line yesterday," Warren says. "Seven bodies. Two of them died in a crash, the rest were shot. One of them was dumped further down the road from the rest. No one heard or saw anything. You know anything about that?"

Tom doesn't answer. He looks back at the sheriff, holding his eye.

"Hmm," Warren says.

"Did you hear about the bodies in Leeport?" Tom says.

"What bodies?"

"Carla Mann and five others. They worked with Tessa Maberry. I guess they haven't been found yet."

"What happened to them?"

"They were killed. By Penney Pharma, same as Tessa. Probably by Lee Giles specifically, but we can't know that for sure."

Warren exchanges a glance with Vanessa. She gave him the broad strokes when she told the story. She didn't mention what had happened to Carla and the others. He turns back to Tom. "You didn't report it?"

"I just did. What else were we supposed to do before now? We couldn't trust anyone on the way here. We're hoping we can trust you."

"I need to look at your bank account," Eric says, holding out the phone.

Warren glares at him. "Are you out of your mind?"

"I need to check for payments," Eric says, not backing down.

"They run this bullshit on you?" Warren says to Vanessa.

"I didn't have anything to hide, Warren," she says.

Warren grumbles, but he opens the app and Eric resumes his search. He turns his attention back to Tom.

"How many deputies are on duty today?" Tom says.

"Six."

Tom thinks. "Vanessa showed us the location of the building online while we were waiting for you. It looks isolated."

Warren shrugs one shoulder. "It's out the way."

"Vanessa says you have an armoury."

Warren doesn't answer.

"Though she says it's not a big one. Shotguns, mainly. No automatic rifles."

"What's your point?" Warren says.

"My point is, Carla Mann knew we were coming here. She knew we were coming to speak to a deputy in Bedfordshire County and, in turn, the sheriff. When I found the bodies last night, there were signs of torture. They wouldn't have been killed before they gave up all they knew."

"What are you saying?"

"I'm saying that the people who killed them are probably already in Bedfordshire County. They're either roaming the streets looking for us, or they've gone straight to your department. Those trees that surround it, they provide a lot of coverage."

Warren looks doubtful. "Rollins, this is a small place. There are no cities in Bedfordshire County. Hell, there are barely any towns. We mostly deal with bored kids joyriding, or a couple of domestic disputes a week. You know who we make most of our bookings on? People from outside the county, driving through too fast because they think there's nothing here. I can count on one hand the amount of major violent crimes we've had here in the last ten years."

"And that could all change today."

"He's clear," Eric says, handing Warren his phone back.

"No one's going to attack in Bedfordshire County," Warren says.

"You've got that armoury for a reason," Tom says.

"Because sometimes we're an overflow holding cell for

nearby, bigger stations. And even then, we've never had any trouble."

"Do you really want to run that risk?"

Warren looks down at his phone. He doesn't put it away. "Well, now that you're all happy I'm clean and trustworthy, we should head into the station and get this whole thing cleared away."

"You didn't answer me, Sheriff," Tom says.

"If you all want my help, then you come with me now and do as I say."

"Warren, I don't think we should take what they say for granted," Vanessa says, "but we can't be complacent either. Maybe there *are* armed and dangerous men lying in wait. The risk isn't just to them, it's to the rest of your deputies, too."

"The station is the safest place," Warren says. "These people will be safe there. We all will."

"So long as you call all of your people in," Tom says. "And you tell them to raid the armoury and be ready."

Warren holds up his phone. "Three of my men will be on patrol. I'll call two of them here to escort us in. The third, I'll tell to go to the station with the others and get ready. That good enough for you?"

"Make sure they're armed and ready, Sheriff," Tom says.

Warren heads toward the kitchen to make the call. He motions for Vanessa to join him.

Tom summons the others closer to him. "Maybe he's right," he says. "And maybe the station is the safest place to be. But when the cruisers get here, I'm not going to travel with you. I'm going to follow in my car."

"In case of an ambush?" Eric says.

Tom nods. "If anyone gets the drop on you all at the

station, I want to be able to get the drop on *them*. If nothing happens, I still want to be able to hold back, keep an eye on those woods, make sure no one tries to sneak up on us."

"Maybe we should all stick with you," Melissa says.

"I'd feel better doing that," Dennis says.

"I don't think the sheriff would go for that," Tom says. "I can see it on his face – he thinks we're blowing this out of proportion. He's not taking us as seriously as he should. You heard him. If he was, I wouldn't be following you all separately. If we all say we're not going with him, he might refuse to help. And if anything does go down, I want you all to be able to get inside that building and under cover as fast as you can. I don't know that they'd be so brazen as to besiege a sheriff's department, but they've attacked us in broad daylight a couple of times already. We can't put anything past them."

"Should I go with them?" Eric says, motioning to Melissa and Dennis.

"I'd feel better if you did," Tom says. "Lee Giles is an ex-Navy SEAL, but I don't think his men are. I'm not sure what walks of life they come from, and there's no denying that they're dangerous and he's probably given them training, but their main advantage has undoubtedly been their numbers and the cops they have on their payroll. They killed Carla and the others, but what kind of threat were those tied-up kids posing to them? If we need to go up against them, especially with the sheriff's men on our side, I think we should be okay."

"We can't take that for granted," Eric says.

"We're not. That's why I'm following."

48

G raham radios Lee. "Incoming."

"Anything of interest?" Lee says.

"Just a cruiser. I don't see anyone else in it. Just the deputy."

"Copy." Lee chews on a piece of jerky, staring at the sheriff's department and silently willing something to happen soon. He's aware of the time passing. At some point, he's going to have to give up on this location and continue the search elsewhere. Every minute that ticks by is a minute against them.

The thought has occurred to him – what if Rollins and the others lied to Carla about where they were going? Had Rollins spotted his tail earlier than it appeared he did? Would he be so callous as to sacrifice the squatters so they could pass on false information, send Lee and his men on a wild goose chase? It's the kind of thing he would do. He's not so sure Rollins and the rest would, though. It doesn't appear to be their style. His concerns are just making him think wild things, he knows.

The cruiser Graham told him about comes into view, parking down the side with the others. The deputy hurries into the building. Lee takes notice of his speed. He squats down and lifts his binoculars, trying to see through the window. The new arrival is talking to one of the other deputies. They seem animated, and potentially concerned. He can't see the other two deputies he knows are inside the building.

"He seemed in a hurry," Josh says, standing nearby.

Lee grunts. He looks back at him. Josh stands, hands raised and clasping his tactical vest at the collar. Before he can say anything, Graham comes back on the radio.

"Heads-up," he says. "More incoming – two cruisers, and another vehicle, civilian, between them."

Lee and Josh exchange glances. Lee gets back on the radio while Josh alerts the others, tells them to look alive.

"What kind of civilian vehicle?" Lee says. He thinks of the Toyota he's seen Rollins and the others travelling in so far.

"A blue Honda."

Lee remembers seeing a blue Honda leave this morning. It belonged to one of the female deputies. "Can you see the people inside?" he says.

"Not yet," Graham says. "They're still distant, but they're coming closer. Give me a second."

Out the corner of his eye, Lee sees Doug sitting up, suddenly alert, aware that something could be about to happen. He watches Lee, then starts to push himself up to his feet.

Graham comes back on the radio. "Okay – jackpot. I've got eyes on Eric Braun, Melissa Ross, and Dennis Kurtley. They're in the backseat of the civilian vehicle. There's another woman in the front. I saw her leave here a few hours ago. She's driving the vehicle. Next to her is the sheriff."

"You're sure?" Lee says, feeling relieved that their wait is finally paying off.

"Rich here, sir, and I can confirm. We have eyes on them right now, and they're coming your way. We recognise the sheriff from the station's website. It's definitely him."

Something niggles at Lee. "What about in the cruisers?"

"One deputy apiece," Graham says.

"You're sure? No one else inside – front or back?"

"No, no one."

"Then where's Rollins?"

There's a pause, then, "We don't have eyes on him."

Doug is standing close enough that he's heard this. He stares at Lee, silently questioning him.

Lee ignores him. "You're certain of that? No sign of Rollins? No other vehicles?"

"No, sir – no Rollins, and nothing else coming up behind this small convoy."

Lee lets his finger off the transmitter. "*Shit.*"

"What does this mean?" Doug says. "Your whole story hinges on Rollins being here."

Lee waves him away, silencing him. "It doesn't matter," he says. "We continue as planned. We strike when they arrive, and we still place the blame on him. This time, he survives – you did your best but he got away. He'll be on the run. We can deal with him later."

"But –"

"I don't have time for you, Doug," Lee says, staring him down. "The second they arrive at that building, we move in. Time is of the essence. We can't give them a chance to make any calls." Lee turns to Val. "As soon as they pull up, hit the jammer. We don't want to spook them ahead of time."

"Got it," Val says.

Lee gets back on the radio to Graham. "Are they clear?"

"They'll be in sight for you soon," Graham says.

"Good. You and Rich stay there, keep watch. If anyone tries to come up the road to the station, put a stop to them."

"Copy."

Lee points to Doug. "Get back, stay out of the way." He gets on the radio to his men in the trees. "Positions. Go on my mark. I want this quick and painless."

He turns back to the station and awaits the arrival of the small convoy, annoyed at the lack of Rollins, but pleased finally that their time here hasn't been a complete waste.

Josh is close by. "No Rollins, huh?" he says. "That's a shame. You promised me I was gonna get my dick wet."

"There's time yet," Lee says. "We deal with this situation, and then we go and find that son of a bitch."

49

Vanessa stops her car directly in front of the station while the two cruisers continue on to park down the side. They left the sheriff's car back at Vanessa's, choosing to all travel together. Dennis and the others hurry out and get inside. Dennis sticks close to Melissa and Eric while Warren starts barking orders to his deputies, Vanessa sticking close to him.

"We're on high alert, people," Warren says. "I don't believe we're under any real threat here, but we need to be prepared regardless. Have any of you noticed any suspicious activity nearby, seen anyone in the trees?"

"No, sir," one of the deputies says. "If we'd seen something like that we would've been straight outside to investigate."

Dennis looks the deputies over. They're armed with shotguns, and they look like they've just been awakened from a deep sleep, and now they're wide awake and wired. Their eyes cut left and right, and their grips are tight on their weapons, trying to keep their hands from shaking. Most of them are overweight and look like they've enjoyed the easy life keeping watch over Bedfordshire County. A threat like this isn't anything they ever expected, or wanted. A couple of the other deputies, like Vanessa, have kept themselves in shape, however. They look more prepared, and they're calmer, too. Vanessa goes to the armoury and puts on a ballistic vest and arms herself with a shotgun. She comes back with four more vests, one each for Dennis, Melissa, and Eric, plus one for the sheriff. She hands them out, showing the three civilians how to put them on.

The two deputies who were parking their cruisers hurry back inside. "What's going on?" one of them says.

The sheriff quickly informs them. "Now get your vests and get armed," he says. He heads through to the back of the station, toward the door marked as his office. "You three, come with me." He points to Dennis and the others. Vanessa accompanies them.

Dennis looks around the building as they make their way through it. There are seven deputies, plus the sheriff. Eight, all told, and yet he'd still feel better if Tom were here with them.

Toward the rear of the building he can see empty holding cells, their doors open. The space in between the front of the building and there is mostly occupied by desks where the deputies work. There's a room to the far right where they take emergency calls to the station.

Dennis can feel his heart beating hard. The vest feels heavy on him and he shrugs his shoulders, trying to get comfortable. It constricts him, makes him feel compressed. Makes his chest tight.

Melissa notices. She places a hand on his back. "Breathe, Dennis," she says.

Dennis swallows. He tries to take a deep breath. It almost chokes him. "Y'know," he says, leaning close to her. "I'm starting to regret ever pulling myself out of the gutter."

He thinks he means it as a joke. Thinks he's trying to bring some levity to the situation, and to make himself feel better. Instead, he sees a deep sadness in Melissa's eyes when she hears this statement. "Oh, no, Dennis," she says, holding onto his arm. "Don't say that. You did the right thing. All along, you've done the right thing. This isn't how it's supposed to be."Dennis wants to apologise for making her feel bad, but before he can say anything he hears Warren curse loudly. He's looking at his cell phone. "No signal," he says.

"What's it usually like here?" Eric says.

"Full bars," Vanessa says.

"Shit, could there be a jammer out there?"

Warren has a landline on his desk. He picks it up but before he can dial, he holds it to his ear. "Silent," he says, looking at Vanessa. "The line's been cut. Damn it, they must be close–"

Then, the power goes out. Melissa grabs Dennis, holds him close to her. The next thing he knows, he's being pushed down, and Eric is saying, "Get on the ground!"

Somewhere in the station, a window smashes. There's a low explosion, and out the corner of his eye, through the open door of the sheriff's office, Dennis can see smoke filling the main part of the building.

More windows shatter. Bullets strike the building.

50

Tom didn't follow the cruisers all the way to the station. He pulled over at the side of the road half a mile back and continued on foot toward the trees.

As he gets closer, he drops to the ground and crawls through the field adjoining the woods, watching for movement within. He takes his time, moving slowly and carefully.

Then he sees them. Two men, dressed all in black, concealing themselves amid the trees. They're masked. They're wearing tactical vests. They're armed. They're each carrying an MCX Spear, as well as handguns. They're watching the road. They're not looking toward the field.

Now that he's seen them, Tom speeds up his crawl, heading toward where the trees are thickest behind them. He has his Beretta and his KA-BAR. He pulls out the KA-BAR as he nears. Once he gets into the trees he stands and conceals himself. He makes his way toward the two men he saw, knife held low and ready. He scans the ground as he moves through it, watching out for anything that could snap or make a noise, anything that could give away his approach.

The two men come into view. They stand silently and hidden from the road, still watching. Tom creeps closer. One of them pushes up his mask to wipe sweat from his face while there's no one around. Tom realises he's familiar. He recognises him from the composite drawings Dennis described at the station. He's one of the men Dennis saw kill Tessa.

Then, the sound of gunshots splits the silence. Tom freezes. The man on the left begins to turn, glancing back toward the sound, while the man on the right pulls his mask back down. Tom speeds up, no need for stealth any longer. He sees the masked man's eyes widen, his mouth begins to O under its covering, but Tom reaches him and slashes the KA-BAR across his chest before he can make a sound. The knife keeps moving, arcing toward the man on the right, and Tom drives it straight through his chest, into his heart. It's momentarily jammed, so he lets it go and grabs the man on the left by the back of the head, dragging his face down into Tom's quickly rising knee, smashing it into the centre of his face. The man straightens, nose no doubt broken, and Tom drives the flat of his hand upward, under his nose, driving the broken cartilage and bone back into his brain.

The distant gunshots continue. There's a lot of rifles opening fire upon the sheriff's department. Tom was right. They were here. They were lying in wait. The sheriff didn't take him seriously enough. He wasn't careful.

Tom can't dwell on that. He retrieves his KA-BAR, then takes the MCX from the man on the right. He takes his spare magazines, too, and then takes the magazines from the other corpse. He readies the rifle, and then runs through the trees toward the sound of battle.

51

Lee's men have the building surrounded. The deputies are trying to fight back, armed with their Glock 19s and their Benelli M4 shotguns, but Lee has seen the deputies. They're out of shape and out of practice. They're not ready for action like this. They're soft, and they're slow, and they're firing blindly into the trees. They don't pose any real threat, other than to the branches and the bark.

Lee directs his men on the radio. "Sustain fire," he says. "Tear that place apart."

The smoke grenade should have stunned them. The barrage of automatic fire will dull them, drive them from the windows, send them into cover. A couple of them are already dead. Lee has seen them fall. One of them hangs out of a shattered window, shotgun dropped.

The gunfire will deafen them, will pound them into submission. Then, when they're almost broken, Lee and the other ex-SEALs will go inside and make sure the job is finished off completely. This was the initial plan when they

thought Rollins was going to be here and they expected this
to be more of a challenge. They're sticking to it, too late to
change their approach now.

Lee holds back in the trees, watching through binoculars, accompanied by Josh, Shameik, and Val. Doug is close
by, standing now and watching, his face drained of all colour.
He keeps licking his lips like his mouth is dry.

"This shouldn't take long," Josh says. "They're not
putting up much of a fight."

"This is easy money," Val says. "I thought this was
supposed to be some kind of a challenge. Where's Rollins?"

"You'll get your chance with him yet," Lee says without
turning.

"That sounds like it's gonna be two separate paydays,"
Val says.

Lee ignores him. He has no problem with this, but he's
not going to talk about money right now.

Doug wipes his mouth with the back of his hand, then
runs both hands down his face. He's sweating. He blinks. "It's
a massacre," he says, almost a whisper.

Lee hits him in the chest with the back of his hand.
"Don't watch if you can't stomach it. Stay back here and wait
until we're done."

Lee hasn't heard anything from Graham and Rich. This
is a good sign. No one is coming to interrupt them. He gets
on the radio. "Saunders, Roden, I want you both on my position now. You stay with Doug. Everyone else, we're getting
ready to move in. When you see us emerge, hold fire." He
pulls down his mask and readies his M4A1, then turns to the
others. "It's time," he says. "Let's go."

52

Tom runs toward the nearest sounds of gunfire. He comes upon a group of three men, all dressed the same as the two he found at the entrance to the trees – black-clad, and masked. Armed with MCX Spears. One of them is turned away from the building they're firing upon, reloading. He's facing Tom's direction. He looks up as Tom runs toward him. As he raises his head, Tom kicks him in the chest, driving him back toward the other two, knocking them down. Tom raises the Spear and shoots the three men where they've landed on the ground.

Before he moves on, he quickly checks their bodies. He takes a spare magazine from them, but will struggle to carry many more. One of them has a smoke grenade. He takes this and then continues on through the trees, heading along to the next group he can hear shooting. He looks through the trees as he goes, seeing how the building is being torn apart by gunfire. He can see at least one dead deputy, hanging out of a window. Tom tries to discern where the gunfire is coming from. They have the building surrounded. He's not sure what they're thinking, attacking a sheriff's department building in the middle of the day, or how they're planning on talking their way out of this.

He reaches two more men and guns them down without stopping. He keeps running, changing the magazine as he goes. He gets far through the trees before he comes upon another group. There are two of them again, but they've noticed that the gunfire from their left has ceased. They're looking his way. They see him coming. Tom isn't all in black, nor is he masked. They open fire without hesitation.

Tom dives to the ground, firing back at them. He rolls and takes cover behind a tree, their bullets hitting the ground and ricocheting off bark. He throws the smoke grenade in their direction, then pushes himself up and splits to the right while they're blinded, circling them. They're firing upon his old position through the smoke, hoping to hit him. Tom fires upon them once he's parallel and he hears them both fall. He gets close enough to make sure the job is finished, and then prepares to move on.

He pauses, listening. He gets closer to the treeline, looking at the station. It's quiet. The gunfire has stopped.

53

Dennis is flat on the ground still, Melissa next to him, her arm keeping him pinned. He can only raise his head to see what's happening. Eric is by the window, armed with a Glock now instead of his 629. He's ducking down, the gun raised, trying to see out of the window.

"The shooting's stopped," he says.

Dennis tries to look around. There's a dead deputy in the doorway to the sheriff's office, her blood spreading across the linoleum floor. Eric took the gun from her after his 629 ran empty. Dennis thinks three of the deputies have been killed. He sees blood splashed on walls through in the main part of the building, and spent casings and bullets litter the ground. Desks have been pushed over to provide cover. There are holes in the walls. All windows have been shattered, and broken glass coats the ground. Some of it is close to Dennis, and falls off him when he moves. He can see shards of it in Melissa's hair.

"Melissa, Dennis," Vanessa says, ducking behind the sheriff's desk. "Are you both okay?"

"I think so," Melissa says, remaining flat. "Dennis?"

"Yes," he says.

"Is it over?" Melissa says.

"I don't see why it would be," Eric says, trying to keep watch but not wanting to expose himself through the broken window.

The surviving deputies also remain low and behind cover. They reload their weapons and try to risk looking out of the windows from a distance.

"Is Tom out there?" Melissa says.

"I don't know," Eric says. "It's too hard to see anything through all these fucking trees. I'm not even sure if I hit anyone – hell, I can't tell if I was even firing in their damn direction."

Warren sits with his back to the wall, breathing hard. He swallows, and looks like he wishes he'd taken Tom's concerns more seriously. "They've got us pinned here."

"Sir, what should we do?" Vanessa says.

Warren doesn't answer. He stares down at his gun, and then looks up at his broken window. He avoids meeting Eric's eye. He licks his lips, trying to think. "We can't stay here," he says, but it's unclear if he's talking to them, or to himself.

"They've got us surrounded," Eric says. "Gunfire was coming from all directions. They could just be waiting for us to show ourselves right now."

"Or else they're about to move in," Vanessa says.

"Jesus Christ, where's Rollins?" Warren says.

"Don't put this on him," Melissa says, snapping her head around to face the sheriff. "He tried to warn you. You promised him – you promised all of us – that this was a safe place."

Warren doesn't say anything. He's scared. They all are. They're rigidly waiting for whatever comes next. They know it isn't over. They know that if the shooting has stopped, something worse must be coming.

One of the deputies in the next room cries out, "Incoming!"

Dennis looks their way and sees something fly through the air, hitting the ground. A small explosion, just like earlier, and then smoke spills from the grenade, filling the station again.

With their attention distracted, another smoke grenade flies through the window into the sheriff's office. It lands close to Melissa. Dennis sees it before she does. He reaches across her and pushes it away, then covers her body with his own.

Smoke begins to fill the office. Warren gets to his feet. Dennis sees him. Warren turns toward the window. "I see them!" he says, his gun raised.

A shot rings out. A hot spray of blood lands on Dennis's face. Warren wheels away from the window, the bullet having torn through his throat. He spins to the ground, spraying blood.

Eric is covering his mouth and nose with his shirt. "Shit! Brace yourselves – here they come!"

54

Lee studied the layout of the building all night and all morning. This is his first time inside, but he knows where to go. He takes point.

A shotgun blasts blindly, hitting the wall close to the entrance. Lee follows the flare of where it came from and strafes the area with his M4A1. He hears the deputy cry out, gargling as their throat fills with blood.

Gunfire erupts, but the deputies can't see where they're shooting. Lee can hear them coughing, too, and so can Josh and the others, and they use these sounds to direct their fire. Lee and the others wear masks. They breathe just fine.

He makes his way toward the sheriff's office. He's seen this is where his targets are cowering. Nearby, he hears Val and Shameik gun down two deputies, and to his count that should be all of them bar one, and she's in the office with the targets and the now-dead sheriff. She's the one they went to see. The one who brought them here. The one who probably thought she could help.

The smoke is clearing. Inside the office, along with the

one remaining deputy, is Eric Braun, Melissa Ross, and Dennis Kurtley. That is, of course, unless any of them caught a stray bullet during the siege. Lee isn't taking any chances. He has to go off what he's seen.

He signals to the three behind him, holding up a closed fist for them to halt. The smoke is clearing in the office, too. They keep to the side, away from the door propped open by the body of a dead female deputy. They'll be armed in there. Animals backed up into a corner. Lee has to be careful. If they catch a glimpse of something, they're going to start shooting.

Lee throws them another smoke grenade.

55

D ennis feels Melissa dragging him from the ground as the second smoke grenade rolls into the office. Glass crunches beneath them as they move. She hauls him behind the desk, behind Vanessa.

Eric, his mouth and nose still covered and his eyes streaming now, starts firing through the smoke, aiming in the direction the grenade came from. Earlier, after the first grenade blinded them, Dennis could hear gunfire through in the main part of the building. He could hear people dying. He thinks everyone else is dead now. He thinks they're the only ones left.

There's automatic gunfire. The bullets hit Eric, lacing upwards from his stomach to his chest. He falls back and slides down the wall, blood smearing behind him. Dennis hears Melissa cry out. Dennis doesn't. He doesn't make a sound. He's frozen. He's numb. Stunned by all he's seen and heard, and shocked with the knowledge that he's about to die. They're coming. They're almost upon them, and they're going to kill them. These men are going to finish what they started the night they chased Dennis after he saw them kill Tessa Maberry. Only Tom is left. Only Tom can stop them.

Vanessa fires toward the doorway, but Dennis doesn't hear anyone cry out like they've been hit. His eyes are stinging from the smoke. He can feel them tearing and leaking.

Then, a dark figure appears in the doorway, and it fires into the room. The bullets hit the wall, but one of them catches Vanessa in the shoulder. She cries out and hits the ground, clutching at her wound and dropping her gun.

The man covers Melissa and Dennis with his rifle. The smoke is clearing. As it does so, he removes his gas mask, and then pulls down the balaclava that covers his face, revealing his features. Dennis's blood runs cold. It's Lee Giles.

Lee looks them over, checking their hands, making sure they're unarmed. He enters the room and kicks Vanessa's Glock away from her. He turns the gun toward her, about to finish her off.

"Don't!" Melissa says, hands raised.

Lee grins. He keeps the gun pointed at Vanessa. "Where is Rollins?" he says.

The question is directed at both of them. They don't answer straight away. Melissa's mouth works, like she's wrestling with telling either the truth or a lie, trying to decide which of them could save Vanessa and get them out of this situation alive.

She doesn't have to make a decision. They hear gunfire from the front of the building.

56

Three men are in the front of the station when Tom reaches the door and gets inside. He's come from the back of the building, where the trees are closest to it. The area was clear of men. The ones who were there, firing, have moved on, gone elsewhere. Regrouping, perhaps.

Tom scans the inside of the station, and quickly checks over the dead bodies he can see. They're all deputies. He doesn't see Melissa, Dennis, or Eric, nor Vanessa or Warren. The only people standing are the three in front of him, and he doesn't hesitate. They're in the process of removing their masks. Tom shoots the closest of them in the back, the bullets tearing through his tactical vest and upwards into the back of his neck, blood spraying out.

The other two start to turn. One of them is white and one is Black. Neither of them is Lee Giles. The man Tom just killed isn't, either. He dives to the side, into cover behind an upended desk. The two remaining men fire at him, their bullets destroying the desk.

Tom keeps moving, pushing himself back across the ground while changing the magazine in the Spear, slamming in a fresh replacement. He stops when he reaches the back room where the dispatcher would ordinarily be situated. The door is open. Tom rises behind cover of the doorframe, inside the room. He sees the two men spreading out, armed with M4A1s. They're not carrying Spears like the men outside. They don't move like them, either. There's something more to them. Old friends of Lee's perhaps, Tom wonders. Maybe ex-SEALs, too.

There's no time to consider this. The Black guy sees him and opens fire. Bullets destroy the comms equipment in the room. Tom can't afford to get trapped in here. It's a small room. The window is already shattered, offering him an escape route should he need it.

When the shooter pauses to reload, Tom swings the Spear out and returns fire, causing him to dive for cover. He's lost sight of the other man.

Tom dives out of the dispatch room, rolling through and rising in front of the cells. The white man emerges as if from nowhere, tackling him into the holding area. Tom drops the Spear, bracing himself for the landing.

It's hard and the tackler tries to mount him, but Tom is ready. He raises a leg and uses the attacker's momentum against him, kicking him overhead, grabbing his M4A1 as he does so and twisting it out of his grip. He sees the Black man approaching the cells, gun raised, and Tom sits up and fires at him, bullets catching him in the chest, throat, and face. He falls back, rifle firing into the air, his finger jammed on the trigger.

The remaining man lunges at Tom with an SRK, and Tom's suspicions are confirmed – this man is also an ex-Navy

SEAL. Tom manages to avoid the worst of his arcing slice, but the blade catches him on the right shoulder, tearing through his T-shirt and cutting him open. Tom feels the blood running down his arm.

The dropped M4A1 is on the ground between them. The SEAL keeps the SRK raised and pointed in Tom's direction, his eyes flickering down toward the rifle. Tom keeps his empty hands raised defensively. He could reach back for his Beretta or his KA-BAR, but he knows that the second he lowers an arm the other man will strike. Behind the SEAL, the cell door is open. He thinks the cell door behind him is open, too, but he doesn't chance a look back.

The SEAL makes the first move. He jabs with the knife. Tom is able to bat it away. They fight over the top of the automatic rifle. Neither of them reaches for it. Tom ignores it, forgets it. Right now, it's just he and the knife, and the man holding it clearly knows how to use it. The automatic rifle can't help him. They circle around it. The SEAL jabs and slices a couple more times, but Tom is able to block and dodge his attempts.

They've switched positions, now. The SEAL is where Tom started this standoff, and vice-versa. Tom sees that the cell door he wondered about is open behind the SEAL. As the SEAL comes in for another attack, Tom parries his strike and kicks him back, toward the open door. The SEAL goes through it. Tom follows, reaching for the cell door. The SEAL dives for the door, seeing what he's trying to do, and tries to cut him with the knife again. Tom manages to catch his wrist. He holds it in place and throws the sliding door closed. It slams into the SEAL's bicep, jamming it between the bars and the door, and he drops the knife. Tom pulls the door back and slams it into his arm again while pushing the arm in the opposite direction of its bend. He hears something break. The SEAL's arm flops at an angle it shouldn't. The SEAL grimaces against the pain of bone grating on bone.

He's still fighting, though. He grabs at Tom with his left hand. Tom holds his thumb and yanks it back, snapping it. He grabs the SEAL by his hair and slams his head into the bars, then pins him in place, his neck against the bars, exposed like it's on a chopping block. Tom throws the cell door into his neck with all of his might. The SEAL begins to cough, his throat crushed. He starts to fall back but Tom throws the sliding door into him again and it slams just under the hinge of his jaw and then into his neck. There's a crack. The SEAL drops to the ground, dead, his neck broken.

Tom hears a shriek behind him. It sounds like Melissa. He scoops up the M4A1 and heads toward the source of the sound. It leads him to the sheriff's office. He sees Melissa clawing at Lee Giles's face. Lee punches her across the jaw and sends her sprawling over the desk. He spots Vanessa slumped against the wall, a bloodied hand clutching her shoulder. She's pale and in shock.

Lee has Dennis by the hair. He spins as Tom enters the doorway and presses a Sig Sauer to Dennis's temple.

"Rollins!" Lee says. "Back up – back up *now!*"

Tom has the M4A1 trained on him, but he can't get a clear shot. Lee keeps Dennis in the way.

"Back up right now or I'll blow his fucking head off," Lee says.

Tom looks at Dennis. Sees the fear in his eyes. He keeps the rifle pointing, but he does as Lee says.

Lee side-steps out of the office, over the corpse of the deputy in the doorway. He presses the barrel of the gun hard against the side of Dennis's head. Tom sees how Lee is equipped with an M4A1, too. It's strapped to his back.

Lee makes his way to the door. Tom keeps the rifle on him, covering him. He still can't get a clear shot.

"If you follow, I'll kill him," Lee says. "The only thing keeping him alive is staying right where you are."

57

Lee drags Dennis out of the door, holding him close, his back to the trees and his own men. He lowers the gun long enough to grab his radio. "Marcus – cover the door! Anyone comes out, kill them! Who else is left? Sound off!"

Saunders and Roden reply. Lee feels his stomach sink when no one else does. "Is that it? Is there no one else?"

Marcus, Saunders, and Roden confirm that they haven't seen anyone else.

"*Shit*. All right – Saunders, Roden, come down here and get me."

Lee didn't underestimate Rollins – he brought plenty of men, he called in reinforcements – and yet the bastard still has him on the back foot. And now it sounds like he's killed most of his team. He needs to keep Dennis alive as collateral. It's the only thing keeping Rollins at bay.

Saunders and Roden reach him and take Dennis from him. "We need to get to a car," Lee says.

"What happened in there?" Doug says. He's followed Saunders and Roden from the trees. "Lee! What happened?"

Lee doesn't answer. He's pulling out his phone. Doug persists, following him, questioning him.

"Goddamnit, I need to know!"

Lee kicks him to the ground. He's done with him. He has no more use for him. He hurries and waits until they're out of range of the jammer, then calls Billy. "No time to talk – get a helicopter out here ASAP. Pick up the GPS on my phone and tell the pilot to land in the nearest field when we get close to each other."

"Got it," Billy says. He doesn't ask any further questions. He gets on with his job.

Lee places another call. Behind them, he can hear gunfire again. Marcus is firing upon the station. Rollins must have tried to follow.

Lee gets through to James. "This is important – don't interrupt me, just listen. Get Scarlett and prepare to flee. Things have gone very badly. We need to enact the escape protocol. When I'm off this call I'm going to contact Awais to come and pick us up."

James is not like Billy. He tries to ask questions. "What – what – what do you mean? What's happened?"

"*James!*" Lee roars into the phone. "You heard me. Now fucking get to it." He hangs up. He should have called Scarlett, but he couldn't admit defeat to her like this. There'll be plenty of time for that later.

Doug has picked himself up off the ground. He's trying to follow. He's calling Lee's name.

Lee wheels on him with the Sig Sauer. He fires into the ground at his feet and Doug leaps back. "If you continue to follow us, the next one's through your fucking head."

58

T om ducks behind the doorway, bullets cutting through the space he previously occupied, as well as hitting the wall and frame close to him. The shooter is in the trees. Tom didn't get a good look at his location.

Melissa comes up to join him, crawling along the floor under the windows, through the blood and the broken glass. "What happened?" she says, raising her voice to be heard over the gunfire.

"Lee has Dennis," Tom says. He looks down at her, sees the bruise forming on her cheek and jaw where Lee struck her. He sees blood on her hands, too. "Are you all right?"

She sits up, remaining under cover, and waves a dismissive hand. "I've been hit harder by drunken grandmothers on a Sunday night."

The shooting has stopped, no doubt waiting for Tom to show himself again. Tom points at Melissa's bloody hands. "Is that yours?"

She shakes her head. "Vanessa's," she says. "I got her

wrapped up and then I heard the shooting out here. She's not in any condition to come with us."

"How's she doing? She looked like she was in shock."

"She's not so bad now. She's got some colour coming back to her. What are we gonna do about this?"

Tom presses himself against the wall and looks down the road. He can see Lee and Dennis getting further away, along with two other men. Lee looks like he's making a call. "I can't see the shooter," Tom says. "And he's waiting for me to show myself again. If I try to spot him, he's gonna take my head off my shoulders."

"He doesn't know I'm here," Melissa says. "Pass me the rifle and I'll go to the window in the office. If you run between windows he might open up on you, I can spot where he is and I can put him down."

Tom looks at her. "You're confident?"

"I'm confident that you can move fast enough you won't get hit," she says. "I'm confident enough that this might be our only way out."

She's right. Tom lowers the M4A1 to the ground and slides it toward her with his boot. She takes it and then crawls back the way she came to the sheriff's office. From where he stands, Tom can see Warren's body. He's flat on his back, eyes still open, staring unseeing up at the ceiling.

He waits until Melissa is in position. She looks back at him, readying herself, the rifle raised. She crouches beside the window. She nods at him.

Tom pulls out his Beretta and then steps in front of the shattered window, looking up into the trees like he's trying to see where the shooter could be hiding. He fires a few rounds blindly, then he quickly jumps to the right, behind cover, and as he does so the shooter opens fire.

Melissa fires, too. She squeezes the trigger hard and empties the magazine. "I think I got him!"

Tom steps into the window again, gun raised. He sees movement through the trees, but it's low. The man is falling. He slides face-first down the embankment, his MCX Spear sliding down beside him.

Tom scans the rest of the trees, but no one else shoots. "Grab a gun and let's go," he says to Melissa as he goes to the body of the nearest deputy and searches them for keys.

He hears Melissa talking to Vanessa. "They have Dennis – we need to go," she says. "We'll send help for you as soon as we're out of range of the jammer."

If Vanessa responds, Tom doesn't hear her. He has keys for a cruiser and he's already heading outside, toward the parking lot at the side where the cruisers and their personal cars are parked. He hopes the vehicle he has keys for wasn't damaged in the siege. He presses the unlock button and a cruiser at the end flashes its lights. Tom runs toward it. Melissa follows him with another M4A1. She jumps into the passenger seat while Tom starts the engine. He drives over the small grassy area directly in front of them and then heads down the road.

"Did you see their vehicles on the way in?" Melissa says.

"No," Tom says. "I heard the firefight start and I made my way straight to it."

Melissa starts like she's going to say something else, but then she points ahead and says, "There's someone in the road."

Tom has already seen them. He's also seen that they're armed. They have a handgun. They turn and see the cruiser approaching. They lean forward a little, squinting, and then they raise the gun and start firing.

Melissa ducks. Tom presses down harder on the accelerator. The bullets hit the front of the car. One of them passes through the middle of the windshield. The shooter isn't dressed like the others. Tom recognises him – Detective Sergeant Doug Posey. Tom veers the car toward him. Doug realises they aren't slowing. He tries to run. He tries too late. Tom mows him down, feeling the car rise and bump as it goes over his body. He looks in the mirror and sees Doug's body lying splayed in the middle of the road.

Melissa looks back. "He didn't look like the others."

"He was one of them," Tom says without elaborating. There is steam rising from the front of the car. Air whistles through the hole in the centre of the windshield. Warning lights are flashing on the cruiser's panel behind the steering wheel.

Ahead, as he nears the end of the road leading to the sheriff's department, a Ford speeds past the junction. Tom sees four men inside. He doesn't see any of their faces, but he sees how fast they're going. "I think that's them," he says. He pushes down on the accelerator, but already he can feel that the car is struggling.

Melissa can feel it too. The engine is roaring in protest, and the steam is billowing heavier, almost obstructing their vision. Out the back of the car, the tailpipe is belching black fumes. "I don't think we're going to be able to keep up," she says.

Tom pushes the car, swinging it out onto the road and pursuing the Ford. "I just need it to get us a mile down the road," he says.

"Is that where your car is?"

Tom nods, staring ahead through the rising steam. When he glances in the mirror, he sees that the cruiser is leaving a streak of fluids on the road behind them. He grits his teeth. They don't have to go far.

The Ford is burning them off. He thinks it's noticed them, but it's also noticed how damaged they are.

The cruiser is rapidly losing power. It dies when his car is in view. They dump it and start running. Once they're inside and the engine is on, Tom does a quick U-turn and tries to make up for lost time. They get the Ford back in sight, but it keeps its distance from them.

"There's no other cars on this road," Tom says. "If we get close enough, I'm going to need you to try and shoot out the rear tyres. Do you think you can do that?"

"Yes," Melissa says, but there's an uncertainty in her voice. "But what if they roll? Dennis is inside."

"He has a better chance of surviving that than if they get away with him. But if the driver knows what he's doing, they shouldn't roll."

"I dunno, they're going pretty fast." Melissa side-eyes their own speedometer.

Tom pushes on, trying to close the gap. The engine screams.

Melissa leans forward suddenly, looking into the distance. Tom sees how she's looking up, into the sky. "There's something coming," she says. "A helicopter. It's low."

Tom sees it. It's swooping, like Melissa said. It looks like it's coming in to land. There's no other buildings nearby. There's certainly no airstrips.

"It's with them," Tom says. "It's coming for them."

Sure enough, the Ford suddenly turns off the road, bouncing and then slowing as it cuts across the grass. The helicopter lands. The Ford heads for it. Someone jumps out of the helicopter, armed with an assault rifle. He's watching the road.

Tom doesn't drive onto the grass. It would slow them, make it hard for them to manoeuvre, especially when there's an armed man standing guard for them. He stops the car next to where the Ford turned off onto the grass, and he takes the M4A1 from Melissa. He tells her to stay in the car and then he runs onto the grass.

The man from the helicopter starts firing at him. Tom rolls for cover behind a nearby bush and shoots back. The Ford stops close to the helicopter. The four men get out. Lee is holding onto Dennis again, using him as a shield. Tom can't fire upon him, and Lee knows it. They board the helicopter. It takes off. Tom runs back to the car.

59

I f they didn't know Tom had an assault rifle, the helicopter probably would have fired upon the car as it flew overhead. As it is, they don't want to risk Tom firing back and causing them to crash and burn.

Tom drives fast, trying to keep the helicopter in view. It quickly gets away. It's not beholden to the road system like he is. He grips the steering wheel tight and takes a right.

"Where are we going?" Melissa says.

"Monmouth Beach," Tom says. "The Penney mansion. They must be panicking right now. Their attack on the sheriff's department didn't play out the way they wanted." He can see the helicopter still in the distance as he gets onto the freeway, but it's getting further and further away from them, and soon it'll be just a speck in the distance.

"What if that's not where they're going?" Melissa says.

"Maybe it's not," Tom says through gritted teeth. "But we have to hope it is, we have to hope they're going to the Penneys, and we have to hope we can cut them off before they get away."

They drive in silence, Tom overtaking vehicles. Horns blare and drivers flip him off, but he ignores them. Melissa suddenly scrambles for her phone. "I need to call an ambulance for Vanessa," she says.

She doesn't start dialling. She stares at the screen. "She's already tried to call me," she says. "Twice." Melissa calls her back, putting her on speaker.

"Melissa, are you all right?" Vanessa says. She sounds groggy, but she's alert.

"We're fine – we're in pursuit. A helicopter came and picked them up. We're going to try and catch up to them at Monmouth Beach."

"Thank God. When you didn't answer I thought the worst had happened."

"We've been busy; I never felt it. How are *you*?"

"Tired and sore, but I'm up. I found the jammer and turned it off. I've called in the off-duty deputies and I've put out as many calls as I can on the radio, contacting other agencies, telling them what's happened and who's responsible."

This should be good news, and it is, but it doesn't put Tom at ease. It makes him drive faster. He needs to get to the mansion, to the helicopter, before the State Police or the feds can turn up. They won't know who Dennis is, and they won't be as concerned about him as Tom is. If Lee and his men start shooting, they're going to shoot back and Dennis will be caught in the middle.

"Let me know if you hear anything else, Vanessa," Melissa says. "And call yourself an ambulance!"

"Already done," Vanessa says. "Melissa, people are coming in to deal with this now. You can sit this one out."

Melissa looks at Tom. He doesn't look back at her. He focuses on the road.

"That's a no can do, Vanessa. They have Dennis. We need to get him back. And there's no guarantee that help can reach the Penneys before we can."

Vanessa is silent, likely deliberating whether she should continue trying to talk them out of their pursuit, or if it's a waste of breath. "Just...just be careful," she finally says. "And if you do catch up to them..." She pauses again, wondering if she should finish her thought. "If you catch up to them, make them pay for what they did here."

60

Lee shouts into the headset, communicating with the helicopter pilot. "Just set it down on the fucking road!" he says. "Right in front of the goddamn house!"

The pilot clearly doesn't like it, but he complies. There are cars coming along the road and they have to slam on their brakes or veer up onto the sidewalk to get around the descending helicopter. The protestors close to the gates of the house brace themselves and cover their faces against the wind kicked up by the rotor blades. Lee sees one of them sent tumbling backwards, others trying to catch her and keep her from blowing away. If he was in a better mood, this would make him smile.

"Kill the chopper," Lee says. "We all get out here."

Dennis struggles now that they're on the ground, but Lee punches him in the centre of the face, bloodying his nose. He doesn't have the patience right now, not for anything. He motions to Saunders. "Keep hold of him. Keep him under control."

"Do we still need him?" Saunders says, clamping a hand tightly on Dennis's upper arm.

"We keep hold of him until we're out to sea," Lee says. "Rollins isn't gonna stop. You saw that psychopath back there at the station. You think he isn't coming right now? Let's go."

Lee hates to admit defeat, but Rollins has beat them here today. He's ruined everything. But this? While they may be escaping, they're not running away. It's a tactical retreat. Lee will come back for the son of a bitch. This is a grudge he'll never let go of, and a downfall he'll never be able to swallow. Rollins *will* die. It just won't be today.

He gets out of the helicopter and raises his Sig Sauer into the air. He fires three times and the protestors scatter. The stalled cars quickly turn around and speed off in the opposite direction. They want no part of whatever is happening here.

The helicopter blades have finally stopped. His four men inside, plus Dennis, get out and follow him toward the gate. On the other side, he sees Billy running down to meet them. He's heard the helicopter arrive. The whole neighbourhood has.

Billy gets the gate open for them. His face is solemn. "They're not happy," he says.

Lee doesn't respond. He keeps walking, heading up the driveway, knowing exactly whom Billy is talking about. They're at the top. They've heard his return, too. James hurries to him, looking hot and dishevelled.

"What's happened?" he says, panting. "What did you do?"

Lee pushes his employer aside. "Just get ready to go," he says.

Scarlett is nearby. She blocks his path. She looks like she's dressed in a hurry, pulling on a tracksuit. Her hair is a mess. She slaps Lee, stopping him in his tracks. She jabs a finger into his face. Lee resists the urge to bite it off. "You promised we'd never have to use this contingency plan," she says. She's almost screaming. She looks wild. "You *promised*. You've promised a lot of things lately. And now we're going to lose everything – our home, our lifestyle, our money – *every-thing,* all because you failed at your job!"

Lee slaps her back. She falls to the ground, her lip bleed-ing. She looks up at him in disbelief. James takes a step forward, but Lee shoots him a look and he freezes. "You're keeping your fucking *lives,*" Lee says. "You're keeping your freedom. All you're losing is this house, the yacht, and your names. All the government can seize is what they know about. They don't know anything about the offshore accounts. You're still going to be rich. Does living under fake names on a tropical island with no US extradition really sound like such a bad trade?"

Scarlett remains on the ground. She wipes at the blood on her mouth, smearing it across her chin. "It wasn't supposed to be like this," she says. "We were supposed to be *kings*. We were supposed to become –"

Lee cuts her off. He's tired of hearing it. "I don't give a shit about your wannabe status. Where we're going, you're gonna have more money than the natives could ever imagine. But first we have to make sure no one is going to come after us, so get the fuck up and get moving."

Lee leaves her on the ground, moving away, turning his attention back toward Billy. "Is the yacht ready?"

"Yes, sir," Billy says. "I sent some men straight out there

after you called. Everything's good to go. We were just waiting on you."

"And is it *ready*?"

"Still in process, but it won't take much longer."

"Who's he?" James says, pointing. "Is this *Dennis*?"

Scarlett is back on her feet. "Why's he here? Why's he still alive?"

"Because Rollins is coming," Lee says. "He stays alive as long as Rollins is still out there. He'll be coming whether he thinks this bastard is still alive or not. Having him alive gives us the upper hand. I haven't underestimated Rollins yet, and I'm not going to start now. This motherfucker can die on the boat, along with your pasts." Lee points toward the beach, and toward the anchored yacht in the distance. "Now unless you wanna wait for him to turn up here, *move*."

61

There's a helicopter in the middle of the road outside the Penney mansion. Tom drives around it, seeing that the gates are open, and drives straight up the driveway. He stops the car at the top and takes the M4A1 from Melissa. It looks clear. He doesn't see anyone around. There are empty vehicles nearby. He gets out, rifle raised, sweeping the area. He heads toward the house. As he approaches, he sees that the front door is wide open. This isn't a good sign.

Inside, the house is still. It's empty. He moves through it, prepared for anyone to appear, attempting an ambush, their own weapon raised, but it never happens. Upstairs, he finds wardrobes open with empty hangers inside. They've fled.

But there's no sign of Dennis, either. No body left for him to find. If they were through with him they would have left him behind. One final taunt. He must still be alive. They still have him.

Back outside, he sees that Melissa is no longer in the car. He sees her running up the driveway. "I spoke to some of the protestors," she says. "They said the helicopter landed about fifteen minutes ago, and then one of the men inside got out and started shooting. They scattered after that. Some of them haven't come back."

"Did they see anything else?"

"They said no one came back down. No one's left the grounds."

Tom shakes his head. "They're not here."

Melissa points out to sea. Tom turns and looks. He sees a yacht in the distance. Below that, he sees a speedboat cutting through the water, heading toward it.

"It's coming from this direction," Melissa says. "That must be them. That must be their yacht."

"They're trying to get away," Tom says.

"Do you know how to fly a helicopter?"

"No," Tom says.

She grabs his arm, pulling him back toward the car. "Then we're going to need a boat."

62

L ee drags Dennis below deck once they're on the yacht, and he ties him up in one of the rooms, binding his wrists and his ankles tight. With some satisfaction, he sees how Dennis's fingers instantly redden and begin to turn purple at the tips.

"Do you understand what you've cost us?" Lee says, rolling Dennis onto his back and holding him by the front of his shirt. "You nosy little fuck."

"You killed a woman," Dennis says, defiant. "You killed her in cold blood. You ran her down in the street like she was vermin."

"She *was* vermin," Lee says. "Just like you. In fact, you're less than vermin. You're a goddamn cockroach, and the boot is descending."

Dennis laughs at him. "It hasn't fallen yet."

Lee glares. "You're suddenly very brave, little cockroach."

"Why not? What have I got to lose? I'm sick of being scared. I'm not scared anymore, and especially not of someone like *you*."

"Rollins isn't here anymore, Dennis. You need to behave yourself."

"And you need to go fuck yourself."

Lee blinks. He wasn't expecting this from Dennis. "Well, I'm sure you'll still be brave when the fire starts licking the skin from your bones. You should've just given up the first night I saw you."

Dennis doesn't say anything to this, but he stares at Lee, unblinking, his jaw set. There's nothing left to say between them.

Lee leaves him, closing the door on the room behind him. On his way back to the top deck, he sees Billy coming down.

"Everything should be in place," Billy says. "Awais is en route. I'm just checking everything over to be certain."

Lee claps a hand on his shoulder and nods, grateful for Billy and his foresight. Lee heads up top. He can see James and Scarlett standing at the front of the yacht, close to each other on a rail, talking in low voices. Lee leaves them for now and goes to the pilot, tells him they're ready to go. Lee has given him coordinates. The pilot sets a course for them. The location is out to sea, far out of view of the shore.

When he reaches James and Scarlett, they stop talking. Scarlett still has blood on her chin, and the cut in her lower lip looks fresh and shiny. "Awais is on his way," Lee says. "He's going to need rewarded for this."

Neither of the Penneys says anything to him. Scarlett stares at him with a defiance similar to Dennis's. James looks at the ground.

Lee ignores their sour expressions. "Once we're out of view of the mainland we'll blow the yacht," he says. "It's going to have to be soon, before anyone has a chance to catch up to us."

"Like Rollins?" Scarlett says. She's trying to mock him, Lee knows.

"Like the law," Lee says. "Like the feds. By the time they get out here, all we want them to see is burning wreckage."

"Is this..." James begins, his face still lowered. He's wrestling with something. He raises his head long enough to look around wistfully at the yacht. He winces when he sees the armed men scattered upon it. There aren't many of them left. Eight, Lee thinks. Everyone else is likely dead. Judging from the fact that Rollins came after them on the road, Marcus must be part of that long list of deceased, too.

"*What?*" he says, when it's clear James isn't going to continue.

"Is all of this necessary?" James says. "Do we have to do this? Maybe we should take our chances in the courts..."

Lee looks at him and slowly shakes his head. "You're a fucking moron, James." He walks away from them.

63

Tom and Melissa race down the coast toward the nearest marina, trying to keep the yacht in view.

"It's moving now," Melissa says. "But we should still be able to catch up. A smaller boat will be faster than it."

Tom is thinking. He's not sure what their plan of escape is, and that concerns him. "They have a helicopter," he says, sharing his thoughts, interested in Melissa's input. "They'd be able to get away in that faster, but they just dumped it outside their home and chose to go to the yacht."

"They wouldn't all fit in the helicopter," Melissa says.

"No, but the Penneys and Lee could escape in it. They're going to be the priority. Anyone else with them right now could get away in cars and meet up with them later. They know that things have gone wrong for them, and yet they're choosing to try and get away on a yacht, despite how slow it is in comparison to the smaller boats that the feds are going to send after them."

"What are you thinking?"

"I don't know. This just doesn't feel right. It doesn't feel like the best thing they could do to get away. Maybe they're not really on the boat and it's just a distraction."

"Shit," Melissa says. "What do we do if that's the case?"

"We stay the course right now. We won't know until we get out there."

"Well, the marina's not far from here." Melissa looks out to sea, toward the escaping yacht, then turns back to the road. "Next left."

Tom continues to think. He can hear sirens, likely cops heading toward the Penney mansion to investigate the helicopter dumped in the road. "Or, if they are onboard, they could be meeting someone," he says. "Heading out to sea to get collected."

Melissa curses under her breath as they reach the marina. The gate is closed and locked.

"We're gonna have to climb it," Tom says. He looks toward the guardhouse. It's empty. They dump the car and run to the gate. Melissa starts climbing. She doesn't need a boost. Tom jumps up after her, the M4A1 strapped to his back. They drop down the other side and run toward the docks. Tom follows Melissa's lead. She's scanning the boats as she approaches, seeing which is best for them.

"The deck boat," she says, pointing. "It's our best option out of what's here."

They jump onboard. "Do you know how to start this?" Tom says.

Melissa ducks down under the steering wheel, pulling at the panelling there. "I wouldn't have come to this if I didn't."

While she gets the motor running, Tom stands and searches out the yacht in the distance. It's far out.

The deck boat's engine roars into life and Melissa

straightens, manning the wheel. "I'd prefer it if there'd been a pontoon or a bowrider, but this'll do. Hold on."

Melissa drives them out of the marina and onto the sea. Tom takes the assault rifle off his back and holds it ready, bracing himself on the side of the boat with one hand. Melissa points them toward the yacht and opens up.

64

Lee calls Awais, Billy standing nearby. He's left the Penneys sulking on the other side of the yacht. Lee looks toward the distance, but he sees no one approaching.

"What's your ETA?" he says when Awais answers. He can hear the sound of splashing waves and the roar of an engine in the background.

"About a half-hour," Awais says.

"That long?"

"This is all very sudden, Mr. Giles," Awais says. "We weren't expecting to be called out so abruptly. *And* we had to find the appropriate kind of boat. We're coming to you as fast as we can."

"A half-hour – that's definitive? I need a concrete number. It's important."

Awais converses off the call, probably to the pilot. He comes back on the line and says, "Less than. The pilot says we will reach you in approximately twenty-four minutes."

"You can't get more precise than that?"

"He says he does not want to give an exact time. He's going as fast as he can."

"All right. That'll do. We'll see you then." Lee hangs up and turns to Billy. "They're estimating twenty-four minutes. Set the timers on the explosives for thirty."

"Does that give us long enough?" Billy says, looking doubtful.

"There aren't many of us on the yacht, and we're leaving one behind. I'm also factoring in this conversation. Thirty minutes. Go."

65

As they get nearer, Tom spots one man on watch at the back of the yacht. The man is looking their way, waiting for them to get closer before he decides whether they're a threat or simply a passerby. Tom switches the M4A1 to semi-automatic, lines up his shot, taking the waves into account, and fires. He aims low, into the centre of the guard's torso. The bullet connects and the man's body pitches forward, falling over the railing and splashing into the water. Tom waits, watching, keeping the rifle raised. No one else comes running to investigate. The sound of the sea has disguised the noise.

The yacht is moving slowly, as if it's reached its destination, or is close to it. Tom expected to be greeted by a hail of gunfire, but they've lucked out. He's thinking Lee mustn't have many men left after the siege at the sheriff's department, or else there'd surely be more of them on watch at the back of the boat. Melissa is able to glide them in.

The rear of the yacht is too open, with a space there for people to lounge. It won't conceal the deck boat. Instead,

Melissa sticks close to its rear corner on the port side, hoping to avoid detection. The deck boat is small enough that in order to be seen someone would have to lean over the railing and look down. Melissa finds a piece of rope to moor them to the yacht. She looks up toward the railings as she ties it, watching for patrolling guards.

Tom leaves her the M4A1, setting it back to automatic. "I'll be as fast as I can," he says. "If they spot you, shoot them before they can shoot you." He pauses, then adds, "Just make sure it's not me or Dennis first."

Melissa takes the rifle, but asks, "What about you?"

Tom has his Beretta and KA-BAR. He pats them. "Just stay low and keep watch. If they attack and you have to get away, just do it. Don't worry about us. We'll find another way off. Just shoot me a message so I know you're not here."

Melissa nods. She drops down to a knee and scans the railings while Tom goes to the back of the deck boat, closest to the stern of the yacht, and climbs over, getting onboard. He pulls out his KA-BAR and makes sure the area is clear, listening for any approach. He sees and hears nothing.

Pressing himself to the wall, he makes his way around the yacht. He spots a man on the level above, looking out to sea. He's armed with an MCX Spear, like back at the sheriff's department. Tom wonders if the man was there, if he was part of the siege. Tom keeps moving, side-stepping lightly as he passes under him.

He spots a few other men milling around the boat, all of them armed, but there aren't many of them. Between the firefight on the road yesterday and the men Tom was able to kill at the siege, he's certain now that Lee doesn't have many men left.

He gets close to the front of the ship, remaining

concealed, and sees a couple unlike the rest of the men, leaning against a railing and talking animatedly. The woman looks angrier than the man. She's gesticulating wildly. Tom thinks he can see a smear of something on her chin, maybe blood. There's a cut in her bottom lip. Her hair is wild. It takes Tom a moment to realise that he knows who she is, who both of them are. Scarlett and James Penney.

He doesn't see Lee, and he doesn't see Dennis, either. He goes back the way he came and finds a door leading below deck. Tom slips down the stairs, keeping his knife ready, his eyes focussed ahead and his ears attuned to footsteps or any other noise, especially from behind the closed doors.

The corridor is thin, but wide enough for him to move down without having to turn sideways. Ahead, around a corner, he hears a door close, and footsteps soon after. Tom moves toward the sound, toward the footsteps soon to draw level with his position.

A man appears and begins to turn right, away from Tom. Like the men up top, he's dressed all in black. There's a handgun tucked down the back of his trousers, and in his right hand he's carrying a toolkit. Tom grabs him from behind, lodging his left arm in tight under his chin, digging into his throat, keeping him quiet. The man makes a brief gagging sound as his air supply is cut off, but then he's silent. Tom presses the tip of the KA-BAR into his right temple so that the man knows it's there. Tom drags him back down the corridor he's just emerged from, getting him out of the main walkway should anyone else come below.

"Where's Dennis?" Tom says, speaking into the man's ear.

Tom releases the pressure on the man's neck enough for him to answer in a whisper. "Go fuck yourself," the man says.

Tom doesn't waste time with him. He doesn't need to use

the knife, aware of the mess it'll create. He snaps the man's neck. His body falls limp. Tom drags him down the corridor, recounting the steps he heard the man take. It leads him to the end of the corridor. Tom tries the door. It's unlocked. Peering inside, he sees that the room is empty. He drags the body in, dumps it, and then looks around. It's a storage room filled with cleaning equipment.

A flashing red light catches Tom's attention. It's in the corner of the room. It's not hidden. It's a block of C4. There's a timer attached to the detonator planted inside. The red light is the numbers on the timer counting down. There are twenty minutes and thirty-five seconds left.

Tom backs out of the room, pulling out his cell phone. He doesn't want to use the phone close to the detonator. There's only a small risk the phone could set it off, but it's a risk he doesn't want to take. He makes sure the corridor is still clear and then tests the nearest doors. They're all unlocked. He steps into one. It's a bedroom. The bed is made. The room is neat. No one has stayed in here for a while. He checks it for another explosive but he can't find one. He calls Melissa.

She answers in a whisper. "Tom?"

"How's it looking out there?"

"Still clear right now."

"Do you see anyone approaching?"

"What do you mean – another boat? No, nothing."

"Okay. Melissa, I need you to listen to me very closely. I've found a bomb onboard."

"A bomb? Can you disarm it?"

"There's no point – the whole ship is probably laced with explosives. They've planted them themselves, and obviously they have their reasons. Someone must be coming to get them, so keep your eyes open. And set a timer – if me and Dennis aren't off this boat in fifteen minutes, you need to get clear, or else you're going to get caught in the blast."

"But –"

"No buts, Melissa. Just do it. If it takes longer than fifteen minutes, then me and Dennis will find another way off."

"All right – I've set the timer. Get Dennis and get back to me, Tom."

"I intend to."

66

T om moves room to room, but finds no one. He heads down to the lower deck, moving carefully, aware all the while of the ticking clock in the back of his head.

At the end of the corridor, he hears movement. It comes from behind a closed door. Tom goes to it. There's no one else around. Everyone else seems to be up top, on either the upper deck or the observation deck. They'll be aware of the countdown, and how close it's getting, and they're likely waiting to be collected, eager to get off before the yacht goes boom.

Tom stops outside the room where he hears movement and presses his ear to the door. It's hard to make out what's happening. He can hear banging, but it's low, like it's on the ground. Tom tries the handle, but it's locked. It's the first locked room he's found. He kicks the door open, entering with his Beretta raised.

It's a crew bedroom. The bed is dishevelled, and he soon sees why. On the ground, bound at wrists and ankles, is

Dennis. He's managed to wriggle off the bed and is trying to crawl across the ground. Dennis raises his head and sees Tom.

"What's the plan here, Dennis?" Tom goes to him with his knife to cut him free.

"I thought I could get myself loose," Dennis says. "I was wrong."

Tom starts cutting through the binds, starting at his ankles.

"I think they're gonna blow the boat," Dennis says. "Lee said something about fire – I think they're gonna fake their deaths. They've talked in front of me. Someone's coming to pick them up."

"I found the explosives," Tom says.

"How long do we have?"

"Not long. Melissa is waiting for us. We need to go." Tom gets to his feet and helps Dennis do the same.

"Tom," Dennis says. "You came for me – that – I –"

"There's no time," Tom says. "But I wasn't going to let them get away with you."

They leave the room, but as they do, Tom hears a man shouting. It's faint, coming from the next deck up.

"Billy's dead!" he's shouting.

Tom assumes the man he dumped in the storage closet must have been Billy. They came looking for him.

Tom motions for Dennis to stay behind him. "Looks like we're gonna have to fight our way out."

67

L ee hears Roden calling to him, telling him that the reason Billy hasn't returned is because he's dead.

James and Scarlett hurry over. They've heard Roden, too. "Did he say he's *dead*?" Scarlett says.

"What happened?" James says.

Lee looks at him. "How should I know?"

Roden returns to the upper deck. "Neck snapped," he says. "His body was dumped right next to some of the explosives."

"Had they been tampered with?" Lee says.

Roden shakes his head. "Still counting down."

"What does this mean?" Scarlett says.

Lee ignores the Penneys. He starts barking orders to his men. "Spread out! Guns ready. There could be someone onboard."

He's thinking about Rollins. The goddamn sneaky bastard. How could he have gotten out here? At the same time, he finds himself having to suppress a smile. If it *is* Rollins, if he somehow, magically, managed to get onboard the yacht, then that means Lee hasn't lost his chance, not yet. He can find him. He can kill him.

"Turner's missing, too," Saunders says, looking around.

Two men down, Lee thinks. He considers their options. Should he send his men below deck, to root the killer out? Should he send them to Dennis's room – that's why Rollins would be here, that's who he's looking for. But he doesn't know how long Rollins has been aboard. He could be anywhere on the yacht. And if he sends his men below deck, Rollins could be in a secure position and pick them off. He'd be sending them to a slaughter. But it might be worth it. The slaughter could draw him out, open him wide for Lee to deliver the killing blow.

"Just forget it," Scarlett says, pulling on his arm. "Awais is here." She points. The boat is approaching. When it arrives, they'll have plenty of time to disembark and get away before the C4 explodes. "The ship is going to blow. Whoever it is, just let them die with it."

Lee looks toward Awais's boat. It's getting closer. It's almost time for them to go.

But Rollins could be here. Who else would it be?

Lee checks his watch and how long they have left before the yacht explodes. He looks toward Awais's boat getting closer. He thinks of Rollins. It isn't over yet. The defeat Lee was earlier lamenting, it hasn't come to pass. There's still time to redeem himself.

"Fan out!" Lee says, eyeing his men. "Search the entire ship! Find this motherfucker! Bring him to me!"

68

Melissa sees the boat approaching from the starboard side. She first caught sight of it five minutes ago, drawing nearer with every passing second, clearly on an interception route. She thinks of the explosives Tom told her are on the yacht. This must be the pickup. The people coming to collect the Penneys.

Unless it's not. It's not a yacht. It's a fishing boat. A trawler. A large one. Melissa peers around the back of the Penneys' yacht – the *Feel Good* – keeping herself out of view from the new arrivals as they draw closer. But if they're just fishermen, why are they coming this way, heading directly for the yacht? There's no other reason. Or could they be undercover feds? Melissa isn't sure.

She glances back at the railings above her, making sure no one is sneaking up. The trawler gets closer. She can see men on it now. Three of them. She checks the time. Eight minutes until she needs to go. She looks at the yacht again, silently praying that she'll see Tom and Dennis emerge, hurrying toward her, ready to escape and get far away from here. There's still no sign of them.

One of the men standing at the bow of the trawler is waving to the yacht and smiling. Melissa can see his face. He's Indian. Two men stand close behind him, also Indian, but they're not smiling. They both look very severe and serious. One of them is unsteady, struggling to find his sea legs. Melissa sees him swallowing, like he's trying not to throw up. He turns slightly toward the railing in case he needs to hurry over and let loose.

Melissa sees how the man at the front stops smiling. His waving arm lowers. He looks confused. Melissa looks toward the yacht again, wishing she could see the source of his sudden consternation.

The sickly looking Indian turns his head suddenly, clenching his jaw tight, covering his mouth with his hand. His eyes briefly close. When they open, he sees Melissa.

His sickness is forgotten. He turns to the others and points. The other man with him, the one who wasn't waving, they both pull out handguns. They point toward Melissa's location. They start shooting.

Their aim is terrible. They're not accustomed to being on the water. Melissa shoulders the M4A1 and fires back. Her aim is better. The three Indian men realise this, and they scatter away from the bow, ducking for cover. The trawler tries to turn away. Melissa fires at the boat, keeping it at bay. She doesn't shoot wildly. She only has the one magazine. She looks back up at the yacht, but no one is coming, drawn by the sound. The Indian men try to fire at her, but they only hit the water. Their bullets land nowhere near the deck boat. They're closer to the yacht.

Melissa ducks back into cover, watching the railings and occasionally checking to make sure the trawler remains at a distance. She looks at the time. There isn't long left.

69

Tom can hear gunfire, though he's not sure where it's coming from. It's not on the yacht, and it's too weak to be automatic. It's handguns. For that reason, he doesn't think it's coming from Melissa, or from Lee's men.

As soon as the thought enters his mind, he *does* hear automatic fire from the M4A1, but still he hears nothing from the Spears. He makes his way up a deck, Beretta raised, scanning the area. It's the level where he killed Billy. There's no one here. The man who announced Billy's death is also gone. Tom moves on, motioning for Dennis to follow, to stick close.

They reach the stairs leading up to the main deck. Tom knows they could be covered, waiting to see if they emerge from below. There could be a few men there, barring the way. It's too wide of a space, and too much of a risk to emerge here.

"We go back," Tom says, thinking of how he first came down. "There's more stairs at the rear. We'll take them. It's a smaller opening at the top. If there's anyone there blocking the exit, we have a better chance of fighting our way through that."

Dennis turns without saying anything, aware of the ticking clock. They both are. They need to move fast.

As they retreat back the way they came, Tom hears hurried footsteps coming to the top of the stairs they're leaving behind. He gets Dennis to duck low and then he drops to a knee, Beretta raised. He hears someone coming down the stairs, trying to be quiet now, but it's too late. They've already given themselves away. As their legs come into view, along with the tip of their Spear, Tom fires twice, a bullet for each shin.

The man screams and tumbles down the stairs. Tom runs toward him, putting another bullet in him where he lies prone. As he takes the Spear from his dead hands, he hears running footsteps at the top of the stairs, multiple pairs. Tom aims the Spear up and fires as soon as one of the men makes himself visible, blowing off most of his face. The others – two more of them, Tom thinks – start firing back blindly, aiming down the hole without getting close to it.

Tom backs away, out of range of their bullets, keeping the Spear ready. They could be descending into the lower decks from all points now, cutting off all escape routes. But they know they don't have much time left, Tom thinks. They need to get off this ship just as fast as Tom and Dennis do.

He wonders if Melissa can hear the gunfire on board the yacht. He wonders, too, what she was shooting at earlier. Has someone come to pick the Penneys up, as he suspected they might? Has she kept them away from the yacht?

Tom can find out later. There are no answers now. He points for Dennis to keep going down the corridor. "I need you to be my eyes," he says. "If anyone comes from that direction, tell me."

Dennis nods. They travel back-to-back, Dennis heading for the rear of the ship and Tom watching to see if the other two men descend. He sees no sign of them. They've learnt better from the two men he's already killed.

"Ahead!" Dennis says.

Tom spins and Dennis falls flat. Tom opens fire at the man who has appeared at the end of the corridor. He doesn't get a chance to lift his own rifle.

Seeing him fall, Dennis gets back up and they continue. Tom sees one of the men from the other end try to venture down, drawn by the gunfire going in the opposite direction. He tries to fire at Tom, his bullets going wide and hitting the corridor walls and the ceiling. Tom returns fire and the man scrambles back up top.

"Which way?" Dennis says.

"It's your right," Tom says. "Set of stairs. Don't get too close to them. I'll need to make sure they're clear up top."

70

The Penneys are panicking. They hear the gunfire erupting around their yacht, up top and down below. What panics them most is seeing how Awais and the trawler he's commandeered can't get any closer.

"What's happening?" Scarlett says. She holds onto her husband, and he holds onto her just as tight, his head cowed. "Who's shooting at them?"

Rollins is clearly on the yacht, hence all the gunfire. But there must be someone else, someone nearby. Someone not on the yacht, judging by where Awais's bodyguards are ineffectually shooting toward. One of them looks like he's about to throw up. He turns his head to the side in between rounds. Lee thinks he might *be* throwing up.

"How long do we have?" Scarlett says. "We're going to blow! We're going to fucking blow!"

"There's plenty of time," Lee says, though he doesn't check the time. He follows the direction Awais's bodyguards are firing toward. Another boat, maybe? Did they manage to sneak up on the yacht? Saunders said Turner had disappeared, and he was the one keeping watch at the rear.

Lee pulls out his Sig Sauer. "Stay here," he says to the Penneys.

"Where are you going?" Scarlett says.

"This'll be over soon," Lee says. "Just stay right here and once we can get Awais close enough I'll throw the two of you over there myself."

He leaves them alone, none of his men left spare to guard them. He heads to the port side, seeing at least one of his men already lying dead near to the stairs down. He can't tell who it is. His face is almost completely gone. Blood spreads out around his skull, seeping into the teak floor. Lee reaches the side and presses close to the wall, hearing gunfire across the whole of the ship, impossible to pinpoint where it's all coming from. After he deals with the issue keeping Awais at bay, he can join the others. He can finally deal with Rollins. Even if they only get a few short seconds together, it'll be sweet.

Lee edges toward the rear of the yacht, hearing automatic gunfire coming from there, shooting in the direction of the trawler. Lee gets close, until he's on top of it. He inches closer to the rail and peers over, quickly pulling back in case the person below is ready for him. They're not. They're focussed on the trawler right now.

Lee sees the top of a red head. Melissa Ross. He grins. He steps forward, the Sig Sauer raised. He takes aim, right at her scalp.

As his finger readies on the trigger, he feels a weight barrel into him from behind, almost knocking him over the railing. Below, as the dropped Sig Sauer sails past her head, Melissa looks up and sees what almost happened to her. Lee manages to keep himself from falling. He spins, lashing out with his elbow. His attacker ducks and then rises, driving a knee into his midsection.

It's Rollins. Even as Rollins's fist slams across Lee's face and blood fills his mouth, Lee smiles. *It's Rollins.*

71

T om hits Lee Giles again, and then grabs him by the back of the head and drives his skull into the side of the yacht. As he falls, a bloody print from his forehead is left behind.

With Lee incapacitated, Tom helps Dennis over the side of the yacht and, holding onto his arm, lowers him to the deck boat below. Melissa wraps her arms around him as he lands and keeps him from falling overboard.

"Tom, come on, let's go!" Melissa says, calling up to him, her arms raised like she's going to catch him. "There's not long left!"

Tom looks back at Lee, and he thinks of Tessa Maberry. He thinks of Carla Mann and the others. He thinks of Eric Braun. The ship is going to explode, but it's not enough. The ship is going to explode, but there's another boat here to get them, and there's no guarantee that Lee will be caught in the blast.

This shouldn't take long. All he'd have to do is snap his neck, same as he did to Billy. Or better yet, break his legs.

Stomp down on his ankles. Make him dead weight. There's only minutes left until the yacht blows, and Lee's men won't be able to carry him off and to the trawler. He wouldn't be able to swim. He'll burn, or he'll sink. Either way, it's better than he deserves.

Before Tom can commit, he sees movement to his side, emerging from the same stairs he and Dennis came up just in time to see Lee lining up his shot, about to kill Melissa. Tom scoops up the Spear he dropped and throws himself against the wall, just to the side of Lee's bloodied forehead print. He fires, cutting down the first man to emerge. He runs to the top of the stairs and sees another man fleeing. Tom shoots him in the back and he goes rolling forward, down the rest of the stairs.

From his right, approaching from the other side of the ship, another man appears. He opens fire. Tom ducks down into the staircase, though he doesn't descend. He stays near the top. He looks to the deck and sees the man's shadow as he approaches, his rifle raised. He stops. He doesn't want to get too close to the doorway, knowing Tom could be sheltering there.

"Giles!" the man calls. "Giles, speak to me! Are you all right?"

Lee does not respond. Tom doesn't know if he can. He might be unconscious. He hopes he is.

The man's shouting gives Tom a better location on him. He gauges the length of his shadow and presses the barrel of the Spear against the wall, watching the shadow and trying to get the direction right. He opens fire, bullets tearing through the wood. The shadow begins to dance. Tom steps out through the doorway and puts a few more rounds into the man as he falls.

Tom turns and finds that Lee has risen. He strikes Tom across the face and then kicks him, driving the Spear back across Tom's chest, its impact almost winding him. As Tom tries to steady himself, Lee kicks at him again, knocking the Spear out of his grip and out of reach. Tom falls to the ground.

Lee mounts him, blood running down the middle of his face, and when he smiles his teeth are red with it. "*Rollins,*" he says, and it almost sounds to Tom like he's happy to see him.

72

M elissa's alarm goes off.

"What's that?" Dennis says, neck arced up toward the railing where they last saw Tom. The shooting has stopped, but he hasn't reappeared.

"We need to go," Melissa says, starting the deck boat.

Dennis wheels on her. "What do you mean? Tom is still up there!"

"The yacht is going to blow."

"I know that! We can't leave him!"

"This is what Tom told me to do," Melissa says. She unties them from the side of the yacht. "I don't like it just as much as you, but if we don't go now we're going to get swallowed in the fireball."

Dennis looks desperately up at the yacht. He calls Tom's name. It doesn't help. They don't see him.

Melissa swallows, feeling sick. There hasn't been any more shooting. She knows Tom could already be dead. Why else hasn't he come back to them? If the shooting is done, he should be on the deck boat with them, ready to escape. But then, if the Penney men have killed him, why haven't they turned their guns upon Melissa and Dennis, just like Lee Giles was about to do before Tom stopped him?

There's no time. It's over. They have to go.

"Dennis, hold on," Melissa says. "We need to get clear."

Dennis doesn't listen. He falls back to the ground, landing on his backside as Melissa turns the boat and he doesn't get straight back up. His hands are on top of his head, clutching at clumps of his hair. He turns as the deck boat does, looking back at the yacht. His eyes suddenly widen. He points. "There!" he says. "They're fighting!"

Melissa turns, though she keeps the deck boat moving. She can see Tom. She can see Lee Giles, too. They fight down the side of the boat, toward the bow. She sees the trawler has started up again and is approaching the yacht. The men who were shooting at her remain armed, their guns pointing in the direction of the deck boat, but they're not shooting anymore. They know their bullets won't make it.

Melissa checks the time. There's only a few minutes until the yacht explodes. They can't stop and go back. It wouldn't help. There's nothing they can do. They have to get clear.

73

Tom manages to roll backward and to his feet as Lee kicks at him again. He blocks another kick and then dodges a left hook, but then Lee feints with a right and follows through with another left that lands high on Tom's cheek. Lee quickly hits a right to Tom's chest, knocking him back a few paces.

Lee is laughing. "I knew it," he says. "You're nothing! I could beat you with one hand behind my fucking back! Hooyah, *bitch*!"

Tom knows there isn't long left, but Lee doesn't seem to care anymore. He throws a right at Tom, but Tom sees that it's a feint again, and he feints back like he's trying to block it, and this time when the left comes arcing in Tom catches it, hooking his arm around it and pinning it to his body. He twists his body and draws Lee in and headbutts him, drilling his forehead into Lee's nose. He hits him with a couple of lefts, jabbing at his chest and stomach, then into his face, mashing his lips back against his teeth.

Lee gets desperate. He tries to kick at Tom with his right leg but Tom catches it in his left arm and then sweeps Lee's standing leg out from under him, dumping Lee to the deck.

Lee's eyes blaze. He's infuriated. Tom prepares to follow through, to stomp at his face, but before he can he feels weight leap onto his back and hands claw at his face. He hears Scarlett screeching while she attacks him.

"You've taken everything!" she screams. "I'll kill you! I'll kill you!"

Tom spins with her, getting his hands under hers to keep her fingernails from scratching at his eyes. He throws himself back, crushing her between himself and the nearest wall. He reaches back and grabs a handful of her hair and flips her over his shoulder.

As he straightens, a punch connects with his jaw. It's not strong. It doesn't knock Tom back. He looks and sees James Penney. James is nursing his right hand like he's just broken it, and his jaw hangs slack as he sees how Tom is unaffected.

Tom punches him in turn. James falls straight back, landing flat on his back, out cold.

Tom turns back to Lee in time to see him slashing with his SRK. Tom manages to get a forearm up and stops the point of the blade from penetrating the side of his skull by centimetres. With his other hand, Lee punches him, driving him back.

As Tom stumbles onto the main deck, gunshots come from the trawler. They hit the deck close to Tom, but he hears Lee shouting at them. "*Stop*! He's mine!"

"We don't have time," one of the men calls back. "We need to go!"

"This won't take long," Lee says, turning back to Tom.

Tom reaches for his Beretta but Lee is charging and he needs to use his hands to defend himself. He blocks and ducks and steps back as Lee slashes and slices at him. He sees off to the side how Scarlett crawls toward her unconscious husband, trying to revive him.

The knife cuts close in front of Tom's face, near his eyes. Lee lunges in and Tom catches his right hand by the wrist. Lee grabs Tom's right wrist in turn. They're locked together.

"There's not long left," Lee says through his teeth.

"Are you willing to die to prove who's the better man?" Tom says.

"You have no idea what I'm willing to do. And aren't *you*?"

"I don't need to die," Tom says. "I already know who the better man is."

He stomps down on the inside of Lee's right ankle and he hears the bone there crack and snap. Lee remains standing, but it's clear he's in agony. The strength has instantly left his grip as the pain courses through his body, and Tom can feel it. He breaks his wrist free and elbow-strikes Lee in the side of the head. He follows through and takes the SRK from him. He spins and slams the blade down through Lee's left boot, through the wood below, pinning him to the deck.

Lee tumbles back, his right leg ineffective and his left stuck in place. He roars, and at first Tom thinks he's screaming, but then he realises he's calling his name.

"*Rollins!*"

The Indian men on the trawler start shooting again. Tom sees how Scarlett has abandoned James and is running to the railing closest to the trawler. She's going to try to get aboard. The unarmed Indian man at the front is reaching for her. Tom turns and starts running in the opposite direction. He needs to get off the yacht. There's no time left.

He reaches the railing and launches himself off it, diving toward the sea.

The yacht explodes.

74

The concussive force from the explosion throws Tom through the air, and he hits the water hard. The impact knocks him momentarily unconscious.

He floats face down in the water, then comes to with a start, sputtering water out of his mouth and nose, gasping for air. He spins, trying to work out where he is, where he's landed. He looks back and sees the yacht burning. He never saw how many explosives there were, but he can see from the damage they've done that it must have been a lot. It's a fireball. It's engulfed the trawler, too. It's burning, and both are already beginning to sink.

Tom kicks his legs and circles his arms, floating where he is and watching the two ships burn. He doesn't see any sign of Melissa, Dennis, or the deck boat. He hopes they got clear. He told Melissa when she needed to leave. They must have gotten to safety.

He doesn't see anyone else in the water. Can't hear

anyone screaming, or crying for help. He has no doubt that Lee and the Penneys were killed in the blast. The three Indian men, too. They were too close to the explosion. The fire would have swallowed them all.

Tom tentatively checks his face and head, the back of his neck, making sure there are no burns or other wounds. He doesn't find anything. If any of the fire reached him, landing in the water must have put him out.

He can't stay where he is forever. It's a long way back to the shore, and his strength is already low from the battle on the yacht and the siege at the sheriff's department. He's confident that no one has survived the explosion. He turns and starts swimming.

Tom focusses on his strokes and his breathing. The water splashes into his ears. It takes him a while to notice that his name is being called. Part of him thinks it's in his head, that it's still the sound of Lee screaming while he was pinned to the deck, knowing his death was coming.

Then he realises it's not Lee. It's a woman, and a younger man, and they're both familiar to him. Melissa and Dennis.

Tom stops swimming and looks around. He spots the deck boat and manages to wave his arms. He calls their names, but he doesn't know if they'll hear him. He sees them both as the deck boat slowly crawls through the waves, Melissa at the steering wheel and Dennis at the front, leaning forward. They're both scanning the water, searching for him.

Dennis spots him first. He calls to Melissa without turning, pointing, not wanting to lose Tom again. The deck boat spins in his direction and Tom swims toward them. They pull up beside him, both reaching down to pull him aboard.

Tom lands on the deck, spitting out sea water, wiping it from his face and eyes. Melissa and Dennis both hold him, squeezing him between them, warming him with their bodies.

Melissa kisses him. When they separate she licks her lips and grins, pressing her forehead to his. "You taste like salt."

75

I t's been three weeks since the Penneys blew up their yacht, inadvertently killing themselves and the Indian businessman Awais Choudhury. Tom and the others have learnt his name in the time since. They've learnt a lot of things in the time since.

Tom has avoided talking to the feds. He's left the talking to Melissa and Dennis. The local police are being investigated, and many of the crooked cops have already been arrested. Further investigations are still ongoing, particularly into Penney Pharma. The board of directors are being questioned, to find out how much they knew about the Indian factory, about the fentanyl, about the murder of Tessa Maberry – about all of it.

"The company will be dissolved," Vanessa tells them. "That's what I'm hearing. They can't continue under the same name, no way. It's been stained forever. They can't rebrand this. There's no coming back from it."

Vanessa's arm is in a sling still, but she's been attending physio for it, and she says she's getting better. She wants to get back on duty soon. The sheriff's department in Bedford-shire County needs rebuilding from the ground up. She wants to help with that.

They're in The Corner Spot. Tom, Melissa, Dennis, Stef, and Vanessa. Dennis and Stef sit close together, their shoulders touching, their hands clasped on Stef's thigh.

"I can't believe what you all went through," Stef says. It's not the first time she's said it. Once they were safe, Dennis was eager to get back to her. She was just as eager to see him again.

They've been to a lot of funerals together over the last few weeks. For Carla and the other activists. For Sheriff Warren Hobbs and the other deputies killed. There was no body for Tessa Maberry's memorial. At Monmouth Beach, where the Penneys wanted to build their marina, instead an unofficial monument has been created. There are pictures of her, as well as Carla and the others, and there are flowers and candles.

Needless to say, the marina is not going ahead.

Tom stands with Melissa. She's not working. She leans against him, his arm around her shoulders. They watch the news on the television behind the bar. The Penney Pharma investigation has dominated the news cycle ever since the yacht exploded.

"The feds and the cops aren't asking about you so much anymore," Melissa says. "I think they've given up on you. They think you've moved on."

Tom says nothing.

"Vanessa helped," Melissa says. "She's a hero to them. She told them you were gone and they listened."

"Thanks," Tom says.

Melissa doesn't question why he didn't want to talk to

anyone. She already knows. They discussed it at her apartment. It takes up too much of his time. If they realise who he is, there's no telling how long they'd want to talk to him.

Melissa turns to him. She keeps her voice low so no one else can hear. "How long *are* you hanging around for?" she says. "I mean, I always knew this was just a short-term thing. You blew into town, and you're probably gonna blow out just as abruptly."

Tom nods. "Soon," he says. "But not just yet."

Melissa opens her mouth as if she's going to ask more, but then she decides better of it. She rests her head upon his chest and turns to the television. Dennis and Stef are laughing about something. Their faces are close. They're always close. Vanessa goes to the bar and orders another round of drinks, but tells the bartender he'll have to carry them over, playing on his sympathy by indicating her arm in the sling.

Tom breathes deeply, inhaling the sweet scent of Melissa's red hair. He's not going to stay here forever. He's going to move on. But until he does, he's going to enjoy the time he has left here. He's going to appreciate the people he's here with. And before he leaves, he's going to visit the memorial of Tessa Maberry, and the graves of Carla Mann and Eric Braun, and the graves of everyone else who was killed here in the effort to stop Penney Pharma, to save the lives they were surely going to destroy with Sentit B. He's going to remember them. He's going to carry them with him.

ABOUT THE AUTHOR

Did you enjoy *Deep Water*? Please consider leaving a review on Amazon to help other readers discover the book.

Paul Heatley left school at sixteen, and since then has held a variety of jobs including mechanic, carpet fitter, and bookshop assistant, but his passion has always been for writing. He writes mostly in the genres of crime fiction and thriller, and links to his other titles can be found on his website. He lives in the north east of England.

Want to connect with Paul? Visit him at his website.

www.PaulHeatley.com

ALSO BY PAUL HEATLEY